Dorothea Townshend

Life and Letters of Mr. Endymion Porter

Sometime Gentleman of the Bedchamber to King Charles the First

Dorothea Townshend

Life and Letters of Mr. Endymion Porter
Sometime Gentleman of the Bedchamber to King Charles the First

ISBN/EAN: 9783743401556

Manufactured in Europe, USA, Canada, Australia, Japa

Cover: Foto ©Raphael Reischuk / pixelio.de

Manufactured and distributed by brebook publishing software (www.brebook.com)

Dorothea Townshend

Life and Letters of Mr. Endymion Porter

Life and Letters of Mr. Endymion Porter:

Sometime Gentleman
of the Bedchamber
to King Charles
the First

By Dorothea Townshend

With Portraits

London
T. FISHER UNWIN
1897

CONTENTS

v

LIST OF ILLUSTRATIONS

INTRODUCTORY

WHEN a modern student, searching through the archives of some dusty museum, or poring over the worm-eaten pages of some forgotten volume, happens to light upon a chance word betraying the familiar human affections common to us all, he feels as pleasant a warmth of surprise as though a living hand had been held out to him across the centuries, and he heard a living voice whisper to him, " I, too, am thy brother."

At first it is not easy for us to realise this solidarity of humanity; we think that gaily embroidered doublets and shining armour must have covered hearts as unlike our own as the quaint raiment was unlike our modern clothes. We think that the men who made long-winded speeches, who listened with delight to interminable sermons, who breakfasted and dined at unheard-of hours, without any of the appliances which seem to us almost absolute necessaries of life; that these cannot possibly have been men like ourselves.

It is true that it would be folly for us to seek sympathy or companionship among the prehistoric hunters of the Stone Age, or even among our own ancestral Jutes and Angles. But when we turn to social and civilised man, and can learn to forget mere draperies and accessories, there comes a delightful day when we become suddenly conscious that we, too, have friends in Arcadia, that we have met Prince Hal more than once in London streets, and that King Arthur is in very truth a modern gentleman.

Those who have learned to seek their friends in all ages and under all costumes, may be glad to walk awhile with a pair of King Charles the First's courtiers, and find, when a few impertinent accessories are forgotten, that Endymion and Olivia are vastly like many a man and woman of the nineteenth century.

The English character may have possibly developed, it may have acquired a few novel airs and graces, and have picked up some dearly-bought wisdom in its progress through two centuries, but at the bottom it has altered little, and we are still what our dead fathers were. We still can laugh with them in their joy, and weep with them in their misfortunes, and learn from them, what the old Greek knew, that "there is nothing mightier and nobler than when man and wife are of one heart and mind in an house ; a grief to their foes, and to their friends great joy, but their own hearts know it best."

It has been often said that we owe our English ideal of family life and domestic affection to the teachings of the Puritan party. But it is not easy to prove that any party or creed has the monopoly of human emotions. No doubt the Puritans numbered among them such happy couples as Colonel and Mrs. Hutchinson, and Governor Winthorp and his Margaret. But we cannot forget that the Puritans drew their spiritual descent from such men as John Knox, whose diatribes against women roused even the grave Cecil to protest, "Maister Knox! Maister Knox! non est masculus neque femina! omnes enim, ut ait Paulus, unum sumus in Christo Jesu." We cannot forget that the great English Puritan poet hoped for nothing from his Betty but that she should cook him savoury meat such as his soul loved, and the Puritans of New England set a Boston sea-captain in the stocks for kissing his wife on a Sunday when she met him at his own door on his return from a three years' voyage.[1]

Natural affection was not the exclusive birthright of the Roundheads, and denied to men who wore love-locks. The Earl of Newcastle, Sir Richard Fanshawe, Sir Edmund Verney, and the Earl of Sunderland, were as true lovers as ever adorned the pages of romance, and the hurried notes that Endymion Porter dispatched to Olivia at every pause in a royal progress breathe a devotion as tender as that of John Winthrop's more studied epistles.

The greater part of these letters to his wife appear to have been seized by the Parliament with Porter's other papers, when he left London in the King's train in 1641. Fortunately for us, even the private part of the correspondence was never returned to the family, but has been left safely buried among the Domestic State Papers at the Record Office.

It is strange when turning over draughts of treaties and the formal dispatches of diplomatists to come upon the faded writing of these old love letters ; and it seems an insolent violation of domestic rights to turn them over and pry into their secrets. But as the papers were rummaged through by

---

[1] In 1656. See "Sabbath in Puritan New England," A. M. Earle.

Parliamentary agents in search of treason more than two hundred years ago, we may hope that the "buried lovers," as D'Avenant calls them, may .pardon more sympathetic readers.

A few letters that escaped confiscation were in the possession of the late Viscount Strangford, a descendant of Endymion Porter's eldest son, and have been printed by Mr. E. B. Fontblanque in his "Lives of the Lords Strangford" (Cassell). The originals are now in the possession of Mrs. Russell, of Aden, granddaughter of the sixth Viscount Strangford. A few more of Porter's letters have been found scattered among various seventeenth-century memoirs.

It may interest the curious to know that Mrs. Porter's writing was not more legible than that of other fashionable ladies of her own, and perhaps of our own, day. Endymion's hand is a beautiful copperplate, and his orthography excellent, except on the occasion of a disagreement with his wife, when he shows his agitation by spelling execrably.

I have to return my best thanks to Mrs. Russell for a copy of an autograph letter of Endymion to his wife ; to Mr. E. B. Fontblanque for his kind permission to reprint the information and letters already published in his "Lives of the Lords Strangford" ; to Mr. S. G. Hamilton, of Kiftsgate Court, for valuable information on the Porter family, extracted from deeds in his possession, and parish registers ; and, lastly, to Mr. C. H. Firth, without whose generous and unfailing help the book could never have come into existence.

CHAPTER I

THE PORTERS OF MICKLETON

WHERE the northern ridge of the Cotswold slopes down through orchards and cornfields to the fertile Vale of Evesham there lived, in the fifteenth and sixteenth centuries, a family belonging to the rank of the smaller gentry, named Porter.

Some authorities [1] say that they derived their name and arms—three bells argent, with a portcullis as crest—from an ancestral porter who guarded the gate of some unknown fortress; while others say that the Porter family bore the silver bells on their shields long before such things as bells were hung at castle front doors. Be that as it may, the family lived and increased for many generations in the villages of Mickleton and Aston-under-Hill, two parishes so closely connected that one priest served the two village churches, and the vellum quarto that registers the births and deaths of Aston lies in the Mickleton parish chest. A prudent man was the parson of the two parishes; he succeeded in holding his position through all the changes between the reign of Henry VIII. and that of James I., and

[1] *Notes and Queries*, 6th Ser. x. 209.

although he had been so injudicious as to take to himself a wife during the short and Protestant reign of Edward VI., he managed to escape deprivation therefor under Mary;[1] and indeed it is perfectly possible that neither he nor the Porters, his parishioners, were ever quite clear as to whether in their inmost hearts they held to the old or the reformed faith.

The Porters traced their pedigree from Robert Porter, of Elrington, Warwickshire, whose great-great-grandson, Richard, settled at Mickleton.[2] Richard's son William was Sergeant-at-Arms to Henry VII. and accompanied Henry VIII. to the Field of the Cloth of Gold.[3] His will is extant, dated 1513.

The family owned a considerable copyhold estate in Mickleton, and they also took long leases of Mickleton Manor itself. The Manor was church property, and it belonged to the Abbey of Ensham, on the Thames above Oxford; the suppression of the monastery did not, however, trouble the Porters, as their lease, fortunately for them, did not expire till 1614. All that happened to them was that they had a new landlord, the freehold of the Manor being granted to Lord Lumley, who sold it to a good friend of the Porters, Sir Edward Greville, and he in turn disposed of it to Edward Fisher.[4]

The history of the part of the Porter possessions that lay in Aston is not so simple; there was a

[1] Mr. S. G. Hamilton.
[2] Harl. MSS., 1543, p. 69 b, "Visitation of Gloucestershire."
[3] Burke's Commoners, vol. iii. p. 577. A tabular pedigree of the descendants of this William Porter appears at the end of the chapter.
[4] Mr. S. G. Hamilton.

MICKLETON MANOR HOUSE.

lawsuit over them that lasted through the greater part of Queen Elizabeth's reign, so that it is not surprising to read in the old documents that Sir William's grandson William, "having wasted the property, died in great misery." [1]   But. in some way or other the family fortunes recovered themselves, and in the end of the sixteenth century there were two Porters living who could claim the title of "generosus," *i.e.*, gentleman, although neither of them rose to the rank of "armiger," nor could write himself "Justice of the Peace."   In 1588 Nicholas Porter and Dorothy his wife and ten children were living at the "Mansion House" at Aston, and were also occupying the leasehold property at Mickleton.   There can be little doubt that this Nicholas was the eldest son of the unlucky William who "died in misery" : the pedigree in the Harleian MSS. leaves one generation out ; but it is clear from the deeds of the property, and from the records of the lawsuit, that William had at least one son and two daughters, and he may very well have had more.   There is no doubt about his one son Edmund (probably baptised in 1546), who in 1591 was living in the handsome manor house of Mickleton with its mullioned windows and picturesque gables, while Nicholas lived down among the cherry orchards in the family mansion at Aston-under-Hill.   When Sir Edward Fisher bought the freehold of Mickleton and settled there in 1599, Edmund Porter seems to have moved to another house in the village, but it was in London, ultimately, that he died.

By that time his son Endymion had risen to a

[1] Cal. Dom. S. P., Eliz., 1592.

high position at Court, and had a house in the
Strand, and probably Edmund removed to town,
and spent the end of his life with his son or in
his immediate neighbourhood.

Nicholas Porter, of Aston, must have been a man
of good position, for among the godparents of his
children we find the names of Elizabeth, Lady
Boteler, the favourite sister of handsome George
Villiers, soon to be Duke of Buckingham ; of Fulke
Greville, Lord Brooke, the poet and friend of Philip
Sidney ; and one of the Colepeppers of Kent, that
brilliant and eccentric family, who, so popular tradition says, cannot even now lie still in their graves.[1]
It is curious that no record remains of the lives of
these ten children of Nicholas Porter, but it was
the boast of this loyal family that no less than
twenty-six gentlemen of the name suffered for the
cause of King Charles ; so doubtless the six sons
of Nicholas Porter are numbered in this roll of
honour. Their sisters bore poetical names,[2] Helnor
(probably Eleonora), Philippa, Cartwright, and
Dorita, but they are only names to us. Their
mother, Dorothy, died February 23, 1600. She
was the daughter of one Underhill. A letter to
Edmund Porter seems to indicate that Nicholas
died at Beaconsfield in 1613.[3]

Edmund Porter married his cousin Angela, a
charming and accomplished woman, who seems to
have had much influence over her children's lives.
Her father was Gyles Porter, grandson of Sir
William, the Sergeant-at-Arms. He was attached

---

[1] *Gent. Mag. Lib.*, "Pop. Superstitions," p. 121.
[2] Mr. S. G. Hamilton.
[3] Cal. Dom. S. P., 1613, Denys Rasingham to Edm. Porter.

to the English Embassy at Madrid,[1] and there he wooed and won a Spanish lady of high degree, Doña Juana de Figueroa y Mont Salve, probably a relation of the magnificent old Don Gomez de Figueroa, Count of Feria and Knight of the Golden Fleece, who had accompanied Philip the Second to England and married one of Queen Mary's Maids of Honour, Jane or Joanna, daughter of Sir William Dormer.[2] Another member of this Spanish family is mentioned in the English State Papers, John de Figueroy, who was frequently sent by Philip of Spain to carry messages to Queen Mary's Council.[3]

The Spanish records [4] tell romantic tales of the founder of the family of Figueroa, a heroic caballero of the very ancient house of Suarez, who opposed the Moorish demand of a tribute of a hundred Christian damsels, and rescued the captives at the head of a band of warriors. His spear was broken in the combat; so, tearing down the branch of a wild fig tree, he laid about him with it so valiantly that the unbelievers were put to flight, and the victor assumed the name of Figueroa and bore five green fig-leaves on his shield of gold in memory of the day. The original seat of this valiant family was in Galicia, one of its members was Comendado Mayor of Leon, and another fell in the Vega of Granada fighting against the Moors.[5] But however glorious were the records of the family, the match with Doña Juana did not find favour in the eyes of old Edmund Porter, Giles's father, and it is said that he went so far as to disinherit his son

---

[1] "Lords Strangford," p. 8. [2] Burke's Commoners, Dormer.
[3] Cal. Dom. S. P., 1556. [4] Nobiliario, Baños de Velasco.
[5] Ibid.

for the deed.[1]   Possibly so severe a penalty was only threatened in order to show that Mr. Porter disapproved of Spanish papists, for in 1588 Gyles had returned home, and we hear of him as living comfortably at Mickleton and paying £23 rent a year.[2]   He did not, however, give up his connection with the Embassy to Spain, for in 1605 he was employed as interpreter to Lord Admiral Nottingham's Spanish mission.   The English Ambassador, Lord Cornwallis, mentions that " Mr. Gyles Porter hath behaved himself very well, and with good allowance of all in his employ."   In spite of Gyles having a Spanish wife (or possibly because of it), he seems to have been no friend to the Catholics, and he kept a sharp eye on the movements of the Rector of the English Jesuits in Spain, "a verie busie fellow," who repaired oftener than Mr. Porter thought well to the Lord Admiral's lodgings.[3]   A James Porter is mentioned among the State Papers in 1598 as bringing home from Spain forty poor Englishmen who had been taken prisoners in the wars : very likely this James is a slip of the scribe's pen for Gyles, as we have no knowledge of any other Porter being employed in negotiations with Spain at this period.

Gyles and Doña Juana had three children, Lodowick, Angela, and Lucina (perhaps Lucia).[4]   Lucina probably died young, and Angela married her cousin Edmund Porter.   Lodowick was probably named after a neighbour, Lodovick Greville, of Mickleton.

[1] Harl. MSS., Pedigree, 1543, p. 69 b.
[2] Dom. S. P., Eliz., 1588.
[3] Winwood's " Memorials," vol. ii. p. 76.
[4] Harl. MSS., 1543, p. 69 b, " Visitation of Gloucestershire."

He seems to have been adopted by his Spanish relations, as the only-letter of his which is preserved is signed with the surnames of both his father and mother, Porter de Figueroa. It is written to his sister's husband, Edmund Porter, of Mickleton.

"DEAR BROTHER,—I did at one instant, and in one packet, receive three of yours, the one dated in July, the other in September, and the last in December. I could have been glad that they had come to my hands according to their date and severally as they were written, for then I should have avoided a good deal of unkind jealousy which I held of you; but I see the fault hath not been yours, wherefore I must crave pardon of you, and do promise to repair the wrong I have done you in coming to see you, which I will perform with all diligence so soon as I can by any means get licence as these. holidays are past. I will presently ask leave for some two or three months, which I will, God willing, spend with you. Your hawk I will bring myself; provide your mew ready. She shall be either a goshawk, a tassel of a goshawk, or a lanner; make your choice, and write me word suddenly what your choice is, for I have acquaintance with all the Archduke's falconers, and will fit your turn. I am undone for want of a good water dog, for I have a piece, and here is great store of fowl, and for want of a good dog I lose half the fowl I kill; it is all the entertainment I have this winter to pass the time. If you can make shift to provide me a dog, I will not fail you of a hawk. I could speak of a thousand particularities, which I will refer to my coming, which believe I am as desirous to perform as yourself can wish ; you do, I can assure you, enchant me with speaking of the good music you have, for if ever my humour did like of it, it is now more addicted unto it than ever heretofore it hath been. To my niece? (blotted) and nephew *Nedd?* I pray you remember me very lovingly, and so with my kindest salutations to yourself I ever rest, Brussels, this 3 of January, 1611,

> " Your assured loving brother,
>> " LUIS PORTER DE FIGUEROY."

" *(Endorsed)*

" To his very loving brother-in-law, Mr. Edmund Porter, at his house at Mickletone." [1]

In the year 1587 the eldest son of Edmund and Angela Porter was born at Mickleton Manor House and named Endymion. No parish registers of Mickleton were kept till three years later, so we have no means of knowing to what godfather the boy owed his poetical name. The Cannings of Foxcote, indeed, who were connected with the Porters by marriage, had an Endymion among them, but it is pleasanter to fancy that the name of Diana's votary may have been suggested by the poet and courtier, Lord Brooke, as a happy one for a child born under the queenly sceptre of the " Virgin throned by the West." It may be more than a mere coincidence that gave the boy the name of Lyly's play, the " Endymion," that was first performed before Elizabeth's Court in the year of his birth.

---

[1] Dom. S. P., vol. lxviii. No. 2.

Be that as it may, the name was fittingly bestowed. The boy grew up courteous and handsome, a lover of art and literature, with a certain poetry of emotion that a life of palace intrigue and political anxiety could never quite stifle.

He was fortunate in receiving a better education than fell to the lot of most country squire's sons. Spain was just then the fashionable place of education, and Endymion and his little brother Tom were early sent off beyond seas to their grandmother's Spanish relations. This does not necessarily imply that the boys were brought up Romanists. The Porters were trustees for Anglican charities and left legacies to the national Church; but those who wished for more than the ordinary grammar school training had long resorted to foreign teachers. "Italy begins to grow out of request," so writes a certain learned man about this period, "it being held dangerous to our nation both for health of body and soul," and Spain became preferred as a place for education. The English Ambassador, Sir John Cornwallis, brought a young kinsman with him to Spain, saying that it was "for better trayning up and attayning some perfection in the language," and later on, in 1617, the eldest son of Nicholas Porter's friend, Lady Boteler, was sent to Spain in the hope, vain as it proved, of curing him of a passion for drink that brought him to an early grave.[1]

The Spanish dignity and gravity, the Spanish dislike of duels, the more than elaborate etiquette, all formed a school of self restraint, very unlike the rough joviality of England in the time of King

[1] Chester Waters, vol. i. pp. 144-9.

James, and no doubt the polish acquired by Endymion from his Spanish education did much in later times to gain him the favour of the reserved and dignified Charles I. We know no details of the life led by the boys in Spain; but, if Howell's letters are to be trusted, Tom was placed at Valencia, and yellow-haired little Endymion was honoured by an appointment as page in the household of the great Count Olivares, the rising favourite in the Court of King Philip.[1] The position of a page, in a household where almost royal state was kept, was that of a gentleman in waiting,[2] not that of a servant, and was well fitted to train the boy for the life of a Court, and, it may be, to make him as familiar with secret ways of intrigue as with the ceremonious formalities of diplomatists.

When the brothers returned to England, Thomas was put to the sea, and later on he was in command of various king's ships, but his fortunes did not flourish as did those of Endymion, and we find the elder brother providing furniture and bedding for Tom's ships, and, in the end, paying the expenses of his funeral.

The family at Mickleton had gone on increasing in numbers while the first and second sons were away in Spain; Edmund was born in 1603, and. Gyles in 1611, and besides these were four older sisters, Elinor, Mary, Jane, and Margaret.

[1] Wilson's "James I.," p. 225. Clarendon, "Rebellion," vol. iv. p. 28.

[2] Compare "Peveril of the Peak," p. 107. "I had often feared I must have kept Giles to be the young master at home: and I have too little nurture myself to teach him much, and so he would have been a mere hunting hawking knight. But in your ladyship's household he will have all and more than all the education which I could desire."

PEDIGREE OF PORTER FAMILY.

From Mickleton and Aston parish registers and the Herald's "Visitation of Gloucestershire," 1623. Harl. MSS. 1543, p. 69.b. Arms Sable, three bells arg, a canton dexter erm. Crest. A portcullis or and arg.

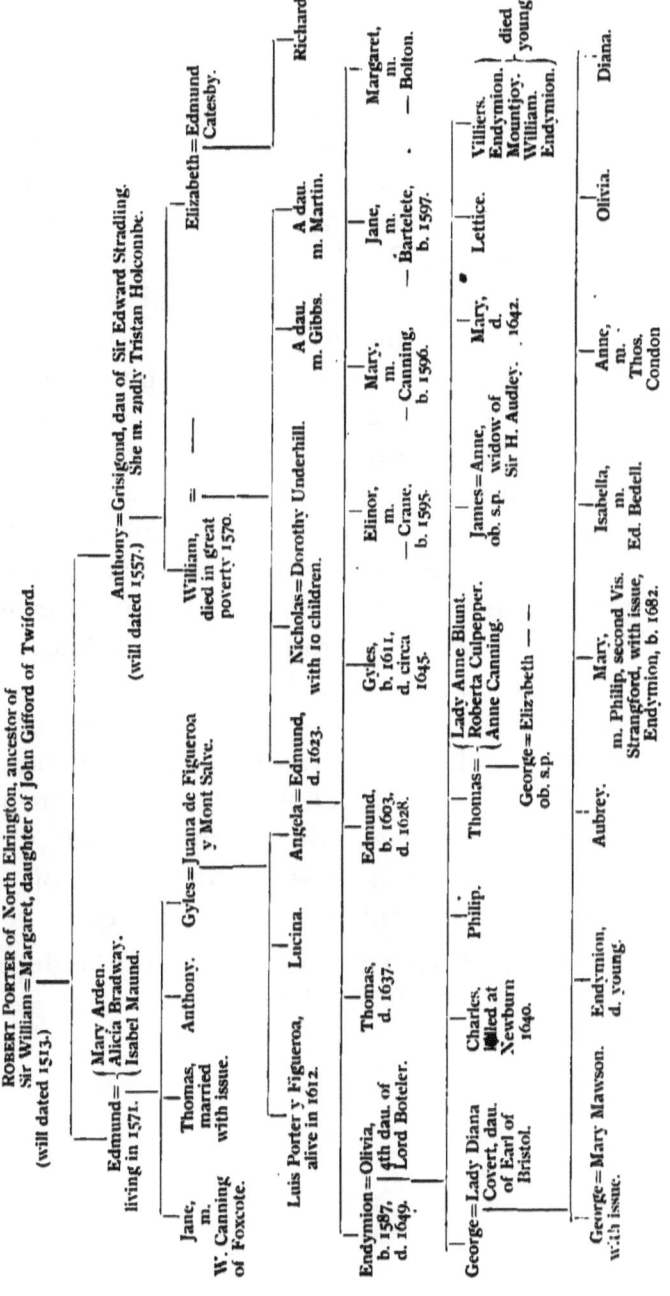

CHAPTER II

GETTING MARRIED

ENDYMION'S handsome face and Spanish education were not destined to be left for long in country obscurity. No doubt it was Lady Boteler's influence that helped the young man to enter the household of her brother, Sir Edward Villiers,[1] and from there he passed on to the service of the brilliant and handsome George Villiers, who soon afterwards became the all-powerful Duke of Buckingham. He promptly made Porter Master of his Horse, and entrusted to him his Spanish correspondence. Probably Porter was still a member of Buckingham's household in 1619, when he was admitted to Gray's Inn ; but he was clearly getting on in the world, for in that year we learn that he received a grant of certain fines and was also able to purchase back the family estates at Aston from his cousin, Richard Catesby.[2] Two years later the King granted him permission to hold a Court Leet for his manor, but a license to preserve game was not given him till the year 1634.

Porter's foot was now on the ladder of advancement, and he climbed swiftly. In 1620, or '21, he

[1] Wilson's " James I.," quoted in Nicholl's " Progresses," vol. iii.
[2] Mr. S. G. Hamilton's Papers.

was taken into the service of Prince Charles, and
was, as Anthony Wood says, "beloved by King
James for his admirable wit, and by Charles for his
general learning, brave style, sweet temper, great
experience of travels and modern languages."[1]
With all these advantages added to his handsome
face, it was natural that Court gossip should be
busy in finding a wife for the Prince's gentleman.
It was thought that 'he would make a match with
the widowed Lady Roos, who was wealthy and had
friends at the Spanish Court, but he had fixed his
affections on a greater lady still, namely, Olivia, the
young and beautiful daughter of Sir John Boteler,
of Woodhall, near Hatfield, and niece of his own
patron, the Duke of Buckingham. This seems to
have been a very worldly-wise proceeding, but it
was nevertheless as thorough a love match as ever
romance devised ; and for once prudence and love
went hand in hand. Olivia was a girl of much
charm and remarkable spirit, with no small share of
the decision and impetuosity of her splendid uncle.
Of their courtship we get but a glimpse, though
we may well imagine that with so high-spirited a
sweetheart it was hardly likely to be monotonously
smooth. One, and only one, of Endymion's early
letters to "his Mistress Olive" has been preserved,
but that one raises the curtain for a moment upon a
lover's quarrel that doubtless proved in the end,
according to the adage, to be but the renewing of
love.

[1] Ath. Ox., Edit. Bliss, vol. iii. p. 2.

Endymion Porter to his Mistress Olive.

" DEAR HEART,—I assure you that nothing could have prevented my writing to you but want of health, which hath been the cause I have not troubled you all this while with my letters.　I make no doubt that your careless disposition will not let you perish with any want of my lines, for I think that my presence affords you no more joy than my love obliges you to, nor my absence no more sorrow than you not caring whether you ever see me again or no, however you profess otherwise ; and this I gather by the salutation I had in the Park from you when I was last there, which strikes in my mind, but cannot any whit diminish that resolution I have so constantly settled in my thoughts to love you, for now I find that neither scorns from you, nor favours from any other creature can alter

　　　　　" Your servant,

　　　　　　　　" ENDYMION PORTER." [1]

The registers of Hatfield do not extend back so far as 1620, but it was probably in 1619 or '20 that Endymion Porter and Olivia Boteler were made man and wife.

Sir John Boteler was descended from the barons of Overstey, Wem, and Sudely, and he had been so fortunate as to marry the favourite sister of the Duke of Buckingham, whereby he had become a sharer in the benefits showered on the Royal favourite, without having, according to Bankes, "any merits, defects, or services" to account for

---

[1] Dom. S. P., James I., vol. cxviii. 74.

his good fortune. He was knighted in 1607, and was created Baron Boteler of Bramfield in the first year of King Charles's reign. But his good fortune did not descend to his family; his five elder sons died before him, and his heir and successor, William, was an idiot from his birth. We may anticipate the future for a moment to say that upon the death of this unhappy being the property passed away to his cousins, the Botelers of Walton Woodhall, and the rest of his family wealth was divided among his sisters as co-heiresses. The eldest, Audrey, married Francis Leigh, Earl of Chichester; the second, Eleanor, was wedded in succession to Sir John Drake of Ash, Devon, and to Sir Francis Anderson; she was ancestress of the great Duke of Marlborough. The third daughter, Jane, married James Ley, Earl of Marlborough.

> " That good Earl, once president
> Of England's council and her treasury,
> Who lived in both unstained with gold or fee,
> And left them both more in himself content." (1)

Olive, as we know, married Endymion Porter; Mary became the wife of the notorious Lord Howard of Escrick, and was ancestress of Lord Chatham; and Anne married Mountjoy, Earl of Newport.[2]

. The mansion at Woodhall, which had been bought by the grandfather of the first Baron Boteler, stood close to the royal palace of Hatfield. Hatfield was given by King James I. to Lord Salisbury in exchange for Theobalds; and later on, in 1690, Lord Salisbury bought Woodhall and pulled it

---

[1] Milton, "Sonnet to Lady Margaret Ley."
[2] Chester Waters, "Chesters of Chicheley," vol. i. pp. 144-9.

down.   No remains of this house are left now but a
brick wall and gateway.

Endymion and Olive began their married life
with good prospects in a pecuniary point of view ;
his name occurs repeatedly among the State Papers,
and always in connection with some grant of Crown
lands or of monopolies.   In forwarding a petition
of Endymion's to Lord Treasurer Middleton,[1]
Secretary Conway significantly reminded him
whose servant Porter had been and whose he
was then, and the world at Court never forgot
that he had been the favourite of the all-powerful
Buckingham as well as of Prince Charles.   But
Endymion's popularity at Court caused many sad
and lonely days to be spent by his young wife.   His
duty called him to attend the King on the many
royal progresses which were made throughout the
country, and in spite of his frequent love letters
Olive felt the separation bitterly, and seems to
have constantly echoed the complaint of the Duchess
of Buckingham to her husband, " Till you leave this
life of a courtier I shall ever think myself unhappy."

She passed most of these periods of solitude at
Woodhall with her father and mother, where she
not only had the company of her family, but was
within a ride, though a long one, of two Royal
residences (Royston and Theobalds), and was,
moreover, on the direct road from London to Newmarket, a situation which gave her the opportunity
of receiving not a few flying visits from her husband.

But to be parted at all so soon after they had
been made one was indeed a cruel lot, as witness

----

[1] Cal. Dom. S. P., 1619-23, pp. 78, 95.

the following letter, the first that we possess from Endymion to her after their marriage.

Probably her eldest son, George, was born at Woodhall. The registers of Hatfield do not begin early enough to give the needful information, but he died in 1683, aged sixty-three, so he must plainly have been born in 1620. He was named George after the Duke of Buckingham.

"*To my dear Wife, Olive Porter, these.*

"AT WOODHALL BY HATFIELD.

"MY DEAR OLIVE,—All the pleasure I can take now is in thinking on thee, and the best way to vent these thoughts in absence is by writing. Sweet love, I entertain myself with the prettiest delusions my fancies can afford, for I make a thousand means to represent thee unto me, and do assure myself many times I see that all happiness of mine, thyself. Wherewith I am infinitely contented, but not satisfied, nor ever shall, till God bless me with the continual being in thy company.

"At Woodstock I have commanded Charles to meet me, that I may hear of thy good health, which I pray for on my knees; and, best love, I intreat thee not to forget how much it concerns me thy preservation. For should thou do otherwise than well, I could not live, and let Him that is the punisher of all sins, lay some plague on me if I speak not as I think. Farewell, my soul's joy, and assure thyself I will live and die

"Thy ever-loving husband,

"ENDYMION PORTER.

"From RUFFORD, *this 12th of August*, 1621.

3

" Remember my service to your father and mother and to your sisters." [1]

" *To my dear Wife, Olive Porter, these.*

" MY SWEET OLIVE,—I can attain to no content till I be made happy in the sight of thy pleasing countenance.   Therefore do not again imagine that I will make the time longer than necessity may force me, but rather shorten it with all the hopes and desires these two days can afford.   Friday is the good one that will increase mine, by seeing myself owner of so much goodness and virtue as is in thee.   Be thou still so religious that thy prayers may preserve me from dangers, then shall I have two good angels to keep me from the inconveniences my bad one would draw me in ; and so shall you also be sure to enjoy the fruits of it in making me

" Your true, loving husband,
" ENDYMION PORTER." [2]

" *To my dear Wife, Olive Porter, these.*

" MY DEAREST LOVE,—Thy care in sending to me shows me how truly thou lovest me, and thy fear of my inconstancy argues no want of affection, but of faith, which if any good works of mine may strengthen, I will come on my knees to see thee, and put out my eyes, rather than look with an unchaste desire upon any creature whilst I breathe ; and to be more secure of me, I would have thee inquire if ever I was false to any friend, and then

---

[1] Dom. S. P., James I., vol. cxxii. 73.

[2] Dated in pencil, March 16, 1622.   Original in the possession of Mrs. Russell.

to consider what a traitor I should be, if to a wife, such a wife, so virtuous and good, I should prove false and not to my friends. Dear Olive, be assured that I strive to make myself happy in nothing but in thee. And therefore I charge you to be merry and to cherish your health and life the more, because I live in you. But what can I say, or what is the least little I can do? Love you. That I do and ever shall, as he that vows never to be anybody's but

" Your husband,

" ENDYMION PORTER.

" I have sent you a bribe which this progress hath afforded me, and I pray you remember my service to your father and mother and to the right honourable parties, and to Mall [1] and Nan and Jack, and to my sister Lee and my brother." [2]

Perhaps written in August, 1622.

" *To my dear Wife, Olive Porter, these.*

" MY DEAR HEART,—I cannot go farther and farther from you but with an infinite desire to hear of your amendment, although the sergeant told me that he left you much better, which was more welcome news to me than any other worldly happiness I could have heard of. Mend apace, my sweet love, and send me word of it, that you may keep me alive with that cordial.

" Your husband,

" ENDYMION PORTER.

" ROYSTON, *this Saturday.*"

---

[1] Mall, probably Mary Boteler, afterwards Lady Howard of Escrick. "Nan" is Lady Newport, "my sister Lee" Lady Ley.
[2] Dom. S. P., James I., vol. cxxii. 104.

"MY DEAR OLIVE,—Every time I part with thee I discover in myself more love than I have patience to live without thee; and am sorry for nothing but that I cannot be always with thee, but that God out of His divine wisdom thought it too great a happiness to give me thee and thy company, lest I should forget there were any other glory. Sweet Olive, I thank you for your kind letter, and I protest to God I love you so as this last absence seems to me more than any I have hitherto . endured, therefore believe that Friday shall be the festival day of the greatest joy this world can afford me, till when and ever I will be

"Thy true loving husband,

"ENDYMION PORTER." [1]

" *To my dear Wife, Olive Porter, these.*

" BEST LOVE,—Thy grief is but a copy of mine, for our absence, though marriage divides it, yet the whole share of discontent for the same belongs to me; and therefore I beseech thee be merry, and do not meddle with that which is mine, that dull sorrow, that can find no remedy for itself but thy sweet company; let it alone for me. Your mother's ill council cannot corrupt your goodness, but your obedience shall tie me to be ever

"Your most faithful loving husband,

"ENDYMION PORTER.

" I pray commend me to Mr. Hukeley." [2] .

---

[1] Dom. S. P., James I., vol. cxxiv. 140-1.
[2] Ibid., vol. cxxiv. 142.

" *To my dear Wife, Olive Porter, these.*

"AT WOODHALL.

" DEAR HEART,—Let all the true friendship that ever was between friends, and all the best affection that hath been in the world betwixt man and wife, present my unfeigned love to thee, and let that love enjoy so much happiness as for my sake you would be merry and believe that I am not absent. For whenever I go to sleep I send my soul to watch with thee, and whatsoever waking I can see with mine eyes, I look on it, through thee ; for if it be a beauty it is none to me, my thoughts do so prefer thine, that I see nothing but thy goodness and love, which makes me happier in thee than the world can with all the rest of the pleasures it can afford. I have sent thee three shirts, and the fourth I keep back to make it an occasion of another letter betwixt this and Friday next, till when I shall not enjoy thy pretty desired company, but I hope in God (by thy good prayers to Him) we shall come to take our rest together and to give Him many thanks for having made thee my wife and me

" Thy loving husband,

" ENDYMION PORTER.

" Do not trouble yourself to answer my letters, but forget not to love me."

" *To my dear Wife, Olive Porter, these.*

" This day, my sweetest love, I write unto thee, and make no doubt but that you are as well acquainted with my heart as with my hand, yet because I received one from you, I thought it want of true love to send this messenger without a letter, although so many may weary and clog you, and you may think that I overtell you that I love you, because it is no new thing but the very same affection, your old friend, grown somewhat bigger since you first knew it : nor would I have your thoughts to seek out answers for my lines, but when you can afford me news of your health in one, I will esteem it as a large epistle of your love ; let it therefore suffice that you know that neither fortune can make me rich without you, nor misery make me poor, so long as I enjoy you and give myself the title of

"Your husband,

"ENDYMION PORTER.

"Send me word if it be so."[1]

"*To my dear Wife, Olive Porter, these.*

"MY DEAR OLIVE,—God of heaven bless thee and send thee a very safe delivery ; my lord will by no means consent that I should come unto you, which grieves me extremely, and for God's sake believe it, there never happened a thing that doth so much trouble me. Good sweetheart, show thy love to me now in excusing to thyself the wrong I do thee to thyself, in not leaving the commands of a master to see so good a wife, at such a time. I protest to God, I am distracted with discontent and know not what to say more than that I love thee as my life and will ever be thine both friend and your husband,

"ENDYMION PORTER."[2]

---

[1] Dom. S. P., vol. cxxiv. 145.
[2] Ibid., vol. cxxiv. 144.

" To my dear Wife, Olive Porter, these.

"My only Love,—This night will divide me from the happiness of seeing thee, but to-morrow I shall enjoy that company of thine which indeed I must confess I' do not deserve ; for my man tells me you say I might have lost a wife ; I do confess I might and such a one, as the world hath not the like. But since God hath preserved you as a greater blessing for me, I give Him thanks and acknowledge my unworthiness, praying to the Almighty to bestow on thee as many graces as He can, that thou mayst be blessed and thy posterity and that I may never forget to be

"Thy loving husband,
"ENDYMION PORTER.

"On Wednesday your young gentleman will be Georgified : pray God bless it." [1]

" To my dear Wife, Olive Porter, these.

"My sweet Love,—Although it be very ill news to hear of George his being not well, yet the good news they bring me of thy health makes amends for that, or any misfortune that can come to me, and, dear Olive, believe me, that I love George for having such a mother, as well as for being my own flesh and blood. I hope it is nothing but breeding of teeth, and when they come forth he will be well. In the meantime if you love me, be not overmuch discontented with anything that may happen, for God who is the giver of all good things can take them away when He pleaseth, and His divine will be done.

[1] Dom. S. P., vol. cxxiv. 147.

"And, sweetest Heart, I thank you for your letter, although I perceive by that, you mistake mine, for I protest to the Almighty that I believe thy love to me to be serious and thy tears unfeigned, and think myself happy in nothing but thee.

"Farewell, and God bless thee and George.　I will live and die thy faithful loving husband.

"ENDYMION PORTER." [1]

"*To my dear Wife, Olive Porter, these.*

"MY ONLY SWEETHEART,—The great desire I have to see theé keeps alive thine image in me, and the extraordinary love which I receive from thee makes me discover mine with as much zeal as my poor understanding will afford, for I am sure I do outlove you, and will be a precedent to all mankind if ever I have occasion to show how a husband ought to love so good a wife.　Be happy in all thou thinkest of me, if any deserts in me can make thee so, for be assured that I will never change. God bless thy child and make him a Saint George, and let not your prayers be wanting for your true friend and your loving husband,

"ENDYMION PORTER." [2]

"*To your Sister, my Wife, Olive Porter, these.*

"MY GOOD OLIVE,—What with the grief of parting with you and the weariness of the way, I came to Newmarket sick and tired; but since, I have been very well, and am like to continue so, unless I shall hear that you want health, which I hope never to do as long as I live, for if I should,

---

[1] Dom. S. P., vol. cxxiv. 148.
[2] Ibid., vol. cxxiv. 149.

I know poison cannot take a speedier course to
shorten my days than that. sorrow would finish
them.   Therefore, as you love me, make much of
yourself, and cherish with care that on which all my
happiness depends, and still remember to pray for
me that God may bless us both with such love
to one another, as neither diseases nor age may
alter our affection.

"The Lord bless little George, and give him
grace to be good and virtuous.   I will never forget to be thy

"True loving husband,

"That will not go to Saxum,"

"ENDYMION PORTER."[1]

It was jealousy, jealousy and nothing less, that
caused his good Olive to wish her true. loving
husband not to go to "Saxum."   Saxham was the
house of Sir John Crofts near Newmarket, and Sir
John had three lovely and witty daughters, who
were great favourites with King James.[2]   The fair
sisters invited the whole Court over to a Masque in
1620.   In 1622 it is recorded that the King went
a-shroving to Saxham, and that Lady Crofts and
her beautiful daughter Cicily were much at Court.

Cicily married Thomas Killigrew, gentleman of
the bedchamber.   Her sisters made great matches,
Anne marrying Lord Wentworth, Earl of Cleve-
land, while Dorothy married Sir John Bennett, and
was the mother of Ossulton and Arlington.

After Endymion purchased the family property

[1] Dom. S. P., vol. cxxiv. 150.
[2] Nicholl's "Royal Progresses," James I., vol. iii. p. 587.

at Aston, he and Olivia occasionally went down
there, but it seems to have been too far from
London to be visited very often.

Herrick, in several poems addressed to Endymion,
credits him with country tastes, nor need this be
regarded as merely a poetic fiction. Town and
country life were not so sharply separated then as
now. When a good part of a gentleman's food
came from his own farm, and his money was
derived from agricultural rents, it was natural
that he should himself take no small interest in
the management of his land, and that good Robert
Bee, the steward, should go into many small details
in his letters to his master, when he sent him the
Aston accounts at the year's end. But Herrick,
not having a wife's bills for jewellery and Court
dresses to pay, is inclined to take a more romantic
view of country life. He describes how Endymion
may

> "Walk about thine own dear bounds,
> Not envying others' larger grounds,
> For well thou know'st not the extent
> Of land makes life, but sweet content.
> When now the cock, the ploughman's horn,
> Calls forth the lily-wristed morn,
> Then to thy cornfields thou dost go,
> Which tho' well soiled, yet thou dost know
> That the best compost for the lands
> Is the wise master's feet and hands.
> . . . This done then to the enamelled meads
> Thou goest, and as thy foot there treads ,
> Thou seest a present godlike power
> Imprinted in each herb and flower,
> And smell'st the breath of great-eyed kine,
> Sweet as the blossoms of the vine."

But there were livelier proceedings at Aston than
supervising the cornfields and enamelled meads; one
of Endymion's friends and neighbours was the cele-

brated Robert Dover,[1] the founder of the Olympic Cotteswold Games. These games were celebrated on a rising ground above Mickleton, about a mile from Chipping Campden; there, above the broad green vale that stretches away across to the Malvern Hills, the country folk assembled at Whitsuntide, and danced, and raced, and sang, and wrestled, and enjoyed the various sports which Mr. Dover trusted "would imbue the people of the neighbourhood with chivalrous valour."

Mr. Dover was master of the revels, riding about on a fine horse, arrayed in a suit of clothes which had belonged to King James himself, and had been presented by him to Mr. Dover, through Endymion Porter, for the greater encouragement of this patriotic undertaking. And among the assembled gentry around Mr. Dover in his high hat and padded suit, were young Mr. Porter with his Spanish elegance, and a tribe of Porter cousins from the neighbourhood; and more distinguished guests were there; D'Avenant and the great Ben Jonson himself came to honour the sports with their presence, and write sonnets in their praise;[2] and who knows whether a certain Mr. William Shakespeare may not have ridden over from Stratford, through the orchards, on one of those gay Whit-Thursdays, to see Justice Shallow's greyhound outrun on Cotsall.

Even for an ambitious young man it must have been hard to leave this fair western home for the gilded slavery of the Court where a rising favourite

---

[1] A deed witnessed by Mr. Dover is among the Porter Papers (Mr. Hamilton).
[2] "Annalia Dubriensia."

had to work very reasonably hard to keep his position.

Herrick, under the name of Lycidas, reproved Endymion for forsaking that country life, which the poet himself did not love quite so much in reality as in pastoral verse.

> "In this regard that thou dost play
> Upon another plain,
> And for a rural roundelay
> Strik'st now a courtly strain,
> Thou leav'st our hills, our dales, our bowers,
> Our finer fleeced sheep,
> Unkind to us, to spend thy hours
> Where shepherds should not keep.
> I mean the court : let Latmos be
> My loved Endymion's court.
> (*Endymion*) But I the courtly state would see.
> (*Lycidas*)   Then see it in report.
> Break, if thou lov'st me, this delay.
> (*Endymion*) Dear Lycidas, ere long
> I vow by Pan to come away
> And pipe unto thy song.
> Then Jessamine with Floribel
> And dainty Amaryllis,
> And handsome-handed Drosomel
> Shall prank thy hook with lilies.
> (*Lycidas*)   Then Tyterus and Corydon
> And Thyrsis, they shall follow
> With all the rest, while thou alone
> Shalt lead like young Apollo ;
> And till thou canst, thy Lycidas
> In every genial cup
> Shall write in spice, Endymion 'twas
> That kept his piping up."

Once, at least, we know that Endymion went down to Aston without his wife, but his letter to her from thence makes no reference to any errand of business or pleasure ; he mentions neither Lycidas nor Mr. Dover, neither cousins nor stewards' accounts ; with lover-like eagerness all that Endymion notices at Aston is his wife's picture.[1]

"*To my dear Wife, Olive Porter.*

"Do not think it any neglect in me my not coming to see you since my departure, for as I hope to be saved, there is nothing in the world so pleasing as thy sight, nor a greater affliction for me than thine absence. I was at Aston where I had the happiness to see thy picture, and that did somewhat please me, but when I found it wanted that pretty discourse which thy sweet company doth afford I kist it with a great deal of devotion, and with many wishes for the original, there I left it. Now I am coming nearer towards you, but cannot as yet have so great a blessing as these lines shall have, to be seen by you, but when the King comes to Windsor I will hazard the loss of all my friends, rather than be a day longer from thee. In the meantime let our souls kiss and my faith and true love shall never fail to assure thee that though fortune hath not given you a rich and powerful man yet God hath bestowed one on you that will live and die
"Your true loving husband,
"ENDYMION PORTER."

Once, at least, too, Olivia seems to have been left at Aston while her husband was attending on a royal progress, in which it would appear that her sister, Lady Newport, was also taking part and sympathising with poor forlorn Endymion in being thus separated from his Olivia.

[1] Morrison Collect. of MSS.

" To my dear Wife, Olive Porter, these.

" ASTON.

" SWEET LOVE,—Thy welcome letter did revive
me and afforded me more content than all the
pleasures I have seen in this tedious progress ; yet
I must confess that the company of your good
sister represented unto me a good deal of happiness, for she did still wish for you as if she would
outwish me, but I am sure that if our desires were
seen mine would prove much the greater ; but for a
sister's love (to give her what's her due) I think it
reacheth to the skirts of mine and might serve as
a dwarf to my giant love, for I am sure where all
natural love ends there mine begins, and can never
diminish as long as your virtuous thoughts cherish
it : for when my eyes, by gazing after any other
beauty, offend you, let them fall out, and if my
mind shall harbour a thought that is not of you, I
wish it may become as blind with ignorance, as they
for want of light, and when I shall alter from this, I
wish the body may perish with the eyes and mind.

" Some ten days hence I hope to see you, which
seems an age to me, in the meanwhile, take my
soul and let that enjoy your happy company till I
come and give you a true account, how you are
esteemed of by your husband,

" ENDYMION PORTER.

" You sent me word in your letter to Salisbury
that you hoped I did not think what I spoke on the
hill, which subject hath made me a poet, and I have
sent you the fruits of my labour here." [1]

Unfortunately the verses are not preserved.

[1] Dom. S. P., James I., vol. cxxiv. No. 143.

CHAPTER III

AS if the cruel partings enforced on these married lovers by the gay Court progresses round England were not enough to bear, fortune was now preparing to separate them more widely.

Endymion's connections and education had from the first commended him to Buckingham as a fit secretary to carry on correspondence with Spain, and his importance increased as Buckingham and his royal master both fell captives to Spanish fascinations.

The memories of the days of the great Emperor Charles V. still cast a golden veil over the waning greatness of Spain, and the semi-oriental pomp and formalities of the Court of Madrid, still partly concealed its real poverty. In truth, Spain was growing yearly poorer, and she was not really the richer for all the gold mines that dazzled the imagination of King James and the rest of Europe ; she had neither trade nor manufacture, she had nothing but memories.

But there was no veil at all cast over the needs of the King of England. He had an expensive family and magnificent ideas. His parliament was tired of voting funds to be squandered on favourites or muddled away by mismanagement. It was no agreeable task to him to be compelled to beg for more, and in his judgment it was a vile degradation for a monarch by divine right to have to come cringing to his parliament for money.

Further, the old king believed that he had a divine mission to give good advice to all the nations upon earth, and compose their differences with no expense but fair words. He had given England peace with Spain,[1] as the greatest, possibly the only, benefit of his reign, and now a Spanish marriage might be the coping-stone of his pacific designs. "Beati pacifici" is engraved round his portrait as the motto of his choice, and just now he had specially strong reasons to desire peace, for his son-in-law, the Elector Palatine, by a wild clutch at the Bohemian crown had been swept into the vortex of the war that was devastating Germany and driven from his electorate. James hated war, he hated decided action, he hated spending money abroad, and it seemed as if this very inconvenient son-in-law would drive him into all the courses which he most disliked. But to his mind there was one brilliant solution for all his difficulties—marry the Prince of Wales to the Spanish Infanta. Then the two great western nations, England and Spain, would give peace to the world, then Spanish influence would alter the whole course of European politics, and replace Frederick in his electorate, a humbler and a wiser man. Spanish gold would fill the coffers of the English king, and every one would be happy.

The King's ingenious scheme was not, however, very popular in the English Parliament. The

[1] Seeley, "Growth of Brit. Policy," vol. i. p. 329.

country had not yet accustomed itself to look on Spain as an ally instead of an enemy. England would have preferred a more forward policy—to marry the Prince to some Protestant lady and aid the Protestant Elector and his wife, the Queen of Hearts, with English money and English men.

But Gondomar, the Spanish Ambassador, knew how to play the game. With jests and flattery the wily diplomatist won his way with the old King, and made of Buckingham a mere tool to carry out Spanish schemes. The Prince was, on the whole, indifferent ; shy, reserved, refined, he detested the idea of a marriage of convenience, and "wished it were no sin to have two wives, one for purposes of state, and one to please himself." But he was warmly attached to his sister, the Elector's wife, and, since marry he must, he was ready to endure any marriage that might be of service to her cause.

All through these slow negotiations Porter was acting as Secretary, and at last, in October, 1622, it was decided to send him off to Madrid as the bearer of a final proposal. England was weary of Spanish delays and excuses ; the business never advanced ; and now the dispatches which Endymion was to carry to Lord Bristol, the English Ambassador, commanded him to break off all matrimonial nego-tiations, unless the Spanish king declared himself ready in ten days to assist the Elector with a Spanish army, or at least to allow the English forces to march through Flanders for that purpose.

But this very peremptory message was not the only one that Porter bore ; he had secret instruc-tions of a very different character. He was directed to tell Bristol that, rather than lose the Spanish match, he was to offer even better terms than before, and to promise that any children born to the Spanish princess might be educated by their Catholic mother till they were nine years old, a concession that would have raised no slight storm had it been known in England.

This proposal was large, yet Buckingham was devising even more startling schemes. He was personally jealous of Bristol, and sure that no plan could succeed that was not managed by himself; so he absolutely wrote to his Spanish friends that the Admiral was getting the fleet ready, and that he himself intended to take "his friend" (Prince Charles) with him to Spain, to bring home "the beautiful angel."

But the old King and the Council had no hint of this wild scheme, and as Porter left the royal presence, all joined in the farewell cry, " Bring us war, bring us war!" It was " much marvelled that having already in Spain an ordinary and an extra-ordinary ambassador, besides an agent, there should be need of another messenger of his quality," wrote Mr. Joseph Meade in a news-letter.[1] Sir Francis Nethersole also said it was suspected that the King had given Porter private instructions differing from those delivered by the Council, as well as letters written by his own hand, of which none knew the contents.

Endymion probably crossed the Channel in a ship commanded by his brother Tom; certainly Tom was with him at the disastrous close of the short voyage, when the vessel grounded near Calais. The passengers hurried over the side into a boat,

[1] "Court and Times of James I.," vol. ii. p. 344.

but in leaping down Endymion missed his footing
and fell, breaking his shoulder, and his servant
trying to follow him, jumped short, fell into the
sea, and was drowned. There is another version
of the accident which says, that a collision took
place between two vessels as they neared Calais,
and that it was in "throwing himself upon the
larger ship" that Endymion fell; and his ill-fated
servant slipped down and was crushed between the
two ships. "The Roman augurs," remarked Mr.
Meade in his journal, "would have taken this for
an ominous sign of the success of the business.[1]

The unlucky Endymion in his crippled state was
obliged to stay for some time at Calais, where
instructions were sent him not only to forward
his letters to Spain, but to follow himself in person
as soon as he was able, which latter command confirmed the public fears that in very truth some confidential and important messages had been secretly
entrusted to him. Two letters written during this
stay at Calais are preserved. The first shows that,
though he was thoroughly cross and miserable, he
would not frighten his wife by telling her of his
accident till he was quite recovered.

" *To my dear loving Wife, Olive Porter, these.*

"MY SWEETEST OLIVE,—I am on my journey,
and Tom will acquaint you how I do. I am fearful
that the King's favour to you may make you lessen
your care of me, but I know thy everlasting love
will not let thee look upon anything but my return,

[1] "Court and Times of James I.," vol. ii. p. 344.

which the hopes to see thee will be much suddener than otherwise it could. All I can say is that I love thee better than my life and nothing shall alter
"Your true loving husband,
"ENDYMION PORTER."[1]

"MY DEAR OLIVE,—Although I writ you in my last that I was well, it was not being so, for I had my share of the hurt and all the misfortune. My shoulder was broken, which now is as well as ever it was in my life, and Tom and I are very merry, and do heartily drink your health, wishing it were possible to have you here with us.

"On Wednesday, if it please God, I propose to go to Spain, till when I have intreated my brother to stay with me, and then I will write you more at large. My sweet and kind Olive, I protest unto God I am now merry, well, and joyed to think how thy good prayers did preserve me; when I return I will thank thee with as many kisses as thou canst let me take, wherein I know thy bounty will afford an equality to my desires. God in heaven bless little George and make him a dutiful child to thee and his grandmother, to whom I desire to be remembered, for I love her dearly, and I pray you forget me not to Sir John and my Lady, and to Mall, and all the rest of our worthy friends.

"Farewell, dearest love,
"Your true loving husband,
"ENDYMION PORTER."
"CALAIS, *this Monday morning*,
"*the* 14*th of October*, 1622.

---

[1] Dom. S. P., vol. cxxxiii. 40.

" As I hope to be saved, my brother is very weel,
I thank God for itt, and I ame

" Youer trew lovinge brother,

" THOMAS PORTER." [1]

On the 1st of November Porter reached Madrid,
and was told the King was away hunting. King
Philip the Fourth was a mere boy of seventeen, and
not at all eager for the English match. His father,
on his death-bed, had bidden Philip make his sister
an Empress, and, as the poor girl herself detested
the idea of a marriage with a heretic, Philip was
unwilling to force her into it. He was, however,
almost entirely absorbed in his own amusements,
and the real ruler of Spain was the favourite
Olivares, a man both honest, intelligent, and
resolute, but one who, like a true Spaniard, was
unable to realise that any nation or any individual
might hold other views than his own. He quite
agreed with King James that the proposed marriage
might solve many difficulties, but there his agreement stopped. If Spain condescended to honour
England with the hand of the Infanta, she certainly
need not be called on to make any further concessions, or to take any new line about the Palatinate;
but he was, on the other hand, determined that
England should remove the galling and oppressive
disabilities from English Romanists, and he hoped
the marriage might even end in restoring the
heretical Prince of Wales and all his people to the
fold of the true Church.

Buckingham had probably told Porter to consider
himself free to act independently of the stately

[1] Fontblanque, "Lords Strangford," p. 24.

English Ambassador, Lord Bristol. At any rate, Endymion decided to waste no time in the delays so dear to the Spanish Court, "the hospital of hope and the grave of the living," as Cornwallis, a former envoy, had well called it. Olivares was no stranger, as Porter had once been a page in his household, so instead of waiting for the formalities of a tedious etiquette which he remembered only too well, he went straight to his former patron, and asked him plainly for an engagement that the Spanish Army in the Palatinate should support the English troops under Vere. Olivares was startled out of his self-control, and betrayed himself. He exclaimed that it was preposterous to expect the King of Spain to take arms against his Catholic allies, and "as for this marriage," said he, " I know not what it means."

Endymion had got what he wanted. It mattered little to him that next day Olivares sought to cover his blunder by telling Bristol that " Porter was not a public minister and it was unfit to trust State secrets to such a man."

Bristol was unwilling to admit that his work had failed, that the negotiations were at a standstill, and that Spain, even if she wished, could do little in the Palatinate ; thus the solemn farce proceeded, every player in it too much absorbed in himself to guess what his antagonist might do next. The Pope was asked to grant the needful dispensation for the heretical marriage, the arrangements for the Infanta's future household were discussed, and fresh articles were drawn up, with which Porter started back to England on the 13th of December.

No word had been breathed to Bristol of Buckingham's wild scheme, but no doubt Porter

saw that nothing would come of these half-hearted
negotiations unless the Spanish hand were forced,
and so he gladly carried a private message to the
Prince from Gondomar (who was just now in Spain),
welcoming the project of his visiting Madrid.   On
the 3rd of January, 1623, Endymion arrived in
England, and on the 15th of February his second
son was baptised and given the name of Charles, a
clear proof that the Prince, at any rate, was not
dissatisfied with Endymion's diplomacy.

Opposition was by this time beginning to awaken
the natural obstinacy of Prince Charles and give him
some inclination towards the marriage.   It was easy
for Buckingham to make good use of Gondomar's
message and imbue Charles with the belief that the
business must inevitably be mismanaged unless the
bridegroom undertook it himself, and that the really
chivalrous thing would be to go and fetch his bride
home in person, as his father had done before him.
Like a knight of old, he would face the diplomatic
dragons and carry off his lady-love in spite of Pope
or King.

Clarendon's account of the scene that followed
with King James is very dramatic.   The Prince, on
his knees, confessed his desire to journey to Spain,
and urged his request with great importunity, while
the Marquess (Buckingham was not yet made
Duke) stood by for a long time without saying a
word ; at last he joined in, and through their
vehement persuasions "the King, with less hesitation
than his nature was accustomed to, and much less
than was agreeable to his great wisdom, gave his
approbation." [1]   But when the two vehement young

[1] Clarendon, "Great Rebellion," vol. i. pt. i. pp. 17–25.

men were gone out, it did not need any great
wisdom in the King to see upon reflection the im-
prudence of the proposed journey, the risks to
which his only son would be exposed, and the
advantage which the possession of the Prince's
person would give to any evil-disposed councillors
in Spain.

These considerations were so terrible to him, that
the next time the Prince and the Marquess came he
fell into a great passion and told them, with tears,
that he was undone and that it would break his
heart if they pursued their resolution. The Prince
reminded the King of his promise, and the Marquess,
"who knew what kind of arguments were of
prevalence with him," treated him more rudely, until
at last the Prince's "humble and importunate en-
treaty and my lord Buckingham's rougher dialect
prevailed," and the King consented to an immediate departure. The young men then said
that as it had been decided, for the sake of
secrecy and haste, that they should only take two
more in their company, "they had thought (if he
approved of them) upon Sir Francis Cottington and
Endymion Porter, who, though they might safely,
should not be trusted with the secret till they were
ready to be embarked." "The persons were both
grateful to the King, the former having been long
his Majesty's Agent in Spain and was now Secretary to the Prince ; the other, having been bred in
Madrid, after many years' attendance upon the
Duke was now one of the bed-chamber to the
Prince ; so that his Majesty cheerfully approved
the election they had made, and desired it might
presently be imparted to the two gentlemen, saying

that many things would occur to them as necessary to the journey that they two would never think of."

Accordingly Sir Francis was sent for into the ante-room. "Cottington," said the King, "here is Baby Charles and Stenny, who have a great mind to go by post into Spain to fetch home the Infanta, and will have but two more in their company, and have chosen you for one—what think you of the journey?" Cottington often protested afterwards that when he heard the King he fell into such a trembling that he could hardly speak, but he made answer by reminding the King of the most obvious objection to the scheme; upon which the King threw himself upon his bed crying out, "I told you this before," and fell into a new passion and lamented loudly that he was undone, and should lose Baby Charles. At this there appeared displeasure and vexation in the countenances of the Prince and of Buckingham, and the latter exclaimed, angrily enough, that, as soon as the King sent for Cottington, he had himself whispered in the Prince's ear that Sir Francis would be against it, and thereupon he turned upon Cottington with all possible bitterness, and reproached him with a thousand hard words. But this violent outburst on the part of Buckingham only threw the poor King into a new agony on the behalf of a servant who, as he foresaw, was doomed to suffer for having answered his question honestly, and he said with some commotion, "Nay, by God, Stenny, you are very much to blame to use him so! He answered me directly to the question I asked him, and very honestly and wisely ; and yet you know he said no more than I told you before he was called in."

However, in spite of the King's better judgment
and Cottington's warnings, the journey was immediately agreed on, but the King saw plainly
that the scheme was really of Buckingham's devising, and, it is said, never quite forgave him
for it.

The Prince and Buckingham started from
Theobalds, giving out that they were riding to
Buckingham's house of Newhall ; then putting on
false beards they started with all speed for the
coast, calling themselves John and Tom Smith,
servants to Sir Francis Cottington. "But their
fine coats," says the news-letter, "gave suspicion
they were no such manner of men."[1] Buckingham
increased the suspicion with which they were viewed
by giving the ferryman at Gravesend a purse of
gold, so that he, supposing them to be duellists,
intending to cross the sea to fight, gave information
to the magistrates, and they were pursued, and only
escaped by the swiftness of their horses. Porter and
three other gentlemen had been sent to await them
at Dover, with such secrecy that Porter was not
even allowed to say farewell to his wife. As soon,
however, as the party reached Paris, he lost no time
in writing his explanations to her.

"MY DEAR OLIVE,—Since my departing from
you I have enjoyed very little content, although I
have had health and everything I could desire,
wanting nothing but your sweet company, by which
you may perceive in how great a measure I esteem
yours, that can prefer it before a Prince's and a
Lord's, both of whom I honour and love as my

---

[1] "Court and Times of James I.," vol. ii. p. 366.

life, and the worst of whom would serve for company to the best man living. I give God thanks we are all safely arrived at Paris, where it hath pleased his Highness and my lord to stay this day to see the town. To-morrow we set forwards from hence towards Spain, and, good Olive, let us have your prayers every day along with us to help to conduct us thither. I make no doubt but we shall have them the heartier for our return; because I fear there may be a grudge remaining still in you for not acquainting you first with my journey, but I was conjured to the contrary by my master, which I hope will fully satisfy you that I ought not to have done it.

"I would have you send Charles and the Spaniard along with the Prince's servants that come by sea. They are to be allowed as my men to come in the ship, and let them bring me one dozen of shirts, and little George his picture, and yours in the gold case which is at Gerbier's, and half a dozen pairs of silk stockings, three black and three colours, and your chain of diamonds, and let me intreat you to make much of yourself that I may hear of your health, which news will somewhat mitigate the pain of this absence.

"Little George and Charles will serve to put you in mind how much you are to love me, and my own conscience shall make me remember that I am not to do anything that may offend the faith I owe to so good a wife. Farewell, sweet Olive, and God Almighty bless thee and thine. I will ever be thy true loving husband,

"ENDYMION PORTER.

"PARIS, *this 22nd day of February*, 1623.

" You must not let it be known from me whither we are gone, but say you know nothing, nor speak to Charles till you hear further from me of coming, for the Prince will not have it spoken of, and I charge you not to tell anybody whither I am gone. Remember my humble duty to my mother and burn this letter." [1]

In Paris the Prince's lightly worn disguise was soon penetrated ; and he was received with all royal hospitality ; and then,, after making but a short stay, " the sweet boys and dear venturous knights worthy to be put in a romance," to use King James's phraseology, set their faces southward for Spain.

We know less of the Prince's adventures on the way than of those which befell the gentlemen who followed him in a couple of months' time. They described the road as " terribly stoney," part of it a narrow passage two feet broad passing over snowy mountains like a stair. One village Sir Richard Wynn was clear " the devil himself doth inhabit, if he dwelleth on earth." Their lodging there had no windows and the floors " were without a foot that wanted holes." They were provided with neither table nor stools for the supper ; " with much ado we got a piece of timber round which we stood and gave God thanks for what we had."

When all was well over, the old King used to retail his son's adventures with delight, " and all the accidents by the way, how many falls they had, the Lord Marquis seven, Sir Francis Cottington twelve and so on of the rest, only the Prince had never one." Perhaps the Prince's luck was due to his

---

[1] Fontblanque, " Lords Strangford," p. 27.

being mounted on the best horse of the party ; Sir
Richard Wynn and his friends could find nothing
to ride but pack mules with no bridles, so that when
the mule of Dr. Maw, the chaplain, " began with
infinite bounces to teach the churchman how to
prove a good horseman," the lesson ended in the
poor cleric "lighting full on his head and shoulders,
where he lay groaning and his mule went into the
river."

The Prince travelled 750 miles in thirteen days,
an average rate of nearly sixty miles a day.   He
rode, at any rate, like no laggard in love.   As the
party approached Madrid, he left Cottington and
Porter half a day's journey behind, and galloped on
with Buckingham and the guide.   They reached
the Earl of Bristol's house at eight of the night on
March 7th, and desired to speak presently with His
Lordship as having a letter to deliver him from Mr.
Cottington, who was behind and had a mischance
by the way ; they having promised to speak with
his Lordship before they went to their lodging.
The servant said that his Lordship was retired into
his study and there was busy about his papers, yet
upon their importunity the servant went in to him,
who sent for them up.   " The Marquess came in
first," says Howell, " with a portmanteau under his
arm, then the Prince who stayed awhile on t'other
side of the street in the dark."   They were brought
through the Countess' chamber into Lord Bristol's
study and then they made themselves known.   We
may imagine the dismay of the harassed diplomatist,
when his visitors threw off their cloaks and he
beheld the handsome faces of the Prince and his
favourite, radiant with glee at the trick they had

played. Here was the precious heir to the throne of England walking calmly into a trap, and his friend Buckingham bent on nothing but amusing himself and thwarting the unhappy Ambassador whose business it was to represent the English crown. Poor man, he had no course but to make the best of it, and he sent at once to tell Gondomar the news.

Next morning, before the travellers were up, the King of Spain sent Olivares to welcome Buckingham, who, with the Prince, presently arose, yet before they could be ready to admit the favourite, the King himself was come. Great was the joy at meeting, [1] the King exclaiming, " Though it were Lent, it was not now Lent to him ! " When Gondomar first saw the Prince he fell flat on his face crying, " Nunc dimittis," and would not be raised up !

This day, Howell says, Sir Francis Cottington and Mr. Porter came, and towards evening on Saturday, Buckingham went in a close coach to Court where he had a private audience with the King who sent Olivares to escort him back, and Olivares on being introduced to the Prince fell at his feet, hugging the royal knees, and " delivered how immeasurably glad his Catholic Majesty was of him coming, all of which Mr. Porter did interprete."

It was not only his Catholic Majesty and the courtiers who were charmed by the Prince's romantic journey, it exactly suited the Spanish popular taste ; songs were written in praise of it and people cried out that the Prince deserved to have the Infanta thrown into his arms. The poor girl herself

[1] " Court and Times of James I.," vol. ii. p. 379.

took a very different view of the case. A pious, gentle creature, with a round face like a Flemish Madonna, she could think nothing but horror of marrying a heretic. Her confessor worked her up to a pitch of despair. "What a comfortable bed-fellow you will have," he said; "he who lies by your side and who will be the father of your children, is certain to go to hell!" [1] The Prince's handsome face and gallant bearing made no impression on her, and as his compliments had to be all translated for him by Lord Bristol, his conversation was limited, and he was reduced to watching her, so Olivares said, "as a cat watches a mouse." [2]

The English suite were not at all pleased with the Spanish way of living, although Cottington wrote, "we are the braveliest entertained that ever men were." The rest would have agreed with him if entertainment meant processions and ceremonials, but when "the worst chamber to be got was at forty shillings the week, a turkey at ten or twenty, and a hen at five or six," the gentlemen began to grumble. The Prince spent ten days at Lord Bristol's, and then made a magnificent public entry, with a cloth of state held over his head, in the same form that the kings of Spain do at their coronation. [3] But after all this glory when his gentlemen arrived at the Palace, they found he had only two little rooms with a garden, "so nasty and illfavourably kept that a farmer in England would be ashamed of such another." Porter, being used to the Spanish way of living, no doubt was less uncomfortable than

---

[1] Gardiner, "Puritan Revolution," p. 41.
[2] Howells, July 10, 1623.
[3] "Court and Times of James I.," vol. ii. p. 378.

his less experienced companions.   His letters to his
wife though very full do not contain the lamenta-
tions that might be expected.

"MY SWEETEST LOVE,—Although I have so
much employment here at Madrid, that I have scarce
time to dress myself, yet if I should not watch and
lose my sleep to write to thee, I were unworthy of
such a wife and could not deserve the smallest part
of thy inestimable love to me.   Oh, that you did
but know how great a grief it is for me to live
without you, for then you would believe that nothing
but you could give me content, nor any but the
want of you cause sorrow in me.   Had I but
expressions for my love, they should satisfy you and
ease me, but if you can give faith to an honest
heart, then be assured that my life only depends on
that love which I hope for from you, and all the
happiness this world can give me leans upon the
same.   The Prince and my lord are well and have
been the braveliest received that ever men were.
Yesterday the King and Queen came publicly
abroad, and the Infanta with them in the coach,
where my master and my lord with the Ambassador
and myself in another coach (with the curtains
drawn in the street) stayed to see them go by, and
the Prince hath taken such a liking to his mistress
that now he loves her as much for her beauty as he
can for being sister to so great a king.   She deserves
it, for there was never seen a fairer creature.
Although the Prince was private and the curtains of
his coach drawn, yet the searching vulgar took
notice of it, and did so press about the coach to see
him, that we could not pass through the streets, in-

somuch that the King's guard was forced to beat them from it and make way through the multitude. They all cried 'God bless him,' and showed as much affection generally as ever was seen among people, only they took it ill he showed not himself to them in a more public manner. Last night the King of Spain had a great desire to see the Prince, and in a coach only with the Conde Olivares, my lord Marquess and myself, he came privately at eleven of the clock at night, and met the Prince in the fields without the town, who came with the two ambassadors only, and there they discoursed in the coach above an hour, and the King used him with so much love and respect, giving him the better hand still, that he is as well affected to his Majesty's nobleness and courtesy as to his sister's beauty. Dear Olive, all these things I thought fit to acquaint you withal, that you may not say I never tell you anything, but all these things, compared to the desire I have to see thee, are nothing but vanity, that is the real felicity only which makes me breathe, and God Almighty grant me leave that it may be quickly, and His blessing light on you and George and Charles, and I pray you send me word how you do, and which is the prettiest boy. Good Olive, intreat my mother to pardon me, for the Prince having but me alone here, I have so much to do that I cannot awhile to write to anybody. Entreat her to send me her blessing, and commend me to my sisters. I will never fail to be,

"Thy true loving husband,

"ENDYMION PORTER.

"MADRID, *this 10th day of March*, 1623.

5

" I would have Ned go to Monsieur St. Antoine [1] presently to learn to ride, I have spoken with him already, and Dick Oliver will carry him to him. I pray you remember me to Mr. Oliver, and read the manner of the Prince's being here to him. Let Charles come as soon as he can." [2]

"MY DEAR OLIVE,—Since my coming into Spain I have received four letters from you, and the two first with so much kindness in them, as I thought my love rewarded ; but the two last are so full of mistrusts and falsehoods, that I rather fear you have changed your affection than that you have any sure grounds for what you accuse me of in them, for as I hope for mercy at God's hands I neither kist nor touched any woman since I left you, and for the innkeeper's daughter at Boulogne, I was so far from kissing her, that as I hope to be saved I cannot remember that I saw any such woman. No, Olive, I am not a dissembler, for I assure you that the grief which I suffered at the parting with you gave me no leave to entertain such base thoughts, but rather lasted in me like a consumption, increasing daily more and more. But seeing you have taken a resolution without hearing what I could say, never to be confident of me again, I will procure to be worthy of your best thoughts, and study to have patience for any neglect from you.

" I understood that you sent me two kisses by a gentleman, God reward you for them, and since your

---

[1] Monsieur St. Antoine was considered the best master of horsemanship of the time. See " Life of the Duke of Newcastle," p. 195, ed. C. H. Firth.

[2] Dom. S. P., James I., vol. cxxxix. No. 81.

bounty increases, I think it unfit my thanks should diminish. I perceive you would be glad to hear of my kissing of innkeeper's daughters every day, that you might have some excuse to do that which nothing but my unworthiness and misfortune can deserve.

"Alas, sweet Olive! Why should you go about to afflict me. Know that I live like a dying man, and as one that cannot live long without you. My eyes grow weary in looking upon anything, as wanting that rest they take in the company and sight of thine; nor can I take pleasure in sports, for there is none that seems not a monster to my understanding where my Olive is wanting. With thee I only entertain myself and were it not for the force of remembering thee, I know not how my life should have maintained itself so long.

"You have a great deal of advantage of me in this absence, your two little babes, and less affection. They serve to entertain you and it teaches you to forget me. Yet, for pity in this banishment and misery let me hear of your health and theirs, and I assure you it will be no small comfort to me.

"Good Olive, let me receive no more quarrelling letters from you, for I desire but your love, it being the thing that only affords me pleasure in this vile world. Send me word how the children do, and whether Charles be black or fair, and who he is like; but I am sure that nurse will swear that he hath my eyes or nose, and you may perchance be angry and say you never saw anything so like some brother of yours as he. I would to God I could hear thee discourse, I would never come to Boulogne to kiss my host's daughter although you would intreat me.

" The Prince visited the Infanta yesterday, whose beauty gave him a just occasion to like her. The marriage will be, as yet I know not when, but if my desires to see you could hasten it, I assure you I would make bold to trouble you before the two months' end which you allow me in your last letter.

" I have sent my Lady Villiers a tobacco-box, I hope she will esteem it as a token of my love, and that you will deliver it with the best grace your father has taught you, which is, ' Hold up your head, Olive.' Now I am sure you laugh and forget the just cause I have to be angry with you, but till I receive more kisses from you I shall not be well pleased.

" I would have you send me word whether my lady be with child and how my little lady doth.[1] I pray you remember my humble service to my lady and tell her that my lord and I wish you both here very often, for which I hope you will pardon us. We live very honest and think of nothing but our wives. I thought to have sent you a token of some value, but I found my purse and my goodwill could not agree, and I, considering that my letter would be welcome to you, I leave to do it, only this ring which I hope you will esteem if not for love, I think, for charity. The conceit is that it seems two as you turn it, and 'tis but one.

" My dear Olive, be assured that I can love nothing but thee, nor can the times afford a place for one thought that doth not let me know my happiness in having thee. Therefore let me entreat you that there may be a fair correspondance and that

---

[1] " My lady," the Duchess of Buckingham ; " My little lady," Lady Mary Villiers, the Duke's eldest child.

you will call to mind how often you have sworn you could love nothing but me. I hope you continue the same, for all your protesting never to be confident of me again.

"I would have you send me my cutwork bands by the first and send me word what hopes you have to receive any money out of Ireland, which Dick Oliver [1] will inform you, and if Sir Edward Villiers can receive the five hundred pounds of Sir Henry Fines.[2] I would have you pay Bloxum out of that money. Howsoever, let it be paid out of the money from Ireland, which you may advise with Dick Oliver and my brother Canning.

"I pray you pardon me this long letter, if you have patience to read hither. Howsoever, I will always do it till you forbid me, for this is the happiest time I pass in this country. I hope to have some employment that may bring me home before you look for me, and although I should not be welcome, I must needs be glad to come having no other heaven, nor joy, but the hope of seeing you. God Almighty bless you and George and Charles and give you His grace, and I pray you remember to pray for him that will ever be

"Your true loving husband,
"ENDYMION PORTER.
"MADRID, *this 17th of April,* 1623.
"*For yourself.*"[3]

"DEAR OLIVE,—At this instant I received a letter from you wherein you find fault with me for my opinion of you. I hope I shall have no just

---

[1] See page 50.   [2] Fiennes?
[3] Dom. S. P., James I., vol. cxlii. 41.

cause to accuse you, but give me leave till I be better satisfied of some reports (which cannot be till my coming home) to suspect something not that you can be unworthy, but that I may be unfortunate. But, for God's sake, do not put me in mind of any unkindness lest my grief help to make an end of that life which gloried in nothing but you. I sent you the ring enclosed in the letter, therefore I know you could not miss of it, but it may be somebody liked it well and so it lost itself.

" I had no money to send you, but here I send you a jewel which you may pawn if we have no more credit. My lord told me my lady should furnish you with what you wanted. I know not whether he hath done it yet or no, but I am sure he will. The jewel which this gentleman brings you is a very pretty one, therefore I would have you keep it and wear it every day to put you in mind of me ; and be you what you will, the world shall ever know that you had and have in me one that loves you as his soul and as well as you can deserve.

" I have sent my lady and my Lady Denbigh [1] each a box. Remember my humble service to them and assure yourself I will ever be
" Your true loving husband,
" ENDYMION PORTER.
"MADRID, *this 16th of May*, 1623.
" *To my dear Wife, Olive Porter, these.*" [2]

" MY DEAR OLIVE,—This day I writ unto you and sent you by Mr. Knowles a jewel of diamonds

---

[1] Susan Villiers, sister of the Duke of Buckingham, m. Fielding, Earl of Denbigh.
[2] Dom. S. P., James I., vol. cxlv. 8.

worth some hundred pounds and also two boxes for my Lady Marquis of the same work my Lady Villiers' was, and now I send you by this bearer a box with perfumes of another kind, I hope you will esteem as tokens of my love, not regarding the value.

"If you did but know how truly I love you, you would never be jealous of me, and had you such reports of me as you conclude for truths, yet if you loved me half so well as I deserve you would not give credit so easily to them. I know you are not so sorry as you would make me believe for my absence, for I hear you are very merry and can take upon you to command other young men to travel from their wives. Long may you be merry, and if I thought my company would diminish it, I love you with that extremity that to give you as much content as I can, I would bar myself from the happiness of seeing you as long as my many desires would give me leave, and my master's business would keep me here.

"My brother Ned writes that Charles his nose and his are very like, but that he is very pretty. God of heaven bless him and my George and send you as much happiness as I can desire, for myself the chiefest thereof is to be accounted
"Your true loving husband,
"ENDYMION PORTER.
"MADRID, *this 16th of May*, 1623." [1]

"MY DEAR OLIVE,—I wonder why you should find fault with me for not writing by those I never heard of, till they were gone, and God is my

[1] Dom. S. P., James I., vol. cxlv. 9.

witness 'tis true, therefore you have as little cause to be angry with me for that as for kissing the inn-keeper's daughter at Boulogne.

"The other letter which I had writ some eight days past, I thought to have sent by my Lord of Rocheford, who was to depart suddenly from hence, but upon some occasion stayed, whereupon I found means to make over all the four hundred pounds by this bearer, Sir Francis Cottington, and so I send you bills here for that quantity. Three hundred and thirty-three pounds Sir Francis is to pay you, for he received the same of me here, and one hundred and twelve pounds my Lady Cary in Tuttle Street is to pay you, I having lent her son here so much, as appears by his bill, which you are to send presently to her that she may accept it and pay it fifteen days after. But after she hath seen it and set down on the back side the allowance of it, you must keep the bill till you receive the money. The bill that is to Mr. Alexander Stafford is the money that Sir Francis Cottington is to pay, which he hath promised me shall be paid at first sight, though the bill be twenty days after. So you may send him word that you have need of the money presently, as I make little doubt you have ; and assure yourself it hath not little grieved me to think you want, for there can be nothing in this world that I would not do, to make you see my care of you is greater than of myself; and should you do anything that were not fitting your modesty it would grieve me more for the loss you would sustain, than for the shame could come to me of it.

"I have no news to send you, nor secrets to write unto you, for which I am sorry, that you might discourse with the one and tell the other. This last letter you sent me was the kindest I have yet received, with which I am so contented that I can vaingloriously brag of it, and by that means deserve the like hereafter.

"I would have you pay Bloxum out of the monies you receive from Ireland, for they are clamorous people, and therefore I hope you will have a care to see him satisfied.

"Send me word how my little boys do, and whether Charles will be black or fair. I have sent here three purses; if you like them not for yourself, you may send them to Lady Boteler, and to Mall, and the Lady Justice.[1] I took out the toy of gold and little rubies, which was in the purse, and send it apart with the purses, and filled the purse which was for you full of perfumes.

"I would have you give my mother forty-five pounds as a token from me, so there will remain four hundred for yourself, which may serve you to spend till I come home, which, as yet, I cannot tell you seriously when it will be. I have written to my mother that I have sent her that money, therefore I pray you have a care to deliver it to her as soon as you shall receive it.

"I would have you make Ned[2] a suit of clothes, or else give him one of mine, which you shall think fittest for him, and let him go to Mr. St. Antoyne, where if he do not well, I may justly forsake him and let him never hope for anything from me. This is my desire, and I hope you will see it fulfilled.

"I have some hopes that my lord will write to

---

[1] Olivia's mother and sisters.   [2] His brother Edmund.

the King in my behalf, and that he will give order to my lady to succor you with some monies, and you shall do very well to speak to her to write to my lord to favour us with something. Howsoever, be you contented, and although I dig for my living you shall never want, but with our poverty we will love as richly as they that have the greatest plenty; and bread with thy company shall please me better than the greatest dainties of the world without it.

"Sweet Olive, remember what it is to be good, and forget not how often you have sworn you loved me, so shall you preserve my honour and your own, and make your vows true with a pure conscience.

"I take no pleasure in any other thing but you, which makes me write you long letters. If they trouble you, pardon me, and believe that it proceeds from the love of him that will ever be

"Your true loving husband,

"ENDYMION PORTER.

"MADRID, *the 7th of June,* 1623.

"I pray you send this letter to Mr. Cross.

"I will write to all my friends by the next, and how by chance I heard that Sir Francis Cottington did go. Believe me, there be few true friends in the world."[1]

"My Lord of Rocheford," mentioned in the above letter, was the Prince's chamberlain, son of Sir Robert Cary, who carried the first news of Elizabeth's death to the Scotch Court. Prince Charles, when a sickly child, was confided to Lady Cary's care, and it was probably owing to her kind and wise management that he lived to grow up. Henry

[1] Dom. S. P., James I., vol. cxlv. 47.

Cary, Lord Rochford and fourth Lord Hunsdon, was afterwards created Earl of Dover. He was great-grandson of Mary, sister to Queen Anne Boleyn and aunt to Queen Elizabeth. The game of gleek mentioned in the following letter was a favourite card-game for three players. The name probably came from "Gluck," "good-luck," being said when one player held four cards of the same sort, four kings, four knaves, &c., as in our modern bezique.[1] This letter gives the most hopeful account of the negotiations of any in the correspondence; the date of the Infanta's arrival in England is decided; she is to be duly delivered there (like a bundle of goods) in March, 1624.

"How happy was I, dear Olive, when I lived at home, secure of your love, and never did suspect that anything could have made you forget me. But now I see your memory fails and my misfortune increases, and I fear that absence hath made you neglect writing to me, and changed that constant love which in my opinion was wholly mine. But it may be that I lived deceived then, and God hath been pleased with this occasion to open my eyes that you may see how little you esteem me. Here have come two posts and I have received no letters from you. It may be mine have been so long, that because I should not trouble you with so much letter you thought good to forbear writing, thinking I could not be so shameless as to do it without correspondence.

"Alas! sweet Olive, if my love were like yours I could forbear to show it, but 'tis impossible, for if

[1] Singer's "History of Playing Cards."

you did but know how miserably I pass this life from the sight of your eyes, you could not choose but pity me.

"I left my heart within your sweet breast at my departing from you, and am united there with you in spite of this tedious intermission of my joy, which makes me live here like a man without a soul, therefore you ought to love that love which is in me, though you have none yourself. Let me entreat you to have a care to let me know how you and your children do, though you write not to me, for that is some comfort and makes me enjoy myself a little. I wonder my mother would forget me, but sure she knew not of the post's coming.

"I sent you by Dick Grimes [1] a chain of gold which is of the prettiest making that ever I saw. I pray you wear it and let nobody know how kind I am to you, lest they laugh at me for my fondness. By Killegree [Killegrew ?] I sent you a feather, but I fear I shall trouble you with tokens as I do with letters. Yet I would willingly have nobody come without some small remembrance to you, which makes me send you this poor token now. I want a better, but cannot tell where to have anything rich enough for my desire, which could not be satisfied though I were powerful to send you the King of Spain's wealth.

"You never send me word how my lady doth. I pray God send her much happiness, howsoever. I hope to see her mother of many children.

"Our business here is not likely to hold. We are

---

[1] One of the Prince's bedchamber ("Court and Times of James I.," vol. ii. p. 381); also called Gentleman of the Horse to the Marquis (Ibid., vol. ii. p. 387).

to come home suddenly, which I desire for nothing but to see you. And as I was writing this the Prince concluded the business himself with the King, so that it is now finished, and I hope we shall all receive a great deal of comfort in it, for sure there was never a better creature than the Infanta is. He [the Prince] is to be contracted presently, and then he means to go away hence within these three weeks so that we shall be at home suddenly. She is to be delivered in March next. God be praised for so great a blessing as we shall all receive by it. And, sweet Olive, have a care to love me as you have ever professed, it may be I may deserve it ; although you think to the contrary, I am unwilling to trouble you with long letters, although I have much ado to forbear.

" The lady which writes to you is wife to a gentleman that I served, I am much beholden to them. She sends you a token, and I would have you write to her and send her some small toy from thence. I have written the letter and copied hers, for it is so ill a letter that nobody could read it. My mother will help you understand them both.

" And thus with my prayers to Almighty God for your health and your children whose blessing and mine light upon them.

" I kiss thy sweet mouth a thousand times and rest

" Thy true loving husband,
" ENDYMION PORTER.

" MADRID, 17th of July, 1623.

" I have sent you one hundred sixpences for counters to play at gleek." [1]

[1] Dom. S. P., James I., vol. cxlviii. 125.

" MY DEAR OLIVE,—I cannot choose but upon all occasions write unto you, to let you know that I am in health, and I must entreat you to do the like, for you would not believe how great a comfort it is for me to receive a letter from you, and since you writ unto me in your last that you were not well I have been exceedingly troubled, therefore, as you love me, let me know, so soon as you can, that you are mended, otherwise I know my love is such that it will give way to absence to make an end of my life.

" But why should I blame anybody for that which was in mine own hands to have remedied, and had I known we should have stayed thus long I would not have left thee, though the Prince, my master, had given me one of his kingdoms. For what can I wish more than content which I did enjoy in thy company, beyond all that the world can give me. In thee I am rich, and without thee nothing but misery. I curse the slow time that helps to lengthen this bitter absence, and seeks nothing but means to make me despair ; which I am, many times here, but that the remembrance of so sweet a love keeps hope alive in me.

"God of His great goodness bless thee and thy pretty children George and Charles. I have sent thee a handkerchief by this gentleman because I have no other token. I could wish it with all my heart a better thing, but I hope you will esteem of it and my love, which shall never fail, now to be,

" Your true loving husband,

" ENDYMION PORTER.

" MADRID, *this 29th of July*, 1623.

" Remember my duty to my mother and your

father and mother. I could not write, this gentleman
went so suddenly.

"*To my dear Wife, Olive Porter, these. London.*" [1]

The long delays which hindered the marriage
had at last aroused Prince Charles, and out of sheer
opposition he succeeded in working himself into a
vehement affection for the Infanta. The Spanish
diplomatists so far encouraged his hopes that they
provided the Princess with a teacher of English
and with a confessor who was directed to awaken
a missionary spirit in her breast, and teach her to
anticipate her exile to a heretical country with the
pious resignation of a martyr.

But Spanish complaisance could go no further,
and Charles petitioned in vain for a chance of a
single word in private with his future bride.

At last he could stand it no longer, and if
Howell's letter to Tom Porter is to be believed,
"love found out a way." The Prince heard that
his inamorata was used to rise early some mornings
to go to gather May dew with her ladies in the royal
garden. So he took only Endymion with him,
thinking no doubt that he would be a more
sympathetic interpreter than the dignified Lord
Bristol, and the pair crossed the river and reached
the garden. The Infanta was in the orchard, and
"there being a high partition wall between, and
the door doubly bolted, the Prince got on the
top of the wall and sprung down a great height
and made towards her, but she spying him first
of all the rest, gave a shriek and ran back; the
old Marquess that was her guardian came towards

[1] Dom. S. P., James I., vol. cxlix. 90.

the Prince and fell on his knees, conjuring his Highness to retire : he [the marquess] hazarded his head if he admitted any other company : so the door was opened and he came out under that wall over which he had got in."

The Prince's suite were as little pleased as his Royal Highness with the Eastern formality of Spanish etiquette, and wonderful reports were sent back to England of the manners and customs of Madrid.

When a play was performed for the Prince's especial amusement, only the royal party were seated on chairs, the ladies sat on the turkey carpet, and the few gentlemen admitted stood modestly in the background. Hay, the handsome Earl of Carlisle, followed the Prince to Spain, but returned home much astonished at the reception he had met with there. Carlisle naturally did his best to conceal his mortification, but the writer of a news-letter of the time seems to have been as acute as a modern American interviewer, and noted that "somewhat breaks out at times." The Earl had not found it easy to secure an audience at all, and when "with much difficulty and importunity he was brought into a room where the Infanta was placed on a throne aloft, gloriously set forth, with her ladies about her, my lord, with his compliments, motions, and approaches could not draw from her so much as the least nod, she remaining all the while as immovable as the image of the Virgin Mary!" The news-letter continues : "At his coming away the Infanta gave him leave to kneel to her above an hour, whereupon our great ladies begin to consult how they shall demean themselves when she comes." [1]

[1] "Court and Times of James I.," vol. ii. p. 399.

But though the great ladies in England might doubt the charms of such a silent princess, the old king was in raptures with everything he heard ; he began building the private chapel for the Catholic Infanta's use, and discussed the pageants to be exhibited for her welcome.

Nevertheless the efforts of the diplomatists proved as fruitless as the Prince's attempts at love-making. The negotiations dragged on ; the Pope delayed granting a dispensation ; the Spaniards still hoped to convert the Prince ; and the impatient Buckingham chafed and fumed till Olivares had to remind him of the need of fitting behaviour before so great a king as his Catholic Majesty. Buckingham's spirits sank lower and lower as time went on, and in the end of July he wrote a solemn sort of testament and farewell to King James, signed as usual, "Your slave and dog," begging his Majesty, if any evil should befall him, "to take care of the bearer of the letter, your ape," and also of Endymion Porter.[1] Though anything but a model character, Buckingham succeeded in winning the affection of all who were closely connected with him. His wife's letters to him at this time are full of the most devoted affection, and his father-in-law gives a pretty account of the reception of a courier from Spain at York House.[2] The Mr. Porter mentioned is doubtless Edmund.

"Your wife, your sister, Mr. Porter and myself were at supper at York House when news came that Dick Gream was come ; but we were so impatient to see him that some would eat no meat,

[1] Hardwick S. P., vol. i. pp. 432-6.
[2] Harl. MSS., 1581, quoted in Goodman's "James the First."

and when we did see him and your letter, they were
so overjoyed they forgot to eat ; nay, my pretty
sweet Moll as she was undressing cried nothing but
' Dad ! Dad ! ' "

But at Madrid Buckingham was looked on with
greater and greater disfavour. He quarrelled
irrevocably with Olivares. The gentlemen of
the suite followed his example and quarrelled
with some over-zealous priests, every one was
weary and discontented ; even Porter, who was
probably more at his ease among Spaniards than
any one, was by his own accounts very cross
and heartily homesick. When Sir Richard Wynn
was happy enough to obtain leave to return to
England he asked the Prince what he might assure
the thousands who would question him concerning
his Highness's return. " He told me that by the
assistance of the Almighty he would be there by
the 10th of June. I entreated him to take a
further day and then not to fail. To conclude, he
laid with me a purse of forty pieces that he would
be landed by that day, which I told him I would
as willingly lose as ever I won any other wager."

Porter's hopes began to rise as autumn drew
on, and his next letter is in a happier strain.

" My dear Olive,—Now the happy time for me
grows near, for now I am sure it will not be long
before I shall see that face of thine wherein all the
joy and content this world can afford me lieth. Be
satisfied, sweet Olive, that I love thee as my soul,
and although I might say in some other letter that
never man did love his wife as I did you, there is
none lost, so long as you continue such as I imagine

I left you, but rather increased, if to so complete and great an affection anything could be added. And for your suspicion of my having any other creature here, I know you writ that bit to make up your letter. I will have so charitable an opinion of you that I dare swear you have not such a thought nor can be guilty of so much malice. No, dearest love, I cannot forget how much reason I have to be constant to you; what pawns you have of mine to oblige me to be so, and what a George and a Charles, the memory of whom were sufficient to keep me chaste, though mine own devilish disposition might lead me to any unworthy act. Believe me that nothing shall ever have power to make me offend you in a thought, for as I hope to be saved I cannot endure the sight of any woman. And good sweet love, do not find new ways to vex me; let it suffice that I live from you, which is so great a punishment that death cannot be greater, this absence being every hour accompanied with grief enough to make an end of my days.

"The 9th of September we are to set forwards from hence, so that I hope within these six weeks I shall be with thee.

"I had nothing to send you now but my true love which comes in these lines, though with a bad expression, yet with as much affection as my haste can afford. I wonder you never send me word what tokens you receive and I never heard of a picture and two boxes of perfumes that came with the trunks and cabinet that my lord sent my lady: you might take the pains to tell me you had received them although you did not esteem them. I would entreat you to inquire after the picture, for

I would not lose it. It is the picture of a Mary
Magdalene with a pot of flowers by her. I pray
you ask my lady if it came not with the perfumes
and three boxes of china with perfumes for you.
Though they be but trifles I would willingly know
what becomes of them, and that which I sent you by
my Lord of Rochford. I sent you by Sir John
Epsley six little glass bottles with silver chains for
little George, and I make no doubt but he will keep
a terrible stir with them. I pray you send me word
whether he hath ever a great tooth yet or no, and
how many teeth little Charles hath.

" My dear Olive, you cannot believe with what
extremity I am joyed that I shall now come home
and stay there till you bid me go away. I am
resolved never to leave thee now, but to live with
thee free from the troubles of this wicked world. I
protest to God, I am happier in thee than in my
life, and I am sure that nothing can afford me any
content till I see thee again. God of His great
goodness give me leave to come safe home.

" I would have you cut George his hair somewhat
short, and not to beat him overmuch. I hope you
let him go bareheaded, for otherwise he will be so
tender that upon every occasion you will have him
sick.

" I writ to your father and mother and my sister
Marie, hoping they would have answered me, but it
seems the letters were never delivered, which was
no fault of mine. I could not at this time do it for
want of notice of the post's going away, therefore I
entreat you to excuse me to them and assure them
it is not for want of love and respect.

" I pray you remember my services to my brother

Ley and my sister, whom I did hear was very sick and I am extream sorry for it, and am glad to hear that my Lady Ley hath 'scaped her sickness.

"Farewell, my sweet Olive, and I' must entreat you to make much of yourself that I may find you merry and well when I come to you. God of heaven bless you and send you all the happiness He can, and as much content as I wish for my own soul, and believe it that whilst I breathe I will ever be

"Your true loving husband,

"ENDYMION PORTER.

"MADRID, *this 28th of August*, 1623.

"Mr. Secretary Cottington is very sick."[1]

"MY DEAR OLIVE,—I had no leisure to write more than that I am well and to-morrow I am to set forward for that happy place where I shall see thee. God of heaven bless thee and thine, and as you love me, believe I could write no more, for I knew not of this gentleman's departure till it was so late that he could not stay, nor had I time to express my love to thee. Farewell, sweet love, and as my soul's health I wish thine, and will ever be,

"Thy true loving husband,

"ENDYMION PORTER.

"MADRID, *the 8th of September*, 1623."

The happy day of departure at last came. The Prince was heartily tired of Spanish procrastination, and at last accepted the fact that he could succeed no better than other negotiators.

[1] Dom. S. P., James I., vol. cli. 75.

Many courtesies were exchanged on leaving Madrid, and Olivares made splendid presents to the gentlemen in attendance on the Prince, giving jewels of great value and excellent swords " with their furniture," to the keeper of the wardrobe, Mr. Endymion Porter and Mr. Thomas Carey.

The romantic courtship had sunk into a mere farce, but the farce was played out to the end. The Infanta continued her English studies and had masses said for her heretical suitor's safety at sea. The events at least turned out well for her. She was rid of her English bridegroom, and before long was married to her orthodox cousin Ferdinand, King of the Romans, and lived to satisfy her father's dying wish and reign an Empress of Germany.

But one actor had no mind to play out the farce to the end. It was never Buckingham's fashion to conceal his feelings, and he told Olivares very roundly on parting that if ever it was his chance, he would requite him.[1] Two years later an English fleet sailed to wreak Buckingham's vengeance on Spain.[2]

[1] " Court and Times of James I.," vol. ii. p. 423.
[2] Dyer's " Modern Europe," vol. ii. p. 535.

CHAPTER IV

ENGLAND AGAIN, AND A NEW REIGN

THERE were grand festivities throughout the country to celebrate the Prince's safe return from Spain.

It was no disappointment to the people that he had failed in the immediate object of his journey; it was possible that he might now look out for a Protestant wife; at any rate, the bells should be rung and the bonfires lighted, and the future might be left to take care of itself.

But a pretence at negotiations for the marriage still went on, and Don Diego de Mendoza was sent over from Spain to report officially to the Spanish Court that the Prince had arrived at home and that the Infanta's masses for his safety might cease. A curious little peep at manners and Court etiquette is afforded by one of the incidents of Don Diego's stay in England.[1]

Precedence was a very solemn matter in those days; a little later there was a real battle for precedence between the French and Spanish ambassadors, when swords were drawn and men lost their lives for what was considered the honour of their country. But now the chief difficulty lay, not

---

[1] Nicholl's "Royal Progresses," James I., vol. iii. p. 587.

between the jealous representatives of the rival kingdoms, but between no less than three Spanish ambassadors ; for Don Diego being the newest arrival considered himself to be the most important personage, while the ambassador who was already in England, the Marquess de la Injosa, was a man of higher rank ; and by way of complicating matters still further a third Spanish nobleman, Don Diego de Mexia, the Ambassador of the Archduke, was also in England at the time ; and this Don Diego was a very great personage indeed.

Buckingham wished to give a grand banquet in honour of Don Diego de Mendoza, but as it was impossible to settle the respective positions of the three stately dons, in order to solve the difficulty Endymion Porter was sent to propitiate the highest in rank of the trio, namely, the Marquess, in a very quaint fashion, and to induce him to stay at home. For this purpose he was accompanied by " a regale of three large flaskets filled with cates intended for the feast," and he bore this message, " that the Duke kissed the Marquess's hands and would have held it an honour to· have his company at his feast, but as he would be deprived of it, he prayed the Marquess to taste what he had provided." The Marquess does not seem to have been exactly flattered by this very curious message, but answered shortly "that the Duke might have had his company had he been pleased to command it."

We do not know whether Endymion's skill in Spanish compliments enabled him to salve the wound to the great man's pride. The report only tells us that the Marquess bade the company good-night, and supped privately in his chamber.

But Spain and the Spanish Infanta became steadily more unpopular, and in a play called "Gondomar," that Spanish statesman was actually caricatured on the London stage, the actors taking the trouble to procure a suit of his clothes to make the likeness perfect.[1]

Moreover, Buckingham's visit to Paris had turned his weathercock fancy in a new direction; he was too deeply offended with Spain to endure further intercourse with her, and France was now the land he favoured. So, in October, 1624, when the Spanish Ambassador went down to Royston, the King was said to be too unwell to receive him.[2] The excuse, it is likely enough, may have been perfectly true, but it seems to be a curious coincidence that just before the arrival there of the Spanish grandee "the Prince and the Duke went unexpectedly to Royston." This sudden visit of the pair, as it is mentioned by several contemporary writers, seems to have attracted some notice; probably they hastened down as soon as they heard that the Ambassador was going to seek an audience, and arrived there just in time to disappoint him.

Endymion's letters about this time seem to have been written during attendance on the Prince at his various hunting-boxes and on progresses through the kingdom. There was a Midland progress which began in July, 1624, and halted at Burleigh, where there were grand festivities including a pageant designed by Inigo Jones and written by Ben Jonson. It was during this journey that Endymion writes from Rufford. In the spring of 1625 he

[1] "Court and Times of James I.," vol. ii. p. 473.
[2] Ibid., vol. ii. p. 483.

accompanied the Court to Theobalds and Newmarket. The following letter is undated, but must
have been written at earliest in 1624, as it mentions
he had been four years married :—

" MY DEAR OLIVE,—I hope that you have forgotten all the unkindness of last night, although I
must confess I did suspect by your letter there was
something remaining in your mind, for it came not
accompanied with that hearty expression of affection
as at other times, or else it may be my jealousy
let me not see the true meaning of it !

" Olive, believe me, that what so ever I am, being
angry, when it is past I love nothing in the world
near a comparison to you : all the joy and comfort
I have is in you : therefore, blame me not if I desire
to have you according to my own heart, and assure
yourself we shall never agree if we seek not to
please one another.   Be you still to me as I shall
deserve, and let me want that happiness of your
affection, if ever I fail to show myself a careful
friend and a true husband to you.   God knows how
unwilling I am to show any kind of distaste when
you cross me, but to prevent a greater mischief, I
think I had better make show of anger for small
offences than conceal them, and let greater be the
ruin of our loves.

" We have been four years married and God hath
blessed us with children.   Let not our carriages
make the world take notice of so much inconstancy
in us that time should diminish the obligations we
have to love each other.   Before I gave you my
hand of husband, you did engage your word to me,
that in whatsoever I should advise you, nothing

should hinder you from following my directions, and I swore to you that if you did so, no man breathing should love a woman more than I would you. I have kept mine oath, and whether you have your promise, that I leave to you; but, my dearest Olive, I wonder why you should suspect me for Saxum [1] when as I hope to be saved, I think of nothing but thy sweet love, which to me is above all the beauties that ever God created : be careful to preserve the best part of us both, which is our affections, and when I fail let God plague me with thy neglect, which would be the worst of all diseases.

"God bless our babes, and send me the blessing of seeing thee quickly, till then I rest,

"Thy true constant loving husband,

"ENDYMION PORTER." [2]

Olivia seems to have remained in London during the autumn of 1624, as her third son was christened at St. Martin's-in-the-Fields on the 1st of October. The entry in the register calls him "Endymion, filius Sagasissimi viri Endymion Pòrter." The letters show that Olivia felt her husband's absence at such a time very keenly, and found it hard to believe he could not obtain leave of absence from Court.

"Little Dim" as he is called in the letters, only

---

[1] It will be remembered that very early in their married life Olive had heard with anxiety of her husband's visits to the lovely ladies of Saxham. It may be hoped this solemn protest quieted her fears, for we hear no more of the Crofts family. See Chap. II. p. 25.

[2] Fontblanque's "Lords Strangford," p. 45. Original in possession of Mrs. Russell.

lived to be two years old and was buried in London
in November, 1626.

The date of the following letter is uncertain, but
from the references to his babes in it, it cannot be
earlier than 1623 and very possibly belongs to
1624.

" MY DEAREST LOVE,—I write unto you from
Theobalds, but having so fit a messenger, I could
not let this occasion slip without the remem-
brances of my best love to you, for I do as I would
be done withall. If you did but as truly love me,
as I do you, nothing would make a difference
between us, but the want of true affection on
your side, gives way to an easy belief of unworthiness in me without desert. I have no
reason to flatter you, nor do I fear anything
that you can do but wrong yourself, which if I
seek to prevent, you ought rather to cherish me
as a true friend than by unkindness make me your
enemy. I protest to God, I love you as my soul
and as by choice you were pleased to think me
worthy to be your husband, so I desire not to
change the constant resolution I made God
witness of when I took you to be my wife, let
us therefore enjoy one another with that true
content that nothing may make me sorry for
our choice. I will ever endeavour to let you
see that I esteem you above all earthly things,
but still I shall wish that you would know I must
govern you and not you me. My dear Olive,
farewell, and let me hear from you, for next your
. . . company your lines afford me the greatest
. . . I can ever have. In haste, with my blessing

to my babes and praying God would give you His,

"I rest, your true loving husband,
"ENDYMION PORTER." [1]

"RUFFORD, *this* 12 *August*, 1624.

"MY DEAR HEART,—This is the third letter I have sent you, and the first I have received from you. I thank you for it, but I wonder you will urge me to come away sooner than the appointment we had agreed upon. I protest to God I have, appointed to me business of so much importance which cannot be dispatched so soon as I could wish, but if you think my sudden presence might help you to any ease I would leave anything that could import me to see you, for I look upon nothing beyond your health and comfort. You have with your letter amazed me, and I wonder your love could give way to let you tell me that unless I presently depart from hence you cannot live; and, sweet Olive, take heed how you conjure me by such uncharitable means, for, as I hope to be saved, I received your letter but now this 12th of August in the afternoon and it is an impossibility to be with you on the 14th, but so soon as conveniently I can I will leave all and come to you. O how it grieves me to think that you should take it unkindly if I should not be better than the first promise. I protest I thought to have come two days sooner than we had appointed, and now I am sure that will be no kindness, by reason you command me to come sooner than anything can fly. My dear Olive, be assured I miss your company

[1] Dom. S. P., vol. cxxxv. No. 13.

more than you can mine, and desire it as health ; therefore you should not press me so violently to do a thing of so much pleasure to myself, and that which I so heartily desire. My content is not to be got out of your company, nor can the want of that make me forget to love you ; the first foundation of which was an everlasting affection, which I will maintain constant while I live. Had I not those dear pawns of George and Charles, yet I could love you for the first cause, which is yourself, *that* I assure you, wheresoever I be, shall ever make me,

"Your true and loving husband,

"ENDYMION PORTER.

"God's blessing light upon you and my children."

"ROYSTON, *October* 22, 1624.

"MY DEAR OLIVE,—I received the answer of my letter and perceive by it, that I must put off my hat first. Your will be done! sweetheart, for otherwise we shall have but little quiet. You send me word that on Thursday you are to be churched. I intreat you heartily that it may be so, for on Friday (being this day sennet) I purpose to be with you, and, sweet Olive, remember that you love me still with that same affection you gave me first your heart, for I esteem it above all earthly pleasures. The news you send me of my George put me in a great deal of sorrow for a long time, God of heaven bless them all and give thee as much content as He can. I know not any for myself out of thy company. Farewell, my dear love, on Friday night thou shalt have thy true loving husband,

"ENDYMION PORTER.

" My cousin Meutys his papers lie in the study upon the shelf where the singing books are. I pray you make clean the closet, but take heed of my loose papers." [1]

" MY DEAREST LOVE,—I writt unto you by my cousin Meutys his man, and sent you the key of my closet, and now I thought fit to do it, that you might understand that the Prince goeth to-morrow to Amptill and stayeth there till Friday. I must attend him, and therefore (as I have already told you) till then I cannot make myself happy. Good Olive, I have so often told you I love you that I can find no new way to express the same in words, believe that it is true, I do so strive to make myself appear in your opinion kind, that I write *nonsense ;* but could you see the secret of my heart, there you might discover strange conceits all tending to the everlasting affection I bear you, and may I want love of God and man, when I fail to be,
" Thy true loving husband,
" ENDYMION PORTER.
" RUFFORD, *this 24th of October*, 1624.
" God bless my babies.
" *To my dear Olive.*" [2]

" My DEAR OLIVE,—Your kind letter came in good time to accompany me in this place which affords me no comfort but desires to see you, in them I take a great deal of pleasure, and with thinking of you I do lighten the burden of absence which otherwise were unsufferable. I understand

[1] Dom. S. P., vol. clxxiii. No. 75.
[2] Ibid., vol. clxxiii. No. 85.

by Mr. Sheldon that you were well and very merry, which was welcome news to me, for by that means I hope you will preserve your health till I have the happiness to see you again, you have the odds of me much, for the company of the little boys will help you to pass away this tedious time better than if I were with you. I beseech God to bless them and you and make me once able to enjoy you without this curse of absenting myself from you, yet, if necessary, will not give way to it. I must have patience, and hope that God gives it me here as a punishment for my former sins, which have been so great, that if I might live still blest with your company, I should fear that the pains in the world to come would be justly laid upon me having felt none in this. My dearest love, farewell, and believe that whilst I breathe I will ever be,

" Your true loving husband,

" ENDYMION PORTER.

" Send me some cuffs.

" NEWMARKET, *this* 20*th of Januarie*, 1625.

" Commend my service to your bedfellow." [1]

" *To my dear wife Olive Porter, these.*"

" MY ONLY DEAR LOVE,—Having written a former letter by Mr. Saunderson, this gentleman would needs have another, and by cause you may see my judgment I can temper my quarrel so that nothing he brings shall savour of distaste. I know you will approve of me for it, and give me more thanks for my understanding than for my letter. I have been very ill with an ague, which if it continue

I shall come home (cum whome) and trouble you with my company, therefore I hope you will pray for my health.   My dearest Olive, when I fail or slacken my love to you, may I want all that's good, and nothing but misfortune fall upon me ; I know you may sometimes be ill and unfit to write to me, but I presume your affection would be always putting me in mind of you and it, and if I love myself, the chiefest cause is for being

"Your husband,

"ENDYMION PORTER.

"NEWMARKET, *this 25th of Januarie*, 1625.[1]

In March, 1625, Charles succeeded to his father's throne, and in May, the long uncertainties concerning the King's marriage came to an end, and in Howell's words, there arrived "a most noble, new Queen of England, who, in true beauty, is beyond the long-wooed Infanta, for she is of a fading flaxen hair, big-lipped and somewhat heavy-eyed, but this daughter of France is of a more lovely and lasting complexion of a dark brown.   She hath eyes that sparkle like stars, and as for her physiognomy she may be said to be a marvel of perfection."

Endymion was one of the gallant train who accompanied Charles to meet Henrietta Maria at Dover, where the poor girl could hardly get through her little formal address for tears and was consoled as tenderly as the chivalrous King could do it.

On Barham Downs, "a goodly train of choice ladies" received the royal bride, "drawn up in two rows," but Howell thought the country ladies far overshone the courtiers.   Doubtless Olive Porter

[1] Dom. S. P., vol. clxxxii. 51.

7

would have willingly been one among these fair
courtiers, and to see no more of the gay reception
than her husband's account of it did not quite
content her, and she let him know it. She was
probably at this time at Woodhall. She had been
at Aston in the spring when her little son Villiers
was baptised,[1] and there can be little doubt the
baby died soon after, as his name is never mentioned in the letters. Olive was unwell and lonely,
and doubtless fretting over the loss of her boy,
all of which things may partly account for her
" swaggering letter " of which her husband com-
plains. He also was often unwell, overworked,
worried, and liable to ague. It was not much
wonder that both occasionally lost their tempers !

"MY DEAR OLIVE,—I did not think to have
received such a swaggering letter from you, but I
see you can do anything now, for time hath worn
out the kindest part of your love, which I did hope
would have lasted longer. I am glad you had not
the keeping of mine towards you for so we might
have been without by this time, but be it spoken to
your comfort or your grief, I will preserve mine
whilst I have breath, nor shall age nor time make
me forget my Olive. I know my own thoughts
best, and I am not ignorant that you are the best
of them, and therefore do not tell me that you will
not be unworthy, for if you be you will wrong yourself most.

"The Queen is expected this night at Dover, and
on Wednesday we shall be at London ; the King
will not come to Greenwich at all. I pray you

[1] See Aston Registers, April 28, 1625.

OLIVIA, WIFE OF ENDYMION PORTER.

have a care of my children, and suffer not Guittens
to come in the house, for he runs into all the ale-
houses in town.   God bless George and Charles
and Dim and you, and so in haste I rest,

" Your loving husband,

" ENDYMION PORTER.

" CANTERBURIE, *this Sunday.*
" *To my dear Wife, Olive Porter, these.*" [1]

" MY DEAR OLIVE,—This last night the King and
the Queen did lie together here at Canterburie, long
may they do so, and have as many children as we
are like to have.   I have sent you two of the King's
points, one for yourself and another for a friend, and
I have sent you this little ruby ring which I would
have you wear for my sake.   On Thursday I hope
we shall meet at London, and although I desire infinitely to see my children, yet I would not have you
let them come to London, you and I will go to them
on Friday.   God Almighty bless them and you, and
fail me when I fail to be

" Your true loving husband,

" ENDYMION PORTER.

" CANTERBURIE, *this Tuesday morning.*" [2]

It was at his old home at Aston that Endymion
hoped to join his children.   That house seems now
to have been left to the farmer who occupied the
land, for old Edmund Porter had died during
Endymion's absence in Spain in 1623, and Angela

---

[1] Dom. S. P., vol. iii. 56.   Endorsed in pencil, " 12 June,
1625 ? "
[2] Ibid., Charles I., vol. iii. 69.

seems usually to have made her home with her son in his house in the Strand.

But her daughter Mary Canning still lived not far off, and of the many cousins scattered through the neighbourhood, young Fulke Porter and his wife Ellen were settled at Mickleton, close by.

The plague was now so violent in London that the King and Queen were forced to make their State entry by water to avoid the dangers of the narrow and crowded streets. It was small wonder that Endymion wished his children to remain in the pure country air under the tender care of their grandmother, whose charming letter gives a pleasant idea of the life among the "enamelled meads" Herrick sang of.

It may be hoped that Olivia soon recovered her health and spirits in her country home, with the companionship of her husband and children, and of her delightful mother-in-law.

"Angela Porter to Endymion.

"My dear Son,—You have now given me all the consolation that this will give you, and at the same time myself, and if you had communicated good news of my daughter-in-law, nothing of what I most desire would have been wanting; but I hope in God that I shall hear of her health, and I beg of you to order your servant to communicate with me relating thereto on the first occasion, for I am well aware you have other things to occupy your attention, and truly I cannot be so happy as these pretty children give me occasion to be, until I hear she is entirely restored to health.

"I wish you could see me sitting at the table with

my little chickens, one on either side ; in all my life I have not had such an 'occupation to my content, to see them in bed at night and get them up in the morning.

" The little one is exactly like what you were when you were of his age, and if it were not tiring you, I would give you such a sermon, but I take up too much time in speaking of them.

"You may rest assured that you need not be anxious : this situation is healthy, and no care that can be bestowed upon them is wanting to keep them in health. In reference to what you say regarding their food, you must know that they have here butter and cheese in abundance. They have also very good cows, and before the children came they killed a sheep once a week and sent it to market, for beef they do not kill on account of the heat, and veal and lamb sometimes they buy in the market; other times they kill when the cows breed. It would be well to do all that I have talked over with her ; but I can assure [you] that she is well pleased that you have again trusted her.

" I will inform you respecting everything, but I must now go and see my little ones to bed..

" The Lord bless you, and allow me to see you as I would wish.

" Your mother,

" ANGELA PORTER." [1]

<hr>

[1] Fontblanque, " Lords Strangford," p. 48.

CHAPTER V

ENDYMION and Olivia were not the only married pair who had their little squabbles. The course of the King's married life did not at first run smooth, and the differences between him and his bride were so serious as to draw threats of armed interference from her brother the French king.

Henrietta Maria had been promised the free exercise of the rites of her Church, and was deeply hurt by the difficulties that were put in the way of the due performance of the Catholic services. It was also natural that she should be jealous of the overwhelming influence of Buckingham, who was determined that the young Queen should be a mere cypher in her husband's court.

She was surrounded from the day of her landing by the ladies of Buckingham's family, and it is little wonder if she grew occasionally tired of their company, for she was in truth hardly more than a child, and a very self-willed and foolish child to boot.

In the end of 1625, when the King was hunting in the New Forest, the Queen visited Titchfield, as the guest of Buckingham's elder sister, Lady Denbigh. She, like most of the Villiers family,

was a lady of decided character, and was a somewhat
militant daughter of the English Church. It was
owing to her representations that the King desired
Dean Cosin to draw up a book of Anglican devo-
tions for the use of the Court ladies, in order that
their lack of religious observances should cease to
be a matter of jesting among the French courtiers.
Lady Denbigh insisted on the service of the Church
of England being performed daily during the Queen's
stay at Titchfield, and the Queen on her side showed
her religious ardour by frequently passing through
the hall where the heretical service was held and
disturbing it as much as possible. It is characteristic that the only letter preserved from Lady Denbigh to Endymion is one asking for the presentation
to a living. She wrote to him in June, 1627, about
the living of Boxted.

Probably the following undated letter of the Earl
of Anglesea refers to this time in the New Forest.
It is interesting to note that even the brother of the
all-powerful Buckingham was glad to use Endymion's
interest with the King.

" *To my dear Nephew, Mr. Endymion Porter, one of
His Ma^{tics} Bedchamber, these.*

"SERVANT,—Your love and hasty occasions caused
my guns to hail bullets in a shower of rain, but so
discreetly as I hope, if not yourself, your trusty citizen
or Weekes will wish for one of Pharaoh's kine to
eat him withal.[1] If not, assure yourself the ground

---

[1] The best explanation that can be conjectured for this highly
enigmatical sentence is that Endymion had sent in a hurry to
Lord Anglesea for a supply of venison, and that the latter had
gone out with his attendants in very wet weather and succeeded

affords no better, and yet I must be still your debtor, for this morning I left with my brother L'Isle a letter which I would entreat you out of the love you owe my brother William Villiers to procure his Majesty to allow of, because it will be both for the good of his wife, the ward, and rest of their children. I likewise took the advice of Sir Har. Holdcraft and likewise of lawyers, which makes me confident you cannot fail to have it effected. Now, in my one particular, I command you good servant, to make my excuse to our Master for my absence, since such a lameness is the cause of it, as were I rich, I should suspect the gout. But as I am no man can make me doubt it, but to his Majesty I trust you will be as just in your promise as myself, and then I shall hope to see you at Hampton Court, where you may swear yourself to be heartily welcome, and my niece, to whom let my service and wife's be remembered as to yourself. So, rest, good doorkeeper, your loving uncle,

"ANGLESEA." [1]

Although the Villiers family were sometimes glad to use Endymion's interest at Court, Buckingham in

in shooting one of the wild cattle of the New Forest. Lord Anglesea is justifiably proud that in blinding rain they managed to pick out as their quarry one so fat-fleshed and well favoured that it might have ranked with the famous seven that were eaten by Pharaoh's lean kine. Readers of Marryat's delightful story, "The Children of the New Forest," will remember Edward Beverley's shot at the wild bull.

[1] Dom. S. P., Charles I., vol. xliv. 60. Christopher Villiers, younger brother of the Duke of Buckingham, created Earl of Anglesea 1623. He was one of the Gentlemen of the Horse to James I., but gossip said he was banished from Court by Charles I., who said he would have no drunkards of his Chamber ("Court and Times," vol. i. p. 12).

his turn was very ready to help Endymion's relations, and promised his sister Margaret Bolton to forward her requests as those of " his near kinswoman."

The Duchess of Buckingham was frequently writing to the Porters either to ask some trifling service from Endymion, or to send scraps of news to Olivia, as in the following note which is too characteristic to be modernised :—

" DERE CUSEN,—Dockter More will tell you how I am. I have sent the dockter's letter to him. I am in good helthe I thanke God and I hope in the end I shall be as well as ever I was. I pray, pray for me ; remember me to your husband and sonns and I do not doubt but we shall be mery agane in York House.

" Amphill is now sould I thanke God, and we shall, by living here a while, redeeme ourselfs out of debt, I hope in Jesus.

" Farewell swete Cusen

" Your most constant frind

" K. BUCKINGHAM.

" My Co : remember his service to you.

" *July* 28 1625." [1]

Of Buckingham's children we get no news through the Porter family till a few years later, when a story told of the eldest daughter, " my little ladie," as Endymion called her, is so pretty that it is worth retelling on the chance that it may be true. After the Duke's death his children were educated with the royal family and treated by the King with the kindness he showed to his own children. Mary

[1] Dom. S. P., Charles I., vol. iv. 140.

Villiers, the "pretty sweet Moll" of her grandfather's letter, had been contracted when a mere
baby to the son of the Earl of Montgomery, but the
boy bridegroom died in 1635, when Lady Mary, it
seems, appeared with the dress and position of a
widowed Countess, although her behaviour was not
quite so dignified or so melancholy as her dress.[1]
It is not clear if the Mr. Porter of the story was
Endymion himself or young George, a boy of her
own age. However, the story goes, one day my
lady Countess took it into her head to desire some
fruit from the King's private garden. Her ladyship
scrambled up into the tree, but there her black
dress and fluttering veil attracted the King's
attention and made him think some strange bird
had alighted in the garden. He called Mr. Porter,
who was a good marksman, and desired him to take
"his fusee" and secure the bird. But when Mr.
Porter arrived at the tree, he was received with a
shower of fruit, and looking up he saw the laughing
face of the girl above him. "Oh heavens," he
cried, "did you but know the reason that brought
me here! I have promised the King to kill you
and bring him some of your feathers!" "You
must be a man of your word," answered the
Countess, laughing, and she sent off in haste for a
large hamper and got into it, then she made one of
her gentlemen take one end and Mr. Porter the
other, and so was carried to the King, Mr. Porter
saying he had had the good fortune to take the
bird alive. His Majesty, eager to see the booty,

[1] She married second James Stuart, Duke of Richmond and
Lennox, and third, Thomas Howard, brother to Charles, Earl
of Carlisle (Debrett).

opened the basket, when the little lady sprang out and flung her arms round his neck, giving him, we are told, a very agreeable surprise.

But to return to the troubled spring of 1627, when the Commons, led by Wentworth and Eliot, were debating on the Petition of Rights. Even in this busy time Charles seems, from the following letter, to have snatched a brief holiday and gone down to Theobalds and Newmarket, with Porter in attendance.

"MY DEAR LOVE,—I heard by Sir John Carie that you were reasonable well, but that cannot satisfy me, for unless I be assured that you are very well I must be ill; as having my sickness or health depending upon you, for I protest to God nothing can please me but what hath a relation to your content, and therefore be assured that I think myself a miserable man when I am absent from you, as much by cause I think it likes not you, as for want of the sight of you wherein I must joy. Let me, so soon as you can, know how you do, but trouble not yourself to write, for I know the hanging down of your head will hurt you; send me also word how my little partridges (partriges) do, and whether Mun call them still or no. God's blessing and mine light on them and you, and let me not live if I love you not better than I do

"Your husband,

"ENDYMION PORTER.

"THEOBALDS, *this* 21*st of Februarie*, 1627 (*O.S. ?*)
"*To my dear wife, Olive Porter, these.*" [1]

---

[1] Dom. S. P., vol. xciv. 12.

" My dearest Love,—I am extremely troubled that I hear not from you, but that I hope you are well, I could not have patience (patiens) to forbear (forbere) to come to London to you, send me word I beseech you, sweet heart, whether your face mend or no, that I may the better endure this affliction of absence from you, which if you be well, I purpose to suffer till the King return, but otherwise I will endure it no longer, but speedily remedy my own torment by coming to you. I have sent this messenger of purpose to see you, and that I may by him truly know how you are, for nothing else would satisfy me ; send him back so soon as you can for till I see him again I shall not rest well. I thank you for the band you sent me, but it had no cuffs which I also want, therefore I must intreat you to supply all this by bearer. And assure your-self that my affection is such to you that nothing in this world is like it, for every man else loves by chance and I only have reason for it, and I presume you will never give an occasion of the contrary to
" Your true loving husband,
" Endymion Porter.
"Newmarkett, *this 26th of Februarie,* 1627 (*O.S.*)
" Kiss all my little boys for me and ask Mun half a dozen to send me as a token.
" I bade you not write, yet you did it, and I know it hurts you, therefore I will not thank you for it.
" *To my dear Wife, Olive Porter, these.*" [1]

" Mun," young Edmund Porter, was evidently a very devoted uncle to the three little boys and loath

---

[1] Dom. S. P., vol. xciv. 53.

to spare any of his "little partridges'" kisses, even to their father.

He seems to have been an established inmate of the Porter household in London, for it will be remembered there are several mentions of him in the letters from Madrid. He appears, however, to have been put to some business in London, and was receiving a regular salary. But in the year 1628 he died, aged only twenty-five, and no further record of him exists but the following curt business letter :—

"WORTHY SIR,—I have received your letters concerning your brother's things which are all safe in my custody and ready to be delivered when you shall please to send for them, and for the time when he entered into wages his warrant will specify, which is in his trunk. He deceased the 30th of December which I know no other but that his pay runneth on till that time, and for any wages that he hath received in the mean time I know of none nor no debts that he oweth, and so for present resting
"Your obediently to be commanded,
"NATHANIEL GOODLAD.
"LONDON, *this 21st of Januarie*, 1627 (*O.S.*)" [1]

The family in the Strand, however, continued to increase. Mountjoy Porter was christened at St. Martin's-in-the-Fields on the 3rd of February, 1627 ; and Philip Porter in 1628. Mountjoy only survived for two years, but Philip lived to grow up and become one of the reckless cavaliers of Restoration days.

[1] Dom. S. P., vol. xci. 28.

Of the anxieties of public life at this time, the
luckless expedition of Buckingham to Rhé, and the
levy of tonnage and poundage, Endymion, who in
one letter avows himself to be " no politician," says
nothing ; but no man could keep himself entirely out
of public life, however little interest he took in
politics, and Porter's share in all Spanish negotiations kept him before the public mind as one of the
faction of the feared and detested Duke of Buckingham.   In 1626, Bristol, who had been recalled from
Spain and ordered into retirement, craved justice
against Buckingham to whom his disgrace was due.
Charles, alarmed for the safety of his favourite,
ordered the Attorney-general to draw up a counter
accusation against Bristol.   The Lords commanded
that the·charges against Bristol and Buckingham
should proceed simultaneously, in order that it
should be finally decided whether Bristol had made
too many concessions during the Spanish negotiations, and whether he had tried to convert the
Prince to Romanism, and whether everything that
had gone wrong during that foolish expedition was
due to Bristol or to Buckingham.   Bristol was sent
to the Tower, but he soon showed Buckingham that
he was by no means inclined to be made a scapegoat.   He demanded an examination before the
Privy Council, and there he questioned Porter so
closely about the Royal letters which he had carried
and the messages which had been entrusted to him,
that both the favourite and his master saw that it
would be advisable to hush up the whole business
as quickly as might be.   Neither side was ready to
carry matters to extremity, and the project of im-
peaching Buckingham was dropped ; but Bristol's

enmity to the favourite had made him acceptable in the eyes of the popular party, and King Charles's third parliament insisted on his being restored to his place in the House of Lords.

All this time the King had continued his futile endeavours to regain the Palatinate for his sister, and had only succeeded in plunging England into a war with both France and Spain.

But in this eventful summer of 1628, Buckingham set his wandering affections on a Spanish alliance.

When Spanish letters were to be written or Spanish messages carried Porter was usually connected in some way with the business, and it was therefore natural that when the Duke decided to patch up a peace with Spain, the first step should be to dispatch Porter to pave the way with Olivares. But the real object of this journey was not explained to the English public ; they were merely informed that Porter was going to Italy to buy pictures. Salvetti, who represented the Tuscan Court in England, mentioned this report in his dispatches, but added that he thought the journey was of a mysterious character.

Salvetti considered that the general disposition in England at this time was to make peace with Spain, and that all that was needed was a mediator between the countries. On the 12th of July he reported, " Mr. Porter is gone to Genoa, where he will embark for Spain to treat with Olivares. Porter will be accompanied by an Irish Dominican friar who lately came from Spain with a statement of the inclination of Count Olivares to make peace. Probably Porter will send the friar before him into Spain, to prepare the way, while he himself will

visit the Italian Courts." [1] The news-letters got
hold of the name of the Irish friar and were more
convinced than ever that Porter and Buckingham
had been in league with the Jesuits to sell England
to the Pope. Endymion's departure was delayed a
little, and he seems to have been in England at the
christening of his son Philip, on July the 15th, for
Salvetti writes again on the 25th of July, " Mr.
Endymion Porter will go next week to Flanders
on his way to Italy, and was to accompany the
Ambassador of Savoy as far as Brussels." We
hear soon after that Porter was at Brussels, that he
had an interview with the Archduchess Isabella, the
Spanish Regent, and that she sent her Secretary to
act as his escort through France. Still mysterious,
Porter disguised himself, and shaved off his beard
so as not to be known, showing thereby how much
the fashions had changed since the days when he
accompanied the Prince and Buckingham to Madrid
and they bought beards for a disguise. But
although he reached Spain in safety Spanish
negotiations were never rapid, and Buckingham
did not wait for Porter to send him news of a
Spanish alliance before prosecuting the war with
France. The failure of his attempt to aid the
Huguenots of Rochelle the previous year still stung
his pride, and he was resolved to wipe out that
disgrace by taking command of the magnificent
fleet now equipped to relieve that important city.
He went down to embark at Portsmouth accompanied by a brilliant escort of friends. Olivia
Porter wrote her godspeed to the great Duke as
follows :—

[1] Salvetti, Hist. MSS. Com., xi. Rept., Mr. Skrine's MSS.

" My Lord,—When your Grace is at leasure, if you take it (*sic*) is that I have remembered my dutie and respects unto you, it will satisfie mee for you shall not neede to trouble your selfe anie further nor to lose soe much tyme as to reade my letter, my name will suffice. And your noble imagination give you to understand, that the rest can bee nothing but prayers, and good wishes for your happiness and safe returne, a sacrifice of a gratefull hart which owes your goodness all that I and mine have and shall be daylie offered by

"You - - ser - -

"Olive Porter." [1]

But the good wishes of Buckingham's friend s were a poor guard against the hatred of the nation. He was warned again and again of the danger of assassination, but he proudly replied, "We have no Roman spirits now." He did not dream that a new spirit was awaking in England, and that he should be the first of the King's friends to fall before it.

He was assassinated in his inn at Portsmouth on the 23rd of August, and with his death, a chapter of English history closed.

By few could the Duke of Buckingham have been mourned more sincerely than by Porter, for to him Endymion owed all ; his position, his wealth, and his wife. Warm personal affection combined with his gratitude to make the name of Buckingham sacred to him to the day of his death. Only a part of the letter in which he pours out his sorrow to Olivia has been preserved, but even in his las

[1] Dom. S. P., vol. cxi. 57 (Conway Papers).

will the name of Buckingham is mentioned with gratitude.

"Now, my dear Soul, I could wish myself wings to fly unto thee, for this day I set forwards towards the seaside, to seek a ship to carry me for England, and if I find one ready, I shall quickly be there, but if in the port I go to there be none, then you must not expect me so soon and therefore if this letter come to you before you see me, be not affrighted with anything, for by the grace of God I shall come safe to you. You cannot believe what a comfort your letter was to me, for till I saw it I have suffered the ill news of the miserable loss of my Lord Duke, which no man can suffer so much as I, and my very soul hath been sensible of it. Good sweet Olive, make much of yourself that by seeing of you I may receive a remedy for the hurt that grief hath caused in me.

"With a thousand kisses, I rest
"Your true friend and loving husband,
"ENDYMION PORTER.
"MADRID, *the 1st of December*, 1628." [1]

Among the many memorials of the death of the Duke one of the best known is Gervase Warmestry's poem, "England's Wound and its Cure," which he dedicated to Endymion Porter.

---

[1] Fontblanque, "Lords Strangford," p. 51.

CHAPTER VI

DIPLOMACY

THE return of Porter from Madrid was anxiously looked for by all parties in England. Some thought we were bound in honour to support the revolted Huguenots in France, and that a Spanish alliance would give us valuable assistance in the French war. Others, more clear-sighted, saw that the war in France was not really one of religion, and that to ally ourselves with the country of the Inquisition under colour of supporting the French Protestants was a manifest absurdity. Yet peace with any European nation was better than haphazard war with all, so Porter's arrival was looked for and talked of, and expected, but in vain.

The weeks grew into months, and still no tidings came of the signing of a treaty with Spain on the return of the envoy. At last when winter had set in came news that Porter was indeed in England, but only as a shipwrecked waif on the Dorset shore. The Spanish ship in which he sailed had run aground at Burton on the Dorset coast, and had gone to pieces.[1] The crew and passengers reached shore in safety, but the Brutonians, as one of Porter's friends called the men of Burton, stripped

[1] "Court and Times of Charles I.," vol. ii. p. 4.

the shipwrecked travellers of all their valuables, and even of their clothes, and so left them naked for many hours before they would afford them any harbour or courtesy, although Porter cried out to them that he was a King's servant. Not till Sir Thomas Freke was sent expressly from London did these too patriotic wreckers treat the foreigners with any humanity, and even then many things of value were still missing, and the arms that were recovered all needed repair.[1]

Cloth was commanded to be sent for reclothing the soldiers and mariners, and a new glass was procured for the captain, and a letter to the Council says that Porter and his companion Don Antonio were expected to arrive in London on January 5, 1629.[2]

Porter had returned to a new England. Buckingham was gone, and the warlike ambition of England died with him. The King had learned a lesson, and, from this time on, his foreign policy was completely altered. He negotiated, but he would not fight. English interests were more and more concentrated at home, and, for the rest of Charles's reign, England ceased to count for anything in the politics of Europe.

When negotiation took the place of action, there was more work than ever for Porter to do, but the more useful he was to the King, the less he was liked by the people.

It was constantly announced by the Government, as in 1628, that Porter was abroad buying pictures ; but the difficulty of knowing exactly what he was doing naturally increased the suspicion with which ordinary people looked on him. The country had

[1] Dom. S. P., Freke to the Council, Jan. 3, 1629.   [2] Ibid.

no reason to trust the wisdom of the King, still less did it trust this mysterious man who was known to be deep in his confidence, and who was said to be buying pictures, when every one knew he was carrying royal messages. What was kept so secret was hardly likely to be honest. He might even be more dangerous than the King who employed him. The fact that nothing could be absolutely proved against him only heightened the alarm with which his mysterious movements were noted. Was it not too likely that this buying of pictures was but a cloak for selling the country, and that this handsome, plausible courtier was in reality a secret Jesuit, deep in plots against the religion and liberties of England.

Wild as these suspicions seem, they grew apace, and by the time a dozen years had passed, this man, who professed himself to be "no politician," was held by the leaders of the Parliament to be one of the most dangerous members of the royal household, and was excepted by name from every offer of amnesty.

The peace with Spain, which Porter had gone to Madrid to negotiate, was concluded in an appropriate manner by no less an envoy than the great painter Rubens, who arrived in London in 1630.

He came with all the pomp and state of an official ambassador, but the combination of diplomacy and art was too convenient an arrangement to be entirely dropped, and some still believe that he was no envoy, "but onely Rubens, the famous painter, appearing onely in his own quality, and Jerbir [Gerbier], the Duke's painter, master of the ceremonies to entertain him."[1]

[1] Meautys to Lady Bacon. "Rubens Papers," Sainsbury, p. 130.

But "the Duke's painter" was yet another of the diplomatic artists. Balthazar Gerbier had succeeded Porter as a confidential servant of the Duke of Buckingham, had been made the Duke's Master of the Horse, knighted, and finally was appointed British Resident in Brussels. He had visited Paris in Buckingham's suite and there had become acquainted with Rubens, so when the great artist came to London he was lodged in Gerbier's house at the King's expense.

Rubens had already been often employed to correspond with England on behalf of the Spanish Regent of the Netherlands, and his letters had frequently been addressed to Porter. So Endymion was naturally very busy during this visit of the great painter, and was entrusted with most of the presents that were to be carried to the distinguished visitor.

But all the condescension of the King, all the courtliness of Porter, all the hospitality of Gerbier, failed to gain more from Rubens than the peace he had been commissioned to conclude. Spain absolutely refused, as she had done ten years earlier, to champion the cause of a Protestant Elector, and Charles's evergreen hopes of Spanish help in the Palatinate were once more blighted.

The treaty of peace was, however, concluded without much difficulty, as one of the chief obstacles to its settlement had been Olivares' personal dislike of Buckingham, and neither England nor Spain had anything to gain by the continuance of the war.

However, Charles had some compensation for his disappointment about the Palatinate. Rubens was willing to oblige his Majesty in another line, and undertook to paint the pictures to decorate the new banqueting-hall at Whitehall at a cost of £3,000. A good many letters in the Porter correspondence refer to the payment of various instalments of this large sum, which was sent by Porter to Brussels through his agents, two Catholic merchants named Wake. A gold chain was also sent through the Wakes; and before Rubens left London the King loaded him with presents, giving him a diamond cordon and ring, and a sword enriched with diamonds. The envoy was also knighted, and departed for Madrid well pleased with his reception in England.

His farewell to Porter was conveyed by Gage another of the agents employed indifferently to negotiate secret treaties and to buy pictures. The affliction mentioned in the letter is the loss of Porter's little son, Mountjoy, who died aged two years.

"LONDON, *Feb. 20th*, 1630.

"I have been twice to your house to wait on you and to tell you that Signior Rubens parteth very well satisfied of your affection and favour to him, and is very sorry for the affliction which God has sent you, but we hope both that by this time your comfort is well advanced, which I shall be extreme glad to understand, as likewise of occasions wherein I may show myself

"Your most affectionate humble servant,

"G. GAGE."[1]

The death of Buckingham smoothed the way to a peace with France as well as with Spain.

[1] Sainsbury, "Rubens Papers," p. 146.

Now that the favourite no longer stood between Henrietta Maria and her husband, she had no further complaints to send to the French Court, and as the French King had no desire to destroy his Huguenot subjects unless they forced him to it by rebellion, the two causes of differences between France and England had ceased to exist. A treaty was signed at Susa, and there seemed now to be no reason why England should not be the one quiet and prosperous country of Europe.

The sorrows of the Elector Frederick ended in 1632, and many men said it was really of a broken heart that he died. His brother claimed the regency of the electorate as guardian of the young Charles Louis, but no country seemed inclined to take up arms in his behalf, or to try to expel Maximilian of Bavaria, on whom the electorate had been conferred.

Charles, however, lost no opportunity of reminding every one that he would be obliged if they would champion the cause of his nephew, and English foreign policy grew to mean nothing but a series of idle and futile negotiations on behalf of the young Elector.

In 1634 excellent reasons were discovered for sending a mission to Brussels. The Spanish troops had united with the Imperial army in inflicting a crushing defeat on the Swedes at Nordlingen, and the victorious Spaniards, under the Cardinal Infante, had just arrived in the Netherlands.

Porter had known the brilliant young general twelve years before in Madrid as a handsome dark-eyed boy, more popular among the Spaniards than the fair Flemish-looking king. What could be

more obvious than to dispatch Porter from England
to congratulate the Cardinal Infante on his successes.
Incidentally he might also try to obtain some redress
for Spanish robberies on English trading vessels,
for Charles was beginning to look with much
jealousy on any infringment of the English lordship
of the Narrow Seas, and he was not to fail to put
in a word on behalf of the Elector whenever there
was an opening.

Porter was accompanied by his two sons, and
travelled in some state with a train of twenty
gentlemen and a large retinue of servants.

He was received with warm hospitality by
Gerbier, who was now English Resident at
Brussels. Reports vary as to Gerbier's success
in that position. He was a poor man with a
large family of handsome and expensive children,
and his enemies said he had not been able to resist
the bribes offered by the ministers of the Regent
Isabella, and had betrayed English secrets to them.
He certainly did not find his position at Brussels
a bed of roses, and the visit of the Porter family
seems to have made him quite homesick for
England. The following year he wrote an
elaborately jocose letter to Porter lamenting his
life in so miserable a place and saying if only he
could return : " How would the mother sheep and
all the little lambs skip and kiss the happy English
ground!"[1]   One suspects this patriotic letter was
a hint that Porter might use his interest with the
King to get the Gerbier family a comfortable post
in England.

But it was not only Gerbier who was delighted

[1] " Lords Strangford," p. 64.

to welcome Porter to Brussels in 1634; the reception afforded him at the Court was also exceedingly gracious, and the Count de Noyelles was sent to convey him to the palace in one of the royal coaches. But this compliment and a parting present of "a brush sett with diamonds and a diamond ring to each of his sons," proved to be all the satisfaction the English Envoy got at Brussels. His first reports, however, had been very hopeful. He wrote to Windebank :—

"MAY IT PLEASE YOUR HONOUR,—The last week I gave you an account of what had passed till then ; since which time I have had another audience with this Prince, wherein I represented unto him the complaints of our merchants for the laying of new impositions upon our cloths and other commodities here contrary to the articles of peace : and also of the excesses and robberies committed by those of Dunkirk upon our merchants in general and in particular upon the fishing busses, for all of which I hoped his Highness would give order to see his ministers here, that full satisfaction and remedy might be had, and to that purpose (with Mr. Jerbier's advice) I drew a remonstrance, and it is referred to the President of the Council of those countries, who seems to be a wise and an honest man ; and gives me hopes that all shall be done as is desired, which is the only cause of my stay now. I write your Honour no news, for the Resident will do it better than I can : he useth me so extream kindly as I must intreat your Honour to thank him for it, and when it lies in my power to requite it, I will not forget the obligation I have to serve him.

Your Honour may be confident of my love and respects to you, and whensoever you shall be pleased to command me, I will not fail to make my actions run equal to my words, as one that desires to be esteemed

"Your Honour's true friend and humble servant,

" ENDYMION PORTER.

" BRUSSELS, 5 *December*, 1634." [1]

This mission had naturally been watched with some anxiety by the English adherents of the young Elector. But they were too wise to hope for much advantage to be reaped from an empty exchange of compliments with the Spanish General, the brother-in-law of the Austrian whose troops were carrying havoc over the fair fields of the Palatinate.

For her own part, the high-spirited and ardent Elizabeth hoped rather that some lucky chance might disturb the formal courtesies of this reception at Brussels. A trifling misunderstanding might lead to a quarrel and then open war and honest blows should arbitrate the Elector's cause, instead of the feeble requests and idle compliments of hollow diplomacy.

Elizabeth's faithful friend, Sir Thomas Rowe, sharply on the look-out for signs of discord, sent Strafford a very different report of Porter's reception to the one which Porter himself had written to individuals. Sir Thomas says—

" Mr. Porter sent to congratulate the Cardinal Infante has received no great satisfaction, for the Prince never moved his hat or foot. What dis-

---

[1] " Lords Strangford," p. 60.

pleased him we may not guess, and his friends
excuse him that it is the way of Spain, and he never
unveiled to any but the Queen Mother of France,
since he came here." [1]

Spanish etiquette was still what it had been when
the handsome young Earl of Carlisle was presented
to the Infanta during Prince Charles's visit to
Madrid, and the Princess did not even deign to look
at him, but sat enthroned like a waxen Madonna.[2]
Spain was still more Oriental than European.

Sir Thomas goes on : " This is at best a proud
defence, but we think there is more in it, for he
offered to write back, but not giving upon his letters
the due title of Majesty to our King, Porter refused
to bring it ; upon this it was formalised, and a week
was spent, but in conclusion, persisting in the difficulty, Porter has returned without any answer.
Some say his Majesty subscribing 'à mon tres
chère cousin,' and not 'altesse,' from thence grew
the exception, but it is not the style of kings to
inferiors, but that of Majesty is due from all inferiors
to them."

Garrard, writing to Strafford, adds the information
that Mr. Secretary Coke drew the letter in French
and gave the Cardinal the style of " Vous," which
the Spaniard abhors as a kind of thou-ing one,
whereas he expected " Altesse Royale," or at least
" Altesse."

It is a pity that Mr. Secretary Coke did not
consult Porter about Spanish etiquette, but that
great man was somewhat jealous of outsiders

---

[1] Rowe to Wentworth, Dom. S. P., Jan. 1635, N.S.
[2] See *ante*, p. 64.

intruding on his business, and, as it was, he complained not long after to the King of Endymion's interference, so he had to be left to mismanage correspondence in his own way.

Coke's royal master also continued to mismanage his diplomatic affairs after his own fashion, and filled English statesmen with dismay, and foreign Powers with impatient contempt. The war that Elizabeth desired was not declared, but Charles continued to negotiate, and more than once was on the verge of giving material aid to the Elector.

The disastrous European conflict still raged, but the struggle was not now between Protestant and Catholic, Gustavus Adolphus and the Emperor, but between France and Spain, and Charles offered his alliance indifferently to whichever country would help his nephew, though it was obvious that Spain would never have the will, and Strafford[1] doubted if France would ever have the power to place Charles Louis on his father's seat.

One of the most miserably mean of the King's manœuvres has an almost respectable aspect put on it by the elegance of the letters in which Porter conveys his Majesty's wishes.

It was in 1639 that a great Spanish fleet destined to carry on the war against France in the Low Countries was forced by the Dutch under Tromp to take refuge in English waters. Of course the Spanish ships were, for the time, in safety, and the Spanish and Dutch ambassadors both appealed to the English King, the Spaniard for the continuance of his protection, the Dutch for permission to attack the enemy in English waters.

[1] Seeley, "English Foreign Policy," vol. i. p. 395.

This was a situation after Charles's own heart. He desired the rival ambassadors to state what each of their governments were ready to do for the Prince Palatine, and while weighing their proposals he did his best to force both fleets to keep the peace.

But the Dutch Admiral, Tromp, had no fancy to remain idle with his prey within reach, and he soon took the matter into his own hands. He attacked the Spaniards, drove twenty of their ships on shore, and so handled the rest of that stately fleet that not eighteen of the whole reached Dunkirk. Pennington, the English Admiral, protected the ships that had gone ashore in Kent, and the King had already ordered the Lord Warden of the Cinque Ports to provide hospitality for any Spaniards who might take refuge on English soil, as long as they could pay for it. But he considered, if the Spaniards were to be sunk, they ought to oblige him by being wrecked in deep water, so as not to ruin his harbour, "but," Porter comments sadly in his letter to Secretary Windebank, "the Spaniard regards nothing but his own accommodation."

" *To Windebank.*

" 1639.

" MAY IT PLEASE YOUR HONOUR,—Last night, at nine of the clock, I received your Honour's letter, with one enclosed from Don Alonzo de Cardenas, and I acquainted his Majesty with the contents of it, and he commanded me to let your Honour know that he would have you make answer to the Resident (if he require it) that the King hath shewed his care of the Spanish fleet, and that if the wind sit where it doth, it will be impossible for his ships to come to protect them against the Hollander, but his Majesty will do the best he can. Howsoever he would have the Spaniards prepare themselves for the worst, for they cannot imagine but that he will be pressed to limit a time for their abode in his port, and, in the mean time, he shall keep them from hostility if it be possible; and his Majesty hath given the best order he can to that purpose; and your Honour can inform them how great a prejudice it would be to the King if they should fight in the harbour, for if any ships should miscarry and be sunk there it would be the ruin of the best harbour in the kingdom; but it seems the Spaniard regards nothing but his own accommodation, nor will they look about them, until the King assign them a day to set sail, the which will be required from him; and when they are out of the port, they must trust to their own force, for his Majesty will protect them no further. As for their making any proposition, I think they are such dull, stupefied souls that they think of nothing, and when I acquainted his Majesty with their negligence in that particular, he told me that the Resident was a silly, ignorant old fellow. I would I could serve your Honour in anything : I have so many reasons to do it, as I should be accounted by all the world an ungrateful man, if I were not inviolably

"Your honour's most devoted

"ENDYMION PORTER.

"WINDSOR, *this 9th of October*, 1639." [1]

[1] "Lords Strangford," pp. 67, 68, 69.

"*To Windebank.*

MAY IT PLEASE YOUR HONOUR,—His Majesty having taken into his gracious consideration what may happen, if the Hollanders should, in a hostile manner, fall upon the Spaniards in the Downs, and by any such act drive them to run on shore for safeguard of their lives, and thereby those that scape may be much necessitated, both for victual and lodging, and the King's subjects damnified by the unruly carriage of soldiers in want : his Majesty (out of his pious care to prevent disorder on all sides) hath commanded me to let your Honour know that it is his royal pleasure you signify unto the Lord Warden of the Cinque Ports and to the Deputy Lieutenants of Kent that they (in such case of necessity) see provision be made for the billeting of strangers in such places, as for their moneys they may have all necessaries of meat, drink, and lodging, that thereby the world may see his Majesty's christianlike intentions to the subjects of his friends and allies. These are his Majesty's commands : and when I can make your honour any return for the favours I daily receive from you in any particular, I will freely let you see that I have hearty desires to be accounted

"Your honour's most faithful humble servant,

"ENDYMION PORTER.[1]

"WINDSOR, *this 10th of October*, 1639."[1]

Porter's next letter on the subject of the Spanish fleet, is to ask the English Admiral's help for a Spanish officer.

---

[1] "Lords Strangford," p. 69.

"NOBLE SIR,—I am so confident of your love to me, as I proclaim to all the world the many obligations you are always ready to lay upon me, and having occasion at this time to make use of your favour, I could not desire you to shew it to one I honour and respect more than this gallant gentleman Senor don Simon de Mascarenas, one whose birth and quality claim from all the world kindness; he is Coronell of a regiment of foot which was passing into Flanders in English ships, but by misfortune the Hollanders lighted of the great part of them, but those few that remain he is to embark in the Downs. Let me conjure you by all our friendship to assist him in what you may, and to advise him the best way and the securest for his own person and his men; and not doubting of your love and care in this, I commit you to God, and rest

"Your true friend and humble servant,

"ENDYMION PORTER.

"LONDON, *the 20th of July*, 1639.

"This noble gentleman tells me that one Captain Fletcher had in his keeping the chains and jewels which did belong to the Sargeant-Major and other Captains. I beseech you let him be arrested, for it is a dishonour to our nation that he should go away and cozen (cousen) poor strangers of their goods; he is now in the Downs, and I hope you will not let him go without restoring what he most unjustly detains." [1]

A month later Porter wrote again [2] to Pennington with many compliments and apologies, to beg him

---

[1] Dom. S. P., vol. ccccxxvi. 10.
[2] Ibid., vol. ccccxxix. 20.

to convey another Spanish gentleman to Dunkirk in some merchant ship.

Again in October he writes :—

" You see how the Spaniards believe that I have power with you, for though this bearer, the Veedor, have my lord Admiral's warrant for a convoy, yet he thinks himself not safe without my recommending him to your care ; and believe me, sir, he is a very honest gentleman, and I hope for my sake you will use him with that love you have ever shewed to my friends, and let me assure you that I shall make you hearty returns whensoever you shall find an employment for

"Your most obliged humble servant,

"ENDYMION PORTER.

" WHITEHALL, *this 30th of October*, 1639." [1]

Porter had soon an opportunity of showing his gratitude to Pennington, as the Admiral was imprisoned to mark the King's anger at his failure to protect the Spanish fleet ! [2]

We know little more of Porter's missions to foreign Powers. The bare fact is recorded that he was once sent to Brussels with the eccentric genius Sir Kenelm Digby, but no letters mention the object of the visit or describe its incidents.

It is also believed that later on, during the Civil War, Porter was more than once sent to the Continent to sell or pawn royal jewels and plate. He was the most likely person to be dispatched on such errands, but there is no documentary evidence

[1] Dom. S. P., vol. ccccxxxi. 73.
[2] Dyer, " Modern Europe," vol. ii. p. 607.

of them to be found, and possibly the rumour may have arisen from the sale of royal jewels by the Duke of Buckingham during the early days when Porter was in his service.

Porter certainly was in Paris during the course of the Civil War, for Lord Digby, writing to Henry Jermyn from France, mentions that he had sent his letters to England by the hand of Porter.

It cannot be doubted that Porter was employed in more foreign negotiations than we are ever likely to trace, for as his missions were always confidential and generally secret, some pains were doubtless taken to hide the evidence of such negotiations. A guarded tongue is an important part of a diplomatist's equipment, and if Porter was no politician, he had not a few of the qualities that make a good diplomatist. Unfortunately, the caution and reticence which made him a valuable servant to the King make him also a tantalising subject for his biographer, and we can only collect scattered hints of the most interesting part of his varied career.

CHAPTER VII

THE custom of Royal Progresses seems to have gone out of fashion under Charles, and as time went on Endymion was evidently able to spend more time at home, and the letters to his wife grew proportionately fewer.

The blank left in the history by the absence of letters is, however, filled up to a great extent by the bundles of bills and accounts which were confiscated with the rest of the Porter correspondence. From them we learn that Mr. and Mrs. Porter sat in winter by wood fires, and lit their rooms with candles costing five shillings for the dozen pounds. When Mr. Porter was in attendance on the King at Oatlands and tore his scarlet coat it cost him a shilling to have it mended, and once when he was unlucky at the bowling green and had forgotten his purse, he had to borrow five and sixpence from his groom to pay his debts. The groom also sends in his account for shoeing the horses, and a cousin, George Boteler, did some horsedealing for Endymion, but he wrote that horses were hard to come by and he could not get one for less than thirty pounds.

The bills which the tailor sent in for Mrs. Porter's

dresses enable us to realise how that handsome lady looked in her every-day life, when she was not sitting in white satin and pearls to be painted by Vandyke.   Ladies seem usually to have worn some sort of short jacket with a stomacher or waistcoat which generally matched the skirt of the gown in colour.   Mrs. Porter and little Marie, her eldest girl, both had cloth of silver waistcoats, and Mrs. Porter had a "Tabby Rose coulered pettycoat and wastcoate" and also ones of black and of "sky colered satin."   The petticoats were sometimes trimmed with "gold and silver parchment"— evidently parchment lace—and also with bone lace. A petticoat and stomacher of incarnadine satin were "lased with two broad silver laces about."   There were also a petticoat and "hougerlin"[1] of black "pudesaw," probably paduasoy, and a waistcoat of "aurora colered satin."   The bodices seem to have been stiffened in the fashion of Queen Elizabeth's days, for there is an entry of half-a-crown for fustian "to lay between the stiffening and the outside." Sometimes the bodices seem to have been cut low and laced across the stomacher, and were then called "stays."   "A black mooehaire sut" had stays to match ; and a "zebelah coulered satin sut" was made with satin stays.   "Zebela colour" is obviously Isabella colour, a shade of tan.   A pair of red baise sleeves were covered with sarsenet, and there were an unlimited number of pockets at one and sixpence each.   Six holland coats cost a guinea to make, including "fustian and tape to them."   Making a dress cost one pound two shillings.   Mrs. Porter

---

[1] Possibly the "Hungerland bands" mentioned in Massenger's play, "The City Madam."

seems to have supplied the dress materials, so only the linings, buttons, &c., are charged in the bills. However, a few details on prices may be collected from them. Black satin was fourteen shillings a yard, black Taffety sarsenet nine shillings, and black velvet only eight and eightpence. One of these dressmakers' bills amounts to twenty-two pounds twelve and elevenpence, and sad to relate, Mrs. Porter only paid one pound towards it. Her shoes came most appropriately from a maker named Heele and cost three shillings a pair.

Her goldsmith's bill is marked "reseved in foell." It included gold earrings that cost twelve pounds, two head pieces at seventeen pounds, and a "cullett" for a hatband setting that cost a pound. The high crowns of the hats seen in portraits of James the First seem often to have been surrounded by a hatband of jewels. A diamond hatband was given by King Charles to the painter Rubens, and long afterwards a diamond hatband was given as a bribe to Lord Howard of Escrick.

One of the beautiful satin "suts" and "hattband setting" mentioned in the bills was probably worn by Mrs. Porter at a gay meeting at Hatfield, described by a correspondent of Lord Conway's in 1636.[1] He tells how Lord Salisbury's guests all rode out on horseback to meet Mrs. Porter, who was expected to dinner at Lord Boteler's house, Hatfield Woodhall. The Countess of Arundel was there, the wife of that stately nobleman who was said to go to Court because there only was a greater man than himself, and who went thither the seldomer because there was a greater man than himself.

[1] G. Garrard to Conway, Dom. S. P., 1636.

Among the party, too, was Sir J. North, as well as
the famous Sir Toby Matthews, who was so mixed
up in all the Roman Catholic matters, and had that
morning arrived from Wrest.   Lord Salisbury killed
a deer in the woods, which was presented to Lord
Cottington, who was "bravely horsed and wearing
a white beaver hat with studded hatband, his coach
attending him."   Then they went to see the deer
called, and a bow was put into Lord Cottington's
hands, but he bungled and shot thrice before he
killed, all the ladies standing by to see his failures.
If he was a bad shot, he was a successful gardener,
for the next morning he sent a present of nine
melons, and six more in the evening, of brave
kinds, some white as winter melons.   The mention
of melons reminds us of the great advances that
were made at that time in gardening under Tradiscant
and Parkinson.   At another date is an entry in the
Porter accounts of ten shillings given "to one that
brought a present of Spanish melons."   Country
gentlemen were proud to send the produce of their
gardens and farmyards up to their less fortunate
friends in London, and substantial presents seem to
have been all the fashion.   Lady Crane sent up
poultry to Mr. Porter, and a buck from the park at
Grafton.   Probably this Marie Crane was some
connection of Endymion's youngest sister, Mrs.
Elinor Crane.

From Burdrop Park, on the Wiltshire Downs,
comes a letter from Sir William Calley telling how
he had met Endymion's brother-in-law, Canning, at
Stow Fair, on May-day, 1628, and rode with him to
his house at Foxcote.   He says he does not mean
to come to London this term, by reason of the

foggy air, but hopes to see Endymion and his wife
in the Long Vacation. Sir William was always
sending up country dainties to his friends in London.
By Richard Harvey, Endymion's trusted servant,
came one time "four collars of brawn, two dozen
hogs pudding, half white and half black, and a fat
young swan. And love and service to good old
Mrs. Porter." For Christmastide, in 1639, came
another two dozen of hogs puddings and six collars
of brawn ; evidently there had been a great pig-
killing at Burdrop in preparation for Christmas.
These good things were sent up to London by the
waggoner, and a week later arrived Lady Calley's
present, a " small rundlet of Metheglin." The good
old knight did not live to see his fair country
overrun by hostile armies : he died in 1641, taken
away while yet peace reigned over his gardens and
farmyards.

But the Porter correspondence ranges over a
fine variety of subjects. Young men starting on
their travels, duchesses and farm stewards, needy
poets and wealthy merchants, all had compliments
to pay and favours to ask. The widowed Duchess
of Buckingham writes to "her good cousin" about
a steward whom "her dear lord had a special care
of." Sir Henry Martin, a man of very different
politics, nevertheless acknowledges Porter's good
offices with the King, and even in the troubled days
of 1640, when the storm of civil war was about to
burst, Porter found time to make jokes in his letter
to the Farmers of the Customs. He writes :—

" Endymion Porter, Esqr., desires a Bill of Stores
for four hogsheads of Graves white wine and half a

hogshead of Rhenish wine, packed up in the dry
cask which came from Amsterdam in the *Elizabeth*,
the Master's name being Michael Jockley, M.ᴰ.
with the mark in the margin, it being for the expense
of his own table.   The ship lieth at Somers Quay.
If you will not allow me a Bill of Store for my wine
I will bring my friends to your houses, and all those
that come home to mine shall drink water, for I live
by your favours, and am

" Your humble servant,

" ENDYMION PORTER.

"*July* 9, 1640."

Stay-at-home parents looked with wonder and
respect on the experienced man who was familiar
with the strange ways of foreign countries ; Mr.
Warmestry, a Worcestershire friend, writes con-
sulting Porter on the advisability of letting his sons
go to Paris with Lord Danby ; and Lord Dorchester
referred to him for advice when Lennox was going
abroad.

Mr. Warmestry's letter is not confined to tourist
business ; he makes suggestions for a smart petticoat
for Mrs. Porter, and winds up with a request that
Endymion will give him due notice if he and Lord
Newport come "through Worcester this summer,
as otherwise" they "may chance to fast !"   The
following very quaint letter is really worth preserving
in full :—

"SIR,—Upon my speedy haste out of Worwick-
shire, I committed a Jewel (juall) of my wife's her
little Dog to the charge of one of my Footmen to
bring after me, who (by reason of the Dogs finding
of a Hare) lost him upon the way.   He not daring

to acquaint me with it, upon inquiry understanding he was taken up by you, came as it appears unknown to me to demand him in my name ; but you denying the delivery he was forced to reveal the truth, and require my letter ; and I must confess, had I sent the Boy, I should have writt howsoever.   But thus much I must *ingeniously* tell you, I esteem'd it over great a curiosity in you to detain the Dog upon those nice terms when the confirmation of so many of my friends and my Hon. Lord that answer'd the truth might sufficiently have satisfied any man ; but since lines (lins) are of greater efficacy with you than your respect to a friend, let these that plead in my wife's behalf, require a restitution of her Dog back, which she highly values.   Thereby you may much indear him that bears you true affection and swear to be

    " Your perpetual friend and servant,

                     " CHARLES SMITHE.

" ASHBY, *this Saturday.*

" To his noble and worthily respected friend,

       Mr. Endimion Porter, at Beauvor present." [1]

The registers of the parish of St. Martin's supply some of the blanks left by the lack of letters, and from them we learn that on July 20, 1632, William Porter was baptised and buried the same day, and in 1634 another little Endymion was baptised, but did not live a year.   London was not favourable to child life in those days.   The gardens of the Strand stretched down to the Thames, and green lanes surrounded St. Martin's Church, but the plague claimed its victims yearly, and the closely fastened

       [1] Dom. S. P., vol. cccclxxv. 88.

windows and crowded houses prevented any real improvement in public health for many a year to come. The following letter tells of the most serious quarrel that we know of between Endymion and Olivia. Probably Olivia was unwell and in bad spirits, just as when she wrote the "swaggering" letter soon after little Villiers' death.

"August 1, 1634.

"OLIVE,—I writt unto you a letter by this gentleman which it seems you take unkindly. As I hope for salvation I know no cause for it, but sure you are apt to mistake me, and are fearful that I should oblige you overmuch to esteem me; wherein, though you show but little love, yet 'tis a sign of a good conscience. God continue it in you, and send me grace to mend my life as I will my manners, for I will trouble you with no more of my letters, nor with any design of mine, yet I will not despair of you as you do of me, for I hope that age and good considerations will make you know I am

"Your best friend,
"ENDYMION PORTER.

"Commend me to the children, and send this enclosed to D'Avenant with all speed."[1]

"Olive Porter to Endymion.

"SWEETHEART,—My brother tells me you are very angry with me still. I did not think you could have been so cruel to me to have stayed so long away, and not to forgive that which you know was spoke in passion. I know not how to beg your pardon, because I have broken my word with you

[1] Dom. S. P., vol. cclxxviii. 3.

before ; but if your good nature will forgive me, come home to her that will ever be

"Your loving and obedient wife,

"OLIVE PORTER.

"*August*, 1634." [1]

Was the brother who acted as peacemaker Captain Tom Porter? Olive had no brother of her own living but poor weak-witted Lord Boteler, so she must allude to one of her brothers-in-law ; and who so likely as the good-natured sailor, Endymion's favourite brother, to say a word in season ? Captain Tom probably made his home with Endymion when he was on shore, for he never married, and Endymion seems to have managed his business for him, even to buying him a feather bed and other bedding. These must have been of uncommonly good quality, as they cost £16, while the usual price of a feather bed and bolster was only £4 10s. Captain Tom, no doubt, stood god-father to Endymion's little son Thomas in 1636. He shared to some extent in Endymion's good fortunes ; in 1630 he was granted lastage and ballastage to the value of £50 a year, and the reversion of Alfarthing Manor was also settled on him. In 1632 there was " much contention between Captain Porter and Captain Plumley, who should be general of four ships royal," and it was popularly believed that Porter would get them.[2] In March, 1635, Captain Thomas Porter was command-ing the *Henrietta Maria*, and he had the " carrying

---

[1] Dom. S. P., vol. cclxxiii. 83.
[2] "Court and Times of Charles I.," vol. ii. p. 189.

ENDYMION PORTER, WITH HIS WIFE AND SONS.

of Lord Ashton to Spain." [1]   The following year,
August, 1636, he was mentioned by Captain Giles
Penn in a letter to Secretary Nicholas about the
Sallee Rovers, whose piratical expeditions were a
terror to the south-western shores of England and
Ireland.   Captain Penn asked that Endymion
should be consulted about his brother undertaking
an expedition against the Corsairs, saying : " Captain
Porter is fittest to be employed on the action, both
for language and other respects." [2] No doubt Tom's
knowledge of Spanish would have been useful in
the Mediterranean, but the expedition did not sail
till 1637, when a civil war had just broken out
among the Moors, and they were glad to purchase
English neutrality by surrendering no less than two
hundred and seventy-one captives. But the expedition was not commanded by Tom Porter ; he had
sailed on his last voyage.   In the autumn of 1637
Sir Wm. Calley wrote regretting to hear of the
weakness of Captain Porter at a time when Endymion also was ill, " labouring under a fever," which
prevented his visiting Sir William at Burdrop ; and
the next mention we find of Thomas Porter is the
bill for his funeral. Endymion had his brother
buried with all due observance ; the velvet pall
cost £1 and escutcheons were £1 7s.   Herrick,
who with D'Avenant acted as a sort of Poet
Laureate to Endymion, wrote a poem on Thomas's
death, but it has no personal interest.

As time goes on the Porter children take their
share in the family correspondence, and their bills
add to the family expenses.   When Charles Porter

[1] Garrard to Strafford, Oct. 3, 1635.
[2] Cal. Dom. S. P., August, 1636.

went to Spain in 1637 he wore a pair of black silk garters with roses that cost eighteen shillings, and five shillings was paid for the carriage of one of his letters. Possibly it may be the one that follows :—

"DEAR MOTHER,—I have received your letter, in which I understand that my father *and are* very angry with me, which hath not troubled me a little to think that I should deserve any anger at either of your h [*torn off*] the ways that possibly can be to retain your loves will do my endeavour to amend any fault you accuse me of. Therefore, I beseech you, sweet mother, not to let your anger continue, for it is the only thing I desire to shun in this world. I am extremely glad to hear that my little brother Tom proveth so fine a child, and that my nurse and you are friends again : I pray you to let it last both with her and me.

"Your dutiful and obedient son,

"CHARLES PORTER.

"MADRID, *the* 16*th of January*, 1637, *O.S.*

"I pray remember my humble duty and service to my lady Duchess and my Lady of Arundel." [1]

George Porter received a safe conduct in a journey to France and Spain in October, 1638. There must have been some hurry in his departure, for Lord Conway writes : "Sir W. Howard is gone into Holland with the Prince Elector, and with him young Mr. Porter, neither of them with any more clothes or shirts but what they had on their backs." [2] George did not return till the following July, so it is to be hoped that his wardrobe followed him. He

[1] Dom. S. P., vol. cccxliv. 24.   [2] Hist. MSS. Com. xii.

travelled home with his aunt, Lady Newport. A letter announcing his landing at Dover to his mother, says, "His aunt will not suffer him to come without her, who will to-morrow morning be coming toward you." [1]   It may be gathered from the following French letter from little Philip Porter (perhaps written as an exercise), that George had been ill while he was abroad.[2]

"MON TRES CHER FRERE,—Je suis fort joyeux d'entendre que vous avez perdu votre fievre. Je seray bien aise de vous voir icy ou a Londres. Ma tante estoit malade hier, mais auiourdhuy elle se porte mieux. Tous se recommendent a vous et ie demeure.

> "Vostre tresaymé Frere,
> > "PHILIP PORTER.

"17 *September*, 1638.

"A son tres cher frere Monsr. George Porter." [3]

A couple of letters from Woodhall tells of the doings of the younger children while George and Charles were on the Continent. While Endymion acted as guardian to poor William Boteler, Woodhall, which was settled on Olivia after her brother's life, seems to have been used as a country house for the family ; it was more conveniently situated than Aston, and Alfarthing never seems to have been a favourite place of residence. In 1638 the two younger boys were at Woodhall with their sister Marie. "Mr. Thomas" was at this time aged three, and "Mr. James" was eight months old.

---

[1] Barter to Mrs. Porter ; Cal. Dom. S. P., 1638.
[2] See Chapter XIII.
[3] Dom. S. P., vol. cccxcviii. 108.

" HONEST MR. HARVEY,—I am very glad to hear
of your good health and of your coming to town,
and more will I be when it is my fortune to see
you, that I may give you thanks for so *many
Courtesy* and good Counsel as I have Received at
your hands. Truly we were here in expectation
to see my noble Mr. and Lady some days of this
week, but I now see our *selfs* frustrated. The bay
Nagg that you writt of shall be taken in, and well
kept and breathed against my Mr. is pleased to send
for it. John Aldridge the Keeper desireth my Mr.
and lady to know that if they will have some does
to be kill'd that it must be within this 7 or 8 days
at the furthest, because this wet weather will make
them fall away. Both Mr. Thos. and Mr. James
are in very good health, God be Thanked, and
Mrs. Mary continues still in her quartan ague, and
is very desirous to go to London if my lady will be
pleased. She gives you many Thanks for your
Kind Commendations and returns to you her kind
love and service, as I do and the rest of our
Company, and wishing you all health and happiness, Resting for Ever

"Your humble servant,

" FRAN. DORVAN.

"Pray do me the favour to present my best
service to Mrs. Dorothy.

"WOODHALL, *October* 22, 1638." [1]

The other letter from Woodhall tells of the early
promise of Philip Porter. The tutor, James Gibbs,
who writes, was probably a cousin, for letters are
extant from Ralph Gibbs to his uncle, Nicholas

[1] Dom. S. P., M., vol. cccc. 77.

Porter of Aston, and from Gertrude Gibbs to her uncle Edmund of Mickleton.[1]   A little later James writes to Harvey that he wants his money matters settled that he may go abroad to Padua or Bologna to complete his medical studies.   He says his only reason for remaining in England had been "Signior Endymion."   It is probable that when he went abroad he took Mr. Philip, his "maister piece," with him, for less than a month after the following letter was written a license was issued to permit Philip Porter to travel abroad with two servants for three years.

"Mr. Harvey,—This is to bid you welcome to London again, and to give you notice that I had, and have a great resentment of the misfortune of not seeing you when you called at Woodhall passing by.   Here we are all alone, and apply ourselves to our books diligently, and so much the better, by how much the less distraction we find, and farther we are from London.   I hope to make Mr. Philip my *maister*piece, according as he proceeds with me, and takes Learning.   I have already shewed his father the profit he hath made to his great satisfaction and joy, of one yt [that] could scarce read a word in English when I first undertook him.   This I speak without any exaggeration, or desire to arrogate more to myself than many that know it will give me.   His Father told us we should shortly be going over Sea, but I fear it will not be before next Spring.   I should be very sorry to come to London to teach him in the interim, for the many occasions *of divertment* that daily present

[1] Cal. Dom. S. P., 1648–9, p. 429.

10

themselves.   So that I mean to write to mi Señor
to know his intention shortly, and if we go not
away this winter, that he would please to let us live
in the Country far enough with some friend or other
of his.   But this with you alone, and under seal.
What you please to advise me, I shall be glad to
follow.

"As for Mr. Charles, no great matter could be
worked with him ; wherefore I should urge (?)
some settled course should be thought on for him."[1]

The tutor's prophecies were not fulfilled.   Charles,
with whom he could do nothing, turned out one of
the best of the family, while poor Philip, the masterpiece, made entire shipwreck of his talents and of
his life.

[1] Dom. S. P., vol. cccclviii. 21.

CHAPTER VIII

POETS AND PAINTERS

THERE are not many references to be found among Porter's letters to his literary and artistic pursuits, so it is only from other contemporary records that we can picture the intellectual coterie that he gathered round him in his house in the strain where Herrick could sing

> "When to thy porch I come and ravished see
> The state of poets there attending thee,
> Those bards and I all in a chorus sing
> 'We are thy prophets, Porter, thou our king.'"

One of the pleasantest offices of Porter's historian is to gather the notices of the generous help which he extended to needy men of letters, painters, and musicians. Hardly a poet of the time can be found who had not to thank Porter for encouragement, and generally for substantial support. In the days of his dependence on the Duke of Buckingham, he carried the Duke's gifts to Ben Jonson ; and when he became a rich man, Herrick, D'Avenant, Decker, and May, all had to thank him for assistance.

Porter was not a mere parvenu who thought the gifts of the muses could be bought with money ; he wrote verses himself that were no worse than those of many contemporary minor poets, and to his literary friends he could, in Herrick's words, give

> "Not only subject matter for our wit,
> But likewise oil of maintenance to it."

He wrote an elegy on the death of the poet Donne. Inspiration will not always come to the writer of memorial poetry, and this "sad inscription," as he calls it, does not perhaps rise much higher than the ordinary level of the tombstone class of literature.[1]   But the verses he prefixed to D'Avenant's poem of Madagascar are pleasanter reading than the funereal apostrophe to the Dean of St. Paul's, and indeed are a good deal livelier than the poem they introduce.

The poem of Madagascar was addressed to Prince Rupert, at the time when there was a wild project of setting him up as a sort of seventeenth century Rajah Brooke in the Island of Madagascar. On the title-page of the book are the words, "If these poems live, may their memories by whom they were cherished, Endymion Porter, H. Jermyn, live with them."

Porter's introduction runs thus—

> "I am compelled by your commands to write
> I'th' frontispiece of this, and sure I might,
> With quaint conceits, here to the world set forth
> The merit of the poem and your worth,
> Had I well fancied reasons to begin,
> And a choice mould to cast good verses in.
> But wanting these, what power, alas, have I
> To write of anything?   Will men rely

---

[1] See Appendix.

On my opinion? which in verse or prose
Hath just that credit, which we give to those
That sagely whisper secrets of the Court
Having but lees for essence, from report.
And that's the knowledge that belongs to me,
For by what's said, I guess at poetry!
As when I hear them read, 'strong lines' I cry,
'They're rare,' but cannot tell you rightly why.
And now I find this quality was it
That made some poet cite me for a wit.
Now God forgive him for that huge mistake!
If he did but know with what pains I make
A verse! he'd pity then my wretched case,
For at the birth of each, I twist my face
As if I drew a tooth; I blot and write,
And then look pale as some that go to fight.
With the whole kennel of the alphabet
I hunt sometimes an hour, one rhyme to get.
What I approved of once, I straight deny
Like an inconstant prince, then give the lie
To my own invention, which is so poor
As here I'd kiss your hand and say no more,
Had I not seen a child with scissors cut
A folded paper, into which was put
More chance than skill; yet when you open it,
You'd think it had been done by art and wit.
So I perchance may hit upon some strain
Which may in time your good opinion gain.
And howsoever, if it be a plot
You may be certain that in this you've got
A foil to set your jewel off, which comes
From Madagascar, scenting of sweet gums
Before the which my lay conceits will smell
Like an abortive chick, destroy'd in the shell.
Yet something I must say, may it prove fit.
I'll do the best I can, and this is it.
What lofty fancy was't possess your brain,
And caused you soar into so high a strain!
Did all the muses join to make this piece
Excel what we have had from Rome or Greece!
Or did you strive to leave it as a friend
To speak your praises when there is an end
Of your Mortality? If you did so,
Envy will then scarce find you out a foe.
But let me tell you, Friend, the heightening came
From the reflexion of Prince Rupert's name,
Whose glorious genius cast into your soul
Divine conceits, such as are fit t'enrole

> In great Apollo's Court, there to remain
> For future ages to transcribe again.
> For such a poem in so sweet a style
> As yet was never landed on this isle,
> And could I speak your praises at each pore,
> 'Twere little for the work, it merits more."

D'Avenant was one of the most grateful and attached friends of the Porter family ; and he was not only a friend, he also constituted himself their poet laureate, and celebrated not only Endymion and Olivia, but also their son George and Captain Tom.

D'Avenant was first introduced to the world by Fulke Greville, Lord Brook. Brook was one of the stately figures that lingered on after the Elizabethan age was past. The schoolfellow and friend of Sir Philip Sidney, and no mean poet himself, he was also, what is more to our purpose, the godfather of little Fulke Porter of Mickleton, and the near relation of Sir Edward Greville of Aston. In one of these old Gloucestershire manorhouses the young D'Avenant probably grew to know Endymion Porter, and when Lord Brook's tragical death in 1628 threw the poet on the world, he found a new patron in Porter, and soon had good reason to write :—

> " Wise love that sought a noble choice,
> To tune my harp and raise my voice,
> Forbids my pinnace rest
> Till I had cured weak hope again
> By safely anchoring within
> Endymion's breast."

Porter did his best to forward his friend's interest at Court, as the following letter to Harvey shows.

" RICHARD HARVEY,—I would have you solicit
my Lord Duke who is now in London, to know
what he hath done with my Lord Keeper concerning Mr. Davnant's Patent : if he hath procured
the passing of it : follow it close and attend the
sealing : It hath already passed the Signet and
Privy Seal, and they are both paid for, there only
remains the Great Seal to pay for : disburse the
money for it, and keep the Patent until Mr.
Davnant send you the money (which by the next
opportunity let me understand how much it comes
to) and until with the money he send under his
hand to whom he shall deliver it : then deliver it.

" Your true loving friend,

" ENDYMION PORTER.

" *April* 16, 1639.

"(*Endorsed*) To my loving friend Mr. Richard
Harvey at Mr. Ondimion Porter's House in the
Strand." [1]

Porter also did a very important service to
D'Avenant when his play " The Wits " was brought
out. Herbert, Master of the Revels, who exercised
the censorship of plays, did not approve of various
exclamations introduced into the play, and bowd-
lerised it carefully before he let it appear.
D'Avenant complained to Porter, who laid the
matter before the King, and the royal critic decided
that "faith," "death," and "sleight" were asservera-
tions and not oaths, and might be replaced in the
text. It is not easy to understand what matters
our fathers strained at as camels and what they
considered as mere gnats. If Herbert could pass

[1] Dom. S. P. vol. ccccxvii. 100.

the plots of D'Avenant's plays it was curious he
should object to the asseverations.

When " The Wits " was printed D'Avenant, as
was due, dedicated it, to Porter in the following
words—

" *To the chiefly beloved of all that is ingenious and
noble, Endymion Porter, of his Majesty's bed-
chamber.*

" SIR,—Though you covet not acknowledgements,
receive what belongs to you by a double title.
Your goodness has preserved life in the author,
then rescued his work from a cruel faction which
nothing but the forces of your reason and your
reputation could subdue. If it became your pleasure
now, as when it had the advantage of presentation on the stage, I shall be taught to boast
some merit in myself; but with this inference,
you still, as in that doubtful day of my trial,
endeavour to make show of so much justice, as may
countenance the love you bear to your most obliged
and thankful humble servant,

                              " W. D'AVENANT."

D'Avenant wrote at least eight addresses to
Porter. Some are mere complimentary *vers de
société* as when he says, if ever Endymion should
prove unkind, he cannot survive the blow, but

> " Olivia then may on thy pity call
>   To bury me and give me funeral."

And when the poet accompanied Porter on one of
his expeditions into the country, he wrote a moving

account of the dangers of Worcestershire lanes in
bad weather when the floods were out, and

> " Each man did wish
> His hands and legs were fins, his horse a fish."

But when the travellers put up for the night at
Wickham, their merry hearts made them forget
their bad accommodation.

> " He, who to-night ruled each delighted breast,
> Gave to the palate of each ear a feast,
> With joy of pledges made our sour wine sweet
> And nimble as the leaping juice of Crete,
> Was the brave Endymion——"

Another of these society verses is a dialogue
supposed to have been carried on between Porter
and one of his Court friends, Henry Jermyn.
Jermyn was the Queen's favourite attendant, and,
in later days, her most trusted counsellor. All the
King's servants were not looked on with favour in
her Majesty's circle, but Porter seems to have been
popular everywhere, except among the Puritans.
In the dialogue, Jermyn and Porter lament the
supposed death of George Goring at the siege of
Breda, and describe Goring as resembling Philip
Sidney in manners as in fate. From what we
know of George Goring's later life he must have
fallen sadly below his early promise!

But the verses addressed to Olivia are too
charming to be merely conventional compliments.
Such, for example, is D'Avenant's New Year's
greeting [1] to " Endymion's love."

---

[1] A copy of this poem is to be found in a commonplace book
among the Sloane MSS. 1792. It has sometimes been alluded
to as a poem by Porter himself, but there seems to be no
authority for the assertion.

"Go! hunt the whiter Ermine and present
The wealthy skin as this day's tribute sent
To my Endymion's love, though she be fair
More gently smooth, more soft, than Ermines are.

"Go! climb that rock and when thou there hast found
A star contracted in a diamond,
Give it Endymion's love: whose glorious eyes
Darken the starry jewels of the skies.

"Go! dive into the Southern sea! and when
Thou'st found to trouble the nice sight of men
A swelling pearl, and such whose single worth
Boast all the wonders that the seas bring forth,
Give it Endymion's love! whose every tear
Would more enrich the skilful jeweller.

"How I command! How slowly they obey!
The churlish Tartar will not hunt to-day!
Nor will that lazy sallow Indian strive
To climb that rock, nor that dull negro dive.
Thus poets, like to Kings, by trust deceived,
Give oftener what is heard of, than received."

D'Avenant also wrote a duet supposed to be
sung by Endymion and Olivia. Olivia begins—

"OLIVIA.

"Before we shall again behold
In his diurnal race the world's great eye,
We may as silent lie and cold,
As are the shades where buried lovers lie.

"ENDYMION.

"Olivia, 'tis no fault of love
To lose ourselves in death, but, O, I fear
When life and knowledge is above
Restored to us, I shall not know thee there.

"OLIVIA.

"Call it not heaven, my love, where we
Ourselves shall see, and yet each other miss,
So much of heaven I find in thee
As thou unknown, all else privation is.

" ENDYMION.

" Why should we doubt before we go
   To find the knowledge that shall ever last
   That we may then each other know?
   Can future knowledge quite destroy the past?

" OLIVIA.

" When at the bowers in the Elysian shades
   I first arrive, I shall examine where
   They dwell who love the highest virtue made,
   For I am sure to find Endymion there.

" ENDYMION.

" From this vext world when we shall both retire
   Where all are lovers and where all rejoice,
   I need not seek thee in the heavenly choir
   For I shall know Olivia by her voice.

But D'Avenant was not the only poet who found
Endymion a haven of refuge from the unkindness of
fortune. Complimentary verses addressed to him
by grateful and expectant authors are preserved in
plenty, and the fashionable craze for anagrams even
enabled one Mr. Jones to turn " Endymion Porter "
into " Ripen to more End " and expand that senti-
ment into a sonnet which reads somewhat like the
beginning of an epitaph—

" The fruit of man at first like blossoms be
   Which pleasing to the eye hang on the tree."

The reader will doubtless spare the rest.

As a patron of so many literary men Porter
received many dedications of books, amongst which
we may mention Decker's " Dream," and in 1631
Thomas May presented his " Antigone " in the
following words :—

" To the most highly honoured Endymion Porter Esq., one of his Majesty's bedchamber.

" To speak of you as you deserve I dare not, since your known modesty would check my pen, but this I dare say, there no wits or any other true abilities that ever had the happiness to know you but will spread your worth, and think you most worthy to stand as you do in the presence of a King, wishing you long blest in his Majesty's favour and the King blest with more such servants as you are."

The critic Edmund Bolton was a far-away cousin to the great Buckingham, and seems to have been intimate with Porter, whom he calls his "good and noble friend" in the dedication of his " Historical Parallel showing the difference between Epitomies and just histories." Bolton is best remembered by his grand scheme of a literary Academy, which was to review and superintend all English secular writings and translations from foreign languages and to publish an Index Expurgatorius for the benefit of the vulgar. It was to be under royal patronage, to meet at Windsor Castle, and, in fact, was to establish an order of nobility for literature. There were to be three ranks in the society, and to the third, the Essentials, Endymion Porter was to belong with Ben Jonson, Drayton, Sir Kenelm Digby, and many other distinguished men. King James was rather pleased with the scheme, and had it been carried out, Bolton's Academy would probably have numbered among its members all the literary men catalogued by Suckling in his Session of Poets. But Suckling's bards were not collected by the fiat of Bolton, nor even by the wisdom of the far-famed

British Solomon. Suckling tells that Apollo in person had descended to select a poet laureate for England. Ben Jonson demanded the honour as his right, but was only elevated to be host of the New Inn; poor D'Avenant, whose beauty was certainly not his strong point, was told that he could not hope for the wreath, as

> "In all their records, either in verse or prose,
> There was not one Laureate without a nose."

Mr. Hales, of Eton, would not compete, but merely sat by, smiling, and Falkland, who might have claimed any honour he chose to ask, had his mind too intent on higher things to care for any earthly fame. Porter was present with many more, but Apollo passed them all over and placed his wreath of bays on the head of an alderman, as he judged that

> "it was the best sign
> Of good store of wit, to have good store of coin!"

The wisdom of the decision was applauded by all, especially by the needier of the poets, who hoped to borrow largely from the well-lined pockets of such a laureate.

It is curious for us to remember that there was one writer who is not numbered among Suckling's poets, but who might have been judged and criticised as a new and not entirely satisfactory author by Bolton's academicians. The passionate Elizabethan age was over and the era of Dryasdust begun. Shakespeare was not then the writer quoted by every penny-a-liner and read in every

boys' school.   To the learned men of that day he
was still

> "Fancy's child
> Warbling his native woodnotes wild,"

and there was some doubt whether "woodnotes
wild" were the proper thing in literature.   There
is a story of a very serious discussion held by Porter
and some of his literary friends, concerning the
amount of Shakespeare's learning.[1]

Porter's own part in the conversation is not
remembered, but D'Avenant, Suckling, and the
learned Ben Jonson were eager in the argument, and
Mr. Hales, true to Suckling's description—

> "Set by himself most gravely did smile,
> To see them about nothing keep up such a coil."

Suckling, who was a professed admirer of "fancy's
child," was defending him with some warmth against
the criticisms of learned Ben Jonson, till Mr. Hales,
who had sat still for some time, interposed, and told
them "that if Mr. Shakespeare had not read the
ancients, he had likewise not stolen anything from
them : and that if the opponents would produce any
one topic finely treated by any one of them, he
would undertake to show something on the same
subject at least as well written by Shakespeare."

But the literary muse was not the only one served
by Porter.   The mention of music books in his
letters makes it probable that he inherited the
musical tastes of his uncle, Don Luis, and he
appears to have been as generous a patron to both
musicians and painters as he was to poets.

[1] Nicholas Rowe.

When Sir Francis Cottington was sent to Spain
in 1629, Porter's commissions to him combined the
purchase of pictures with greetings to an admired
Spanish singer. Cottington wrote from Portsmouth
on the day of his embarkation,[1] promising to do his
best to bring back to Porter some paintings by
Titian, and Porter especially begged him "not to
forget the book of drawings of Leonardo de Vinzi.
It is in Don Juan de Espino's hands, who every one
knows, and Vinzente Juares best, who is the wench's
father who sings so well." Cottington wrote from
Madrid the following April : "I have read your
letter in Spanish to Donna Francesca and her father,
and they are exceedingly glad to · hear from you,
and that his Majesty doth please to remember them.
Donna Francesca's angelical voice has more power
to give life than Orpheus."[2] A good many letters
refer to this admired prima donna : a couple of years
later Gabriel Hippesley wrote from Madrid[3] that he
had heard Endymion's "Mistress," and will ever
commend his taste "for Donna Francesca is the
rarest in the world." It may be remembered that
any lady who was much admired was termed Mistress just as the word Servant was used as a term of
affection to Prince Charles by his own mother on
her death-bed, and by Lord Anglesea in writing to
Endymion.[4]

But music and poetry were after all no new things
in England : for many generations they had been
patronised by great people and loved by small ones.
The really new departure at this time was in painting : pictures began to be valued as works of art

[1] Sainsbury, "Rubens Papers," p. 308.   [2] Ibid.
[3] Cal. Dom. S. P., 1631, April 15.   [4] See Chapter IV.

and not merely as family portraits.   The King led
the way in this awakening of taste, and the example
he set was followed by most of the great nobles;
Buckingham, Arundel, and many others began then
to form the collections of which the country is still
proud.

It is very probable that Porter had learnt to love
Art and had become familiar with great pictures
during his boyhood in Spain.   In his riper years he
was not only a generous patron of artists, but also one
of the King's favourite picture collectors.   Charles
found no small pleasure in being surrounded by cul-
tivated and artistic attendants, and moreover it was
very convenient to him to select as a messenger to
Spain or Italy an envoy whose varied capacity could
combine a little diplomacy with many visits to
studios, and could carry a letter or whisper a word
to a foreign statesman, while he seemed to be absorbed in bargaining for statues or paintings.   As
has been seen, more than once when Porter went ,
abroad, the public were uncertain whether he were
only " buying pictures," [1] or if he were indeed negotiating treaties and every ambassador and envoy
was expected, like Cottington, to keep his eyes open
for bargains in pictures or marbles.

One of the earliest artists invited by the King to
England was Horace Gentileschi, an Italian painter
who arrived in 1625, and was granted an annuity
of a hundred a year, besides furniture for his house
" from top to toe " valued at four thousand pounds.
The Duke of Buckingham shared the King's ad-
miration for Gentileschi, but was so slow in paying
for his pictures that " Mr. Endimion Porter was

[1] See Chapter V.

forcett to solicitt " for the artist.[1] It is said that Porter was handsomely rewarded for this use of his interest, but it must be remembered that acknowledgments of the sort were at that time rather looked on as fees than as bribes.

In 1627, the King made a most important addition to his galleries, for he was so fortunate as to secure the entire collection of the Duke of Mantua,[2] which included twelve Emperors by Titian, the " Mercury instructing Cupid," by Correggio, which is now in the National Gallery, a Madonna by Raphael, and paintings by Michael Angelo, Andrea del Sarto and Tintoret. The pictures were bought by Daniel Nys and Lanier, the Master of the King's music, but much of the correspondence passed through Porter's hands. Money was sorely needed in England just then to equip the fleet for Buckingham's disastrous French war, and Burlamachi, the Rothschild of the day, was dismayed at the large sum that was to be diverted from sterner uses. He writes to Porter, "If it were for two or three thousand pounds it could be born, but fifteen thousand will utterly put me out of any possibility to do any thing in those provisions which are so necessary for my Lord Duke's relief." However, the money for the pictures was found, and a month later Lanier was sent back to Italy to repair them and arrange for their transport to England. Lanier seems to have made purchases for Porter as well as for the King, and was also selecting statues for the Duke, but, like Gentileschi, he had to seek Porter's aid in getting his money matters settled. He writes to

---

[1] Sainsbury, " Rubens Papers," pp. 310–16.
[2] " Rubens Papers," pp. 320–40.

Porter, "I find you still the best friend, to be by me for ever religiously beloved and honoured above all others. . . . Though the Duke of Mantua be dead and a son of the Doge of Venice have murdered a senator in St. Mark's Palace, yet I do not forget to give you infinite thanks for the favour you have done my poor wife in getting her my money." [1]

Mr. Petty, the Agent for the Earl of Arundel, was busy searching for marbles, but Porter's friend, Sir Peter Wych, the Ambassador at Constantinople, secured two statues, which "Mr. Petty desired infinitely," and shipped them home from Scio to Porter for his Majesty's collection, and also announced nineteen statues, great and small, as being already on their way from Smyrna, "some of them I heare are rare peeces."

Those were indeed fortunate days for collectors. The ruined cities of Greece were practically a virgin field for the searcher, and eager agents were ransacking the most remote islands for the treasures of classical days. Mr. Petty, Sir Peter Wych, and Sir Thomas Roe, seemed to have run each other hard in the business, and Sir Peter was a proud man when he could write to Porter of his finds, "There are two men in strife for them, but I shall decide the differences and take them from them both!"

But not only were marbles being shipped from Smyrna, and Titians and Correggios from Italy; there were great artists then living, and Vandyke and Rubens were ready to paint fashionable ladies and plump nymphs for whoever chose to order.

Buckingham was one of the first admirers of

[1] Sainsbury, "Rubens Papers," p. 353.

ENDYMION PORTER

Rubens' work, and bought the master's whole cabinet in 1625. Thirteen pictures by Rubens himself, with paintings, statues, and medals, by other hands, were secured by the Duke for one hundred thousand florins. The King shared his favourite's tastes, and became one of the great painter's most admiring and generous patrons.[1]

But the Flemish artist was not the only great painter who was welcomed at the Court of the art-loving King. William Dobson, " the English Tintoret," as Charles named him, has preserved for us the features of many of the remarkable persons of the time, but it is Vandyke who is so completely identified with the Court of Charles I. that we could better spare most of the memoirs of the time than one of his vivid portraits. His name first comes before us among the Porter papers in March, 1630, when Porter bought one of his paintings, " The Story of Rinaldo and Armida," " and delivered it to the King for seventy-eight pounds."

The artist had already paid a short visit to England in 1620, and in 1632 he returned and settled in London, and was appointed painter-in-ordinary to the King. He became very intimate with the Porter family, and painted them more times than can easily be counted. One cannot help suspecting a little friendly malice in one picture in which the painter introduces his own portrait beside that of Endymion, and makes the literary and artistic courtier look a mere jovial cavalier in contrast to his own refined and dreamy face.[2]

---

[1] See *ante*, pp. 101–103.

[2] This portrait is at Madrid. A tentative list of Vandyke's portraits of Endymion will be found in the Appendix.

CHAPTER IX

BY the middle of the seventeenth century gentlemen had grown too highly civilised to keep their money in an old stocking, or even in a painted money chest with many locks, such as that in which Lord Bacon hoarded his treasures. Like Shylock, men now wished to make their gold increase ; trading was made more aristocratic as well as more profitable by monopolies granted by the Crown to favoured individuals and companies, and many undertakings were now started by Court gentlemen as well as by London merchants. Shrewd Bishop Williams warned Buckingham early in the reign that these monopolies were irritating the public to a dangerous extent, and implored him not to listen to the advice of interested flatterers, " Oh, hearken not to Rehoboam's earwigs ! " But he warned in vain, and the monopolies flourished till the Long Parliament took them into consideration. Then Culpepper rose to protest against the ubiquity of the monopolists. " These men," he said, "like the frogs of Egypt, have got possession of our dwellings, and we have scarce a room free from them. They sup in our cup, they dip in our dish, they sit by our fire ; we find them in the dye-vat, the wash-bowl, and the powdering-tub. They shelter themselves under the name of a corpora- tion." [1]

In more than one of these ubiquitous monopolies Porter had a share, and his soap company involved him in the war with the wash-bowls as his connec- tion with the Yarmouth Salt Corporation did with the powdering-tub.

But it must be admitted that these grants or monopolies were not entirely invented to enrich favourites or to raise money by rents to the ex- chequer. Justices of the peace had long counted it part of their duties to settle the rate of wages and to keep down the price of food ; it was no novelty for a paternal government to supervise trade, to encourage the manufacture of good articles and punish dishonesty. Very good intentions, which conspicuously failed.

The question of the soap monopoly was of more importance than would at first appear, or than Strafford thought when he wrote that "he feared the kingdom was not so cleanly given as to raise the business to any high consideration." A patent had been granted by King James to a company for manufacturing soap by a new process, from materials entirely produced in England. In 1632 Charles erected a new company to buy up these rights and pay £4 to the Crown for every ton sold ; the King helping them by prohibiting the export of tallow and potash. The new company chiefly consisted of the Roman Catholic clique who had attached themselves to Lord Treasurer Portland, and grown rich through his favour ; Endymion

[1] Gardiner's "Hist. Eng.," vol. ix. p. 239.

Porter was one of the shareholders. Naturally, all other manufacturers of soap were very indignant at the new company, and asserted that it was a device of the Jesuits to ruin the country.[1]

They declared their soap was quite as good as this new production, and had only been condemned because the inspector was unfair. So the King's paternal and conscientious Council determined to decide this matter themselves, and sent for two washerwomen, who were directed to bring their tubs and bundles of linen, and then and there, in their lordships' august presence, make trial of the two sorts of soap! But whether the washerwoman who used the Company's soap was the more skilful or not, the Court gentlemen triumphed, their soap was approved of by the Council and they retained their monopoly. When Portland died in 1635, the soap manufacturers made another attempt against the Company, and Laud, who was virtually first in the Council, was inclined to favour them, as he was shrewd enough to see that professional manufacturers were more likely to produce a good article than a company of Court gentlemen. But Cottington was on the Treasury Commission and walked in Portland's footsteps. He only thought of the duty of filling the Treasury and balancing his accounts, and when the Company offered to pay a little more for their right, he threw all his interest into their scale. But when Juxon was raised to the Treasury in 1637 Laud had his own way, and the old soap-makers were allowed to buy out the Company, paying the King £8 on every ton manufactured. Then having got the place of the Company, the

[1] "Commons' Journals," vol. ii. p. 133.

manufacturers proceeded to make exactly the same use of their monopoly that their predecessors had done, to hunt down rivals, and petition for their suppression, while their own soap, being safe from competition, was no better than the article produced before ; and so the soap question vanishes for the time, among subdued murmurs from Court ladies and washerwomen, who mourned together over the havoc wrought by bad soap on laces and lawns. But the matter was not really forgotten nor forgiven, and when the question of monopolies was brought before the Long Parliament, and it was suggested that they were all invented by the Jesuits, the evils of the monopoly of soap were laid at the charge of the Queen s confessor !

But if Court gentlemen could not make money by soap, there were plenty of other projects offered to their choice.

In 1635 a company was formed at Shields for the production of salt, to replace that brought from the Bay of Biscay, and in January, 1638, Endymion Porter was invited to take oath as an associate of the Corporation of Salt Makers of Yarmouth. In 1633 a society for fishing was founded by Portland, his Roman Catholic friends, as in the soap company, being principal shareholders.[1] He himself contributed £1,000, the Duchess of Buckingham £300, and Endymion Porter £100. In March, 1638, Porter petitioned about a harbour light at Filey, perhaps for the convenience of this same fishery company. But the Dutch had hitherto had the monopoly of the fisheries, and were not likely to give up such a profitable matter without a struggle,

[1] Dom. S. P., 1633 ; also Gardiner, vol. vii. p. 349.

while England was so weak at sea that the King
actually debated the possibility of securing Spanish
ships to protect his fishermen! It is not much
wonder that the next year found Parliament
discussing ship money, and that some said the
King had good reason for raising it. If only his
methods had been as good as his reasons and
intentions!

A list of twenty-two men is given in the Domestic
State Papers for March, 1635, who Endymion
Porter desired might not be pressed for service
on the magnificent and ill-fated fleet, which Charles
was preparing with the help of ship money. These
twenty-two men belonged to two merchant ships,
the *Samaritan* and *Roebuck*, which were to sail for
the East Indies the following April. The small
trade carried on by England in the East at this
time was in the hands of the East India Company,
but public opinion seems to have supported the
King in infringing their monopoly, and allowing
Samuel Bonnell and Sir William Courteen to open
a trade in pepper with the Portuguese of the
Malabar coast. The preamble to the license of
the new association states that the East India
Company had accomplished nothing for the good
of the nation in proportion to their privileges and
funds; and authorises the Adventurers to trade at
Goa and other places where the Company was not
already settled before 1635.[1] The Adventurers
were so fortunate as to gain the support of Endymion Porter, who persuaded the King himself to
take a share.[2] In 1637 the *Roebuck* reached Eng-

[1] Rymer, " Fœdera."
[2] " Court and Times of Charles I.," vol. i. pp. 262-4.

land once more and entered Falmouth harbour, bringing news that her Admiral, Captain Oldfield, and most of his crew were dead, having been cast away on an island before they even reached the Red Sea. But as a trading venture the voyage had been a success, every member of the expedition having made £20 a share.

Naturally the East India Company circulated very shocking reports how the *Roebuck* had taken two pinks in the Red Sea, and in them about £60,000 in money, and so tortured the poor Indians by setting burning matches to their fingers to make them confess where their treasure lay, that they had burnt their fingers to the hand. Upon complaint of the great wrong done reaching India, "all our factors at Surat are clapt in prison, and £20,000 seized upon, and our merchants are in great distraction."

The East India merchants,[1] who seem to have been unable to sustain the smallest competition without their trade falling into confusion, went down to Hampton Court to petition the King to send letters to the Great Mogul and the Governor of Surat, to disavow his having authorised such piracies. He granted the letters, saying that he knew of the going of the ships, but that he had of course not given any commission to do such acts. Not content with their petition to the King, they also proceeded to lay an action at law against the Adventurers ; but Endymion Porter at once went to Lord Keeper Coventry "to move that a mild course should be taken in the business." The Company took fright at finding Porter stirring in the matter, and hastened

[1] Mill, "Hist. India," vol. i. ch. iii. p. 71.

to assure him that no action should be brought
against him personally, unless his partners involved
him of themselves. However the Privy Council
treated all the story of torture as a fabrication
(which Mill thinks it probably was), and then
suggested that the terms of Courteen's license
should desire him not to trade with the same
places as the Company. That was such small
satisfaction for the alarmed directors, that they
threatened to abandon the East India trade
altogether, so at last the difficulty was ended by a
promise that if they would raise sufficient capital
to trade on a proper scale, Courteen's license
should be withdrawn.

Some years later Courteen's and Porter's names
are again associated in a grant of Petty Customs,
and, in the beginning of the civil wars, Sir William
did his best to preserve Porter's plate and valuables
from the hands of the Parliamentary party.[1]

In June, 1628, Endymion was granted the lease
of Alfarthing Manor from the Crown. £300 was
paid down for it, and the rent was to be £40
yearly. The mansion stood on a rising ground
near Wandsworth Common : it is now pulled down,
but its name is preserved in Alfarthing Lane close
by. The lease to Endymion was granted with
remainder to his brother, Captain Thomas. There
is no record that any of the family lived there much
during Endymion's life, and when the troubled times
came the property was mortgaged and sold by the
mortgagees. But it was eventually recovered and
held for several generations by Endymion's descendants, John Porter being seated at Alfarthing in

[1] See page 201.

1711.   There is an entry in the accounts for 1638, of wood sold at Alfarthing to the value of £18.

In July, 1628, a pension of £500, granted to Endymion in 1625, was revoked and converted into an annuity for himself and his wife.   The reversion of the keepership of Hartwell Park was also granted by the King to his godson, Charles Porter ; it was to become his after the death of Richard Oliver.   This Mr. Oliver seems to have been a friend of the family.   Lord Mansfield, afterwards Earl of Newcastle,[1] mentions him with Porter, as forwarding business for him with the Duke of Buckingham in 1627, and Endymion sent messages to him from Spain in 1623.

But it would be wearisome to catalogue all the grants that marked the royal favour to Endymion Porter.   A monopoly for the manufacture of writing-paper seems appropriate to such a voluminous correspondent.   He was also collector of fines to the Star Chamber, an office that brought him in some £750 a year.

He had royal grants of land in many places, Hartpury in Gloucestershire, Raby Park in Durham, and Marsley Park in Denbigh, and lands on Exmoor.

The following letter refers to the grant of postmaster, under Lord Stanhope of Harrington, to whom this office had been granted by King James. There had been various infringements of his monopoly of the right of forwarding letters and keeping posthorses for travellers on the principal high roads.   In a petition by George Porter in 1660,

---

[1] "Life of Duke and Duchess of Newcastle."   Ed. Firth, p. 322.

he says the office when he first took it was not worth £5,000 a year, but he and his agents had so improved the business that at the Restoration it was farmed for £21,500.

The office had been formally granted to Endymion Porter with reversion to his son George, in September, 1635, but probably there had been some delay in confirming the grant, and Porter applied to Windebank for help in April, 1636.

The letter is rather a good example of the way in which courtiers spoke of the Stuart monarchs.

" MAY IT PLEASE YOUR HONOUR,—You are best acquainted how long I followed the business of the Postmaster's place, as being one to whom it was referred for the ending and settling of it, and I have made bold to intimate unto his Mat^{ie} in an humble letter his former gracious intentions towards me in the said business, of which I have received so favourable an answer from his sacred mouth, as I assure your honour it hath much lessened my sickness; yet I fear by something his Mat^{ie} said, that he might imagine I was not willing to have the Lord Stanhope's Patent made void; therefore I made choice of your honour to do me the favour as to let his Mat^{ie} know, that I have no disposition nor thought to be averse to any intentions of his, and for this I will hope that his Mat^{ie} doth it for the good of me his poor (pore) servant and creature, and if I be thought worthy by his Mat^{ie} to have the office, I will make it such a one for his honour and profit, as his Mat^{ie} shall have no cause to think it ill-bestowed; but I refer all to his Mat$^{ie's}$ gracious will, for he best knows at what time, and with what place to gratify each servant. And if your honour can pardon me the trouble I have given you in this, your charity is as great as the rest of your favours are to

"Your honour's obliged thankful servant,
"ENDYMION PORTER." [1]

Among Porter's very varied offices we should hardly expect to find him, like John Gilpin, acting as a train-band captain of credit and renown ; but so it was, and when foreign dignitaries arrived, Mr. Porter sometimes met them, not in his Majesty's suite, but on horseback at the head of his "four hundred brave martialists." [2]

More than one band of volunteer soldiers was raised at this time in imitation of the well-known Honourable Artillery Company of London, and in the absence of a standing army these regiments did the office of guards of honour on State occasions.

A letter from Porter to Captain Roydon,[3] of the "Society of the Artillery Garden," expresses his pleasure at the recent readiness of the regiment to assemble to wait upon the Ambassador of the King of Poland. This Ambassador, Racowski, was believed to have come to ask the hand of the eldest daughter of the Queen of Bohemia for the Prince of Poland, but the match came to nothing.

It would seem that in 1631 there was some danger of the Artillery Company itself falling to pieces, and rather sharp messages from the Council showed that it held the Court of Aldermen answer-

[1] Dom. S. P., vol. cccxviii. 26.
[2] See Bindley's "Notes on Pinkerton's Medallic History."
[3] Dom. S. P. vol. cciii. 38.

able for the disorder and lack of discipline of the
City military forces.   Captain Roydon consulted
Porter on the possibilities of reorganising the
regiment as a " Royal Regiment of selected Guards,"
and Porter conveyed to him his sacred Majesty's
gracious approval of the scheme.   But the Aldermen were not at all pleased at their City Company
being turned into a Royal Regiment, and desired
him to proceed no further in the matter.[1]

However another regiment seems to have been
raised in place of that projected by Roydon,[2] as in
1637 four hundred of the "military or trained
bands commanded by Mr. Endymion Porter"
formed a guard of honour on the arrival of the
Ambassador of the Emperor of Morocco.

When the great Lord Vere, the "fighting Vere,"
died, a royal warrant was issued to Endymion
Porter, Captain of the Military Company, and to
the Colonel of the London Artillery, giving the
Company of Trained-bands permission to attend the
funeral of the great soldier.

In 1638 Porter signed a petition to the King to
restore to the gentlemen of the privy chamber the
privilege they had enjoyed under former reigns,
among others that of "keeping the linen of his
Majesty, and that his Majesty may not be put to
needless expense in his linen, and therefore none is
damned without his knowledge and approbation."
The petition also prays that "such parts of his
Majesty's dyett as shall rest when he eateth
privately be served the gentlemen and grooms of

---

[1] "Hist. Hon. Art. Co.," vol. i. p. 70.
[2] Ibid.

the bedchamber, and their leavings to his Majesty's barber and pages who are otherwise unprovided."[1]

It appears that the King's servants made a practice of hunting up any unconsidered trifles that might help to fill the royal purse and leave some reward for the discoverer. Porter discovered defalcations on the part of several public officers and received a part of the money recovered, and he was also granted a reward for the discovery that the dignity of baronet is not "descendable, but that the King may avoid whom he pleases and retaigne only those that deserve his grace and power."[2]

Another valuable addition to the royal wealth was the discovery of waste and unreclaimed lands, which could be claimed as Crown property. A great movement was begun about this time for reclaiming marsh lands in the east of England, and the system seems to have been extended to Ireland. A letter[3] from Porter to Nicholas in 1641, refers to a piece of bog land which he hoped would prove valuable if he could establish his right to it. " I must beg your favour in sending this enclosed letter to Sir Edward Savage, who will present unto you a paper signed by his Majesty, the which concerning me partly, as may appear by the contents. It is a grant which the King was formerly pleased to make to me and Sir Ed. and Mr. Wyndham of certain marsh lands in Ireland. What the Council did with the Irish commissioners, about such things, you may be pleased to inform yourself in every particular, before you put the seal to the letter, for I would not have you put yourself to the hazard of

---

[1] Fontblanque, " Lords Strangford," p. 64.   [2] Ibid., p. 65.
[3] Nicholas Papers, Camd. Soc., vol. i. p. 70.

a censure by our great Secretary here,[1] for more
than twenty such businesses are worth. 'Tis true
I have spent monies in finding the marsh for the
King, and many other reasons which make the
grant very just to me, but, Sir, I beseech you
believe me I love you beyond any benefit, and
cannot deserve anything from good men if I should
desire anything of you which may be inconvenient.
Thus much I thought good to advertise you, not
knowing what the desire of gain may lead other
men to do ; but I pray you take no notice of what
I say here, but do in the business what justly you
may and I shall be obliged to you for it."

But Porter's hopes of wealth to be dug from Irish
bogs soon vanished. In less than a month from
the day this letter was written the storm of war
burst in Ireland and swept the fortunes of great
and small into one hopeless mass of ruin.

The schemes of land reclamation were, however,
more successful in England. In 1626 Hatfield
Chase had been drained by Vermuyden, adding
much valuable land to the country, and driving
away the fevers and agues which infested the
flooded lands, but arousing much ill-feeling among
the men who had made their living by fishing,
fowling, and osier cutting. The beginning of the
great Bedford Level in 1629 aroused even stronger
opposition, and the commoners, as the fishermen
and willow cutters were called, had a hope that the
King would be on their side against the Earl of
Bedford. It was at last decided by commissioners
sent down on purpose, that the inhabitants should
retain their commons till the drainage was com-

---

[1] Sir H. Vane.

pleted, and the work should be undertaken by the King. Porter was granted a tract of marsh lands at North Summercotes, on the Lincolnshire coast, in 1632, on condition of his conveying one sixth part of the reclaimed land as compensation to the commoners, but what value reclaimed meadows could be to fishermen and osier cutters is not explained. In his petition, long after, to the Committee for Compounding, he says the land was 1,000 acres and certain waste lands lying without the banks, but the commoners had resumed possession of them, and he had never got one penny in recompense of his charges of embanking, the banks being now thrown down and the land used in common. Till they were repaired the land was not worth more than £40 a year. The original grant appears to have been of 22,000 acres, but part of that was given as compensation to the commoners, and to the lord of the manor. The entire enclosure is still known as " Porter's March."[1]

Naturally a good many of the letters about land among the Porter correspondence refer to Aston. It appears that the rentals of Aston and Mickleton together amounted to £144 for the half year, and a chief rent of £5 was paid to Sir Edward Fisher. The Aston property consisted of over 640 acres.[2] Among the tenants are Sir N. Overbury, Mr. T. Southerne, and Richard Canning, the husband of Mary Porter. An undated letter from the Aston steward probably belongs to 1625, when Angela had George and Charles staying there with her,

[1] See *Globe*, Jan., 1881. I have to thank E. Endymion Porter, Esq., of Easthill, Frome, for the above information.
[2] Cal. Dom. S. P., 1648, p. 432.

for the writer, the steward Richard Bee, says, " My old mistress and Mr. Porter's children are in good health." Bee's letter is chiefly concerning his letting of land ; a tenant, John Huyns, was going to give up a house and some land to Richard Canning, and Bee advises that Endymion should insist on the outgoing tenant paying the rent he owed £40. There was constant trouble about that piece of land. In July, 1641, a new tenant was going to take it, but there was some difficulty about Mr. Canning, and Bee wrote that it were best to give Mr. Canning the satisfaction he demanded, as he had not £5 worth of goods in the house to distrain upon, and the new tenant wished to enter into possession peaceably, or not at all. Perhaps Aston was settled on Olivia, certainly she took the management of the business there, as in November, 1638, Bee sends an account of his mistress's last half year's rents. Angela Porter was always called " my old mistress " in the steward's letters.

CHAPTER X

POPISH PLOTS

PORTER'S mysterious visits to Spain and Italy and familiarity with foreign courts had made him an object of suspicion to the Puritan party from the earliest days of King Charles's reign, and as time went on these suspicions were greatly strengthened by the doings of Porter's friends in England.

Europe was at that time divided into two great camps, Protestant and Roman Catholic, and ever since the King's marriage with Henrietta Maria she had been looked on with fear and dislike because she represented the Roman Catholic party. Behind her pretty figure might lurk Spanish Armadas and Roman Inquisitors and the masked conspirators of a new Gunpowder Plot. The Queen took no sort of pains to quiet these Puritan alarms; on the contrary, she was exceedingly proud of her intimacy with Con, the special envoy sent from Rome to recall England to the fold of the Church. She was not greatly interested in the theological difference between the Churches, but she was flattered at finding persons of fashion inclining to embrace her religion and looking to her for protection against disagreeable consequences. Naturally every concession made to the Queen and her Roman Catholic friends filled the opposite party with fresh alarm, and even the principles of the King himself began to be doubted.

Porter was in attendance on his Majesty in 1636, when he paid a solemn visit to Oxford in order that a compliment to that ancient and orthodox university might reassure the public on the Royal loyalty to the Church.[1]

The Queen was never able to claim Porter as one of her converts, but Olivia followed the fashion, was received into the Roman Catholic Church, and became a valuable acquisition to her Majesty's party. Mrs. Porter's vehement energy and warm feeling made her an admirable agent for spreading her new opinions among her friends and relations. Such activity on Olivia's part confirmed the suspicions that were felt of her husband, and very possibly some of his serious words of warning found in his letters may refer to her imprudent enthusiasm. More than once he writes : "You must be ruled by me"; "you will find me your best friend"; but such caution was too foreign to Olivia's nature to be readily adopted. She did not confine herself to arguments when active deeds were needful ; when her father, old Lord Boteler, was drawing near his end, Mrs. Porter saw that no time was to be lost in withdrawing him from heretical influences and reconciling him with the true Church. So she drove down to Woodhall and hurried the old man into her coach, and carried him off in safety ; but only just in time, for her elder sister, Lady Newport,

---

[1] Wyane to Nicholas, Aug., 1636, Cal. Dom. S. P.

who was a very vehement Protestant, had heard of
this Popish plot, and also drove down to Woodhall,
with all haste, to rescue her father, but she was too
late ; Lord Boteler was in the Porter coach, Olivia
triumphed, and Con gained one more convert of
quality.

The lovely young Marchioness of Hamilton was
Olivia's next object of attack. She was the
daughter of Lord Denbigh, and her uncle, the
Duke of Buckingham, had been proud to make her
a Marchioness. But the grand match was a loveless
one on the part of the bridegroom, and now the
beautiful and amiable young creature's short life
was drawing to a close. Con was very anxious to
secure such a distinguished convert, and found her
cousin, Mrs. Porter, a most valuable assistant. He
wrote in October, 1637 :—

"We have here, laid up with a hectic fever, the
Marchioness of Hamilton, who, being brought up
in Puritanism, has shewn great violence against the
Catholic Religion, until some months ago she began
to walk with much moderation. Besides some talks
I have had with her on the occasion of visits, I have
several times had speech with her through her
cousin, Mrs. Porter, who informs herself daily of
what should be said to her, furnishing her with
books and discourses, Catholic manuscripts, but her
father, who is a Puritan Ass, being afraid, makes
the pseudo Bishop of Carlisle come to her, who
avoids holding any conference in the presence of
the Marchioness, to whom he says in order to fortify
her, that he would give his soul for hers, but Mrs.
Porter has well replied, ' Little will it help you, my

sister, that the soul of that old man shall be with you in the Devil's House.'   I visit her daily, God knows what will follow."[1]

However, Olivia did not succeed entirely, for, at any rate, the conversion of the Marchioness was never openly announced.   There must have been very strong counter-influences in her family, as not only was her father a " Puritan Ass," but on the outbreak of the civil wars her brother joined the Parliamentary side, so it cannot be doubted that he must have viewed the visits of Con and Olivia with extreme disapproval.   .

But if the Marchioness disappointed the prose-lytisers, they soon got an even more striking convert, namely, Lady Newport herself!   She was so unwise as to engage in a controversy with some Romanist priests, and her knowledge not being equal to her zeal, she was soon worsted in argument and admitted herself vanquished.   No time was lost ; one evening, after the play, she got into a coach with the Duchess of Buckingham and Mrs. Porter, and drove off in secret to the house of a priest, and was there received into the Church of Rome.

Lord Newport was exceedingly angry and appealed to the King, who shared both his vexation and his helplessness.   He did make some endeavours to moderate the childish vehemence of Henrietta Maria, but with so little effect that he was unable to prevent her from holding a public parade of her distinguished converts at a grand Christmas Eve service, of which Con writes, " Such a concourse had seldom been seen."

---

[1] Add. MS. 15390, 1637, from Sig. Georgeo Coneo, Oct. 23rd.

Her Majesty was triumphant, and when she returned to her apartments she ran up to Con in an ecstasy, crying, "Now you see the effects of the King's proclamation!"

The agent himself had to admit that his flock were imprudent and very difficult to manage ; so far from trying to avoid giving cause of offence to the Puritan party, on that very Christmas evening while he was talking to the Queen, they rampantly insisted on keeping their chapel open and most brilliantly illuminated, in order to outdo the Christmas solemnities held at the Spanish Ambassador's!

The names of many of these fashionable converts may be found in the Middlesex Sessions Rolls, with the amounts they were fined for recusancy and not coming to their parish churches during a whole month. In 1641 there is a long list of fourteen hundred and thirty persons who were proceeded against, and among them is " the wife of Endymion Porter, Esq., being late of St. Martin's-in-the-Fields."

When so many Romanist "alarums and excursions" were occurring, it was small wonder that Porter got the credit of many of his wife's sayings and doings.

The danger of his position was increased by the inevitable connection between the King's favourite servant and the King's favourite Minister, Archbishop Laud ; the growing public hatred of Laud heightened Porter's unpopularity, while Porter's mysterious comings and goings increased the suspicions that Laud was intriguing with the enemies of the English Church and people.

An example of the way in which Porter and Laud

were connected in men's minds may be found in the story of Sir Matthew Mennis.   Sir Matthew was a gentleman of litigious disposition who held various pieces of land in lease from the Archbishop of Canterbury.   He was a disagreeable neighbour, and a country gentleman who lived near him could not refrain from expressions of pious thankfulness when he wrote to tell Laud that "it hath pleased God that Sir Matthew Mennis should lately fall into the reach of the law and that the leases he holds from you are forfeited."[1]   But although it was the Archbishop who profited by Sir Matthew's downfall, it was Porter who got the credit of the deed, and Sir Matthew tells in his will of "the great plot and conspiracy against me by Endymion Porter and his agents wherein I suffered in my estate seventeen hundred pounds."[2]

A little later Parliament was informed by two of the official searchers of the Port of London that many Popish books and relics had been rescued from them by the Archbishop of Canterbury and Mr. Endymion Porter.

So the suspicions grew, and it was not long before people were convinced that Porter was as dark and dangerous a Papist as Laud himself.   These rumours received a tremendous confirmation on Laud's arrest, when Prynne, searching among his papers at Lambeth for materials to prove the Archbishop's guilt, found (or said that he found) a letter from Sir William Boswell, the English Ambassador at the Hague, which charged Master Porter, of the King's bedchamber, with being "most addicted to

---

[1] Sir R. Honeywood to Laud, Dom. S. P., 1640.
[2] *Notes and Queries*, 3rd Ser. iv. 144.

the Popish religion and a bitter enemy of the King.
He reveals all his greatest secrets to the Pope's
Legate, although he only rarely meets with him, yet
his wife meets him so much the oftener, who being
informed by her husband, conveys secrets to the
Legate. His sons are secretly instructed in the
Popish religion : openly they profess the reformed.
The eldest is now to receive his father's office under
the King which shall be [*i.e.*, under Charles II.].
A cardinal's hat is provided for the other if the
design shall succeed well. Above three years past
the said Master Porter was to be sent away by the
King to Morocco, but he was prohibited by the
Society [*i.e.*, by the Jesuits] lest the business should
suffer any delay thereby."[1]

By the time this astounding accusation was
printed the civil war had broken out, and Porter
was far away from London, so it remained un-
criticised and unanswered, and it cannot now be
known if it was built upon any shred of actual fact.

Porter's real religious opinions will probably never
be discovered. It was an age when every one had
religious opinions, but it is possible that every one
did not formulate these opinions with logical clear-
ness. The Porter family had always belonged to
the National Church ; various members of the
family had held office in it as churchwardens of
Mickleton and Aston, and had left legacies under
the care of the clergyman of these parishes.
Endymion's own office was that of gentleman in
attendance on King Charles, who prided himself on
his loyalty to the Anglican Communion, and who,
at the end, persuaded himself that he died its

---

[1] " Rome's Masterpiece," W. Prynne, 1644, p. 20.

martyr. A Roman Catholic convert would have been far more in place in the household of Henrietta Maria than in that of the King.

On the other hand, Porter's Spanish relations and Spanish education can have hardly failed to influence his mind at the most receptive age, and he cannot have looked on alien faiths with the horror felt by ordinary Anglicans or Presbyterians. England is the country of compromises, and we may imagine that a genial man of the world like Porter would succeed in devising some *via media* that satisfied his own conscience, and did not wound either his Anglican master or his Catholic wife.

A curious letter to his confidential servant, Richard Harvey, shows that whatever may have been the nominal views of the Porter household, they were ready to make use of any religious ceremonies that might help on their business.[1]

The writer, Wych, tells that a chest of Mr. Porter's, from Madrid, had been stolen "out of my chamber at Bilbao." Instead of sending for the police the messenger invoked the means employed by the Cardinal in the "Ingoldsby Legends," when

> "The Cardinal rose with a pious look,
> He called for his candles, he called for his book ;
> In holy anger and pious grief,
> He solemnly cursed that rascally thief."

In Bilbao the measures taken were, "I had an excommunion and paulinas read in churches and other places where I suspected."

It was the custom to invoke the help of St.

[1] George Wych to Harvey. Dom. S. P., 1638.

Paulina, virgin and martyr, as a protection against thieves, but no exact parallel for the excommunication seems to be known.[1] Porter's servants seem to have shared their master's ingenuity and readiness for emergencies!

[1] I have to thank Canon E. T. Quinn, P.P., Ballybrack and Cabinteely, for this information.

CHAPTER XI

THERE were sharp religious controversies in England, and vague fears of Jesuits and Papal plots, but such differences were trifling compared to the tempest that was now raging in Scotland.

The King had been for some time engaged in trying to introduce uniformity of doctrine and the use of a prayer-book into Scotland, with the result that in February, 1638, all classes were signing the Solemn League and Covenant with wild enthusiasm, as a national protest against royal tyranny.

Charles could not realise that his own countrymen of Scotland were actually on the verge of a rebellion. He condescended to make various proposals, which seemed to himself vastly gracious, and to the angry Scots seemed to be adding insult to injury, till at last even he was obliged to realise that his fair words were wasted, and that he must prepare for action.

It was not easy for the King to get troops together without the help of Parliament, but a parliament would be an even worse adversary than the Scots; so he made shift to gather together an army composed of raw recruits and Court gentlemen. With these hasty levies, half starved and ill-appointed, he marched to meet the Scots, hardy and enthusiastic northerners, officered by veterans who had learnt their business under Gustavus Adolphus.

Endymion Porter was in attendance on his Majesty, and seems, from his letters to his servant, to have left home at short notice.

" RICHARD HARVIE,—I thank you for remembering my gauntlets, and I pray you see that they be finished with all the haste you can, and send them to me with the pistols, if Mr. Courteen have as yet procured them, likewise I would have you furnish me with half a dozen of quires of paper, for we can get none here, and all my store is spent. . . . These pernicious rebels are very insolent, but the English are not afeared of them ; I have sent my wife a proclamation which the King hath now sent into Scotland, I would have you read it, and with my hearty commendation to you I rest

"Your true friend,

"ENDYMION PORTER.

" DURHAM, *the 3rd of May*, 1839.

"I pray you send me truly your opinion of Charles.

(*Enclosed*) "To my very loving friend Mr. Richard Harvie these, London."[1]

" RICHARD HARVIE,—I must intreat you to send me by this bearer two pair of calsons of shamwayes made to come low beneath my knees, and I pray you give order that the seams be curiously sewed so as they do not hurt me, and if Tom Kenistone give you a small piece of fine calico I pray you let it be

[1] Dom. S. P., vol. ccccxx. 34.

brought likewise with him ; the messenger is in haste, and therefore I say no more, but rest

"Your true friend,

"ENDYMION PORTER.

"NEWCASTLE, *the* 18*th of May*, 1639.

"I left a watch with Este to make for the King, and he had a curious case of gold enamelled of me, so that he makes nothing but the intrails.   He is to have seven pounds for it, I pray you let him be paid for it, and see that you send it me safe.

"*To my loving friend, Mr. Richard Harvie, London.*" [1]

Mr. Fontblanque believes this watch to have been the one afterwards worn by the King at his execu-- tion, and deposited as a precious relic in Ashburn- ham Church.   But, he says, "one of the pious pilgrims to the church not believing, perhaps, in the efficacy of touch alone, carried it away with him." [2]

While Endymion was busy over warlike matters Olivia was trying to get in rents.   There is a long and lamentable letter to her from Butler, the tenant of Summercotes, the reclaimed land in Lincoln, at this time. [3]   His letters were always lamentable and generally long, and he signs himself in one "your poor kinsman," so that it would seem that the poorer relations of the Botelers turned into plain Butlers. Richard Harvey generally wrote the business letters, but Olivia herself had added some sharp words to his letter this spring, and Butler writes that he knows she expects money, but he has not been able to sell

---

[1] Dom. S. P., ccccxxi. 75.
[2] Fontblanque, "Lords Strangford," p. 58.
[3] Cal. Dom. S. P., 1639.

his oats, the keel being pressed for the King's
service, and also a command had been issued in
view of the King's march to the north that no oats
should be sold away from those parts. He therefore resolved to sell at Newcastle, but the weather
was too stormy for a ship to go there, " Wherefore,
good Madam, do but consider how the times are,
but by the time the carrier comes to London again
you shall receive both my account and such moneys
as can be made of your corn." In the following
September things seem to have come to a crisis ;
we find Richard Harvey going down to take up the
accounts, with eleven-years-old Master Philip to
represent his parents ; and poor Butler wails that he
is just thrown out of service when he had got the
harvest in. Another tenant, Mr. Cutteris, is described as a good tenant who, though he had paid
no rent, had spent £160 on buildings and improve-
ments, but the Council's commands had prevented
his selling a singular good crop. Endymion wrote
from the camp that both tenants were cozening
knaves to whom he sent a sharp letter.

From the camp, on June 3rd, Thomas Windebank
writes to his father, the Secretary, that "never was
such confusion seen in business of so great weight.
Porter presents his services and is very ready, I am
confident, to do you service, but he says he is not
so able to give so quick despatch to your business
as he desires by reason that Secretary Coke has
made a complaint of him to the King for intruding
upon business, which makes his Majesty slow in
despatching anything that passed not by Secretary
Coke's hands." [1]

[1] Cal. Dom. S. P., June, 1639.

The Scots were not anxious to take such a decisive step as invading England, and the King's army was so plainly unfit for a campaign that he was not disinclined to come to terms, and on June 10th his Majesty agreed to a treaty.

Both sides felt, however, that there was no stability in this patched-up peace, and Strafford came over from Ireland and advised the King to call a parliament.

But, when it met, Parliament proved to have more sympathy with the Scots than with the King, and his Majesty dissolved it after only three weeks' service, and began once more to try and construct an army.

George and Charles Porter were now lads of nineteen and eighteen respectively, and received their commissions,

A friend from Brussels writes to Harvey, " I wish Captain George Porter all happiness, as I do the noble Cornet. I long for to have the gloves and riband."

What the last enigmatical reference means cannot be said, unless it refers to George Porter's wedding. He certainly did marry somewhere about this time, and made a good match, marrying the widowed Lady Diana Covert, daughter of the Earl of Norwich, and sister of George Goring. Of Lady Diana herself we know nothing except that she had lands in Suffolk and Kent. But George Porter and George Goring suited each other only too well.

In April an order was signed by Conway, the general in the north, to Captain George Porter, to repair to Newcastle-on-Tyne with his troop of horse, to pay for what they needed on the road, and to

commit no disorder.[1]   It was easy to sign orders!
but the men, who were raw recruits, angry at having
to serve at all, and very uncertain if they would ever
get their pay, were not at all inclined to be obedient
to their inexperienced commanders.   Mutinies and
outrages were common, and it is not surprising that
the next notice of George Porter is a complaint from
one Christopher Pyburne, of Darlaston, supported
by the local constables, that the "lieutenant, Cornet,
and others of Captain Porter's troop of horse, beat
me, my wife, and children."[2]

What was almost worse than the state of the
army was the state of the fortifications, the towns in
the North were practically unguarded.   In vain did
Lord Conway point out the necessity of protecting
Newcastle whence London brought its supply of
coal.   When the Scots were preparing to cross the
Tweed on the 19th of July, the fortifications of that
important city were still only in a condition to offer
a couple of days' resistance.

Charles Porter was already in the North.   In
April one of his kinsfolk, George Boteler or Butler
(probably the cousin who wrote about a horse in
1628), wrote to Conway, " I suppose your young
officer, Charles Porter, has arrived before this.   He
was with me two days, and I brought him on his
journey as far as York ; I thank you for your noble
care of him."[3]

The next letter is from Charles himself to his
father.

"DEAR SIR,—This is only to let you know how

unwilling I am and have been since my coming hither to let slip any occasion of writing to you, for yesterday I did present my duty to you and to my mother in another packet which I sent by the post, and knowing for certain that this will be safely delivered, I will give you an account of those things which I wrote (writt) in the other packet, for we hear say that all the letters that come from hence are broken open.   My lord uses me extreme kindly, for which I must intreat you to give him my thanks, and this last week he saw me exercise the troop, and was very well pleased with me. I hear, Sir, that you have received the trunk and swords out of Spain (Spayne). Pray, Sir, if you please, make that sword of Luis de Ayala to be put into such a hilt as my brother's black (blake) one, and let it be deep enough that I might thrust both my fingers into it, for I like a good sword extremely.   I have not had the happiness to hear from you since I came from London but once, which hath not troubled me a little, therefore I beseech you to let me hear from you as soon as you can, for there is nothing can be so welcome to

    "Your dutiful and obedient son,

       "CHARLES PORTER.

 " *The 20th of May,* 1640.

 "Pray, Sir, remember my most humble duty to my mother.

 " *To my dear father, Mr. Endymion Porter, these present at his house over against Durham House in the Strand.   London.*   Pay the post." [1]

    [1] Dom. S. P., vol. cccclv. 41.

On the 20th of August the King set out from
London, and that same night the Scots crossed the
Tweed at Coldstream. On the 23rd the King was
at York, which remained for some time the royal
head-quarters, and it is from there that Porter's
letters are dated.

George seems soon to have found out that the
hardships of campaigning were not to his taste.

"GEORGE,—I have sent you your breeches and
your drawers, but I cannot find your gloves, I have
sent you an old pair of mine, which I am ashamed
of, but I have no better, your bottle of diet drink
and your electuary likewise goeth along with Mr.
Jares, he is a very honest gentleman and the King
will cure his daughter to-morrow. I have sent you
a letter from your mother, and if you continue in the
desire to come off the employment, send me word
truly what you would have, and it shall be done ; in
the meantime God preserve you, and I wish you
had lighted on the happy occasion Lieutenant
Smithe did, for then you should have come away
to-morrow. Howsoever I wish you at home with
your mother ; here your hounds are, and this is the
letter which Mr. Smithe hath sent with them. Let
me know what you will have done ; I have given
Hobdie an angel, and whatsoever he needs shall
not be wanting, but send me word what you will
have done with them ; and God of Heaven bless
you.

"Your best friend and most loving father,

"ENDYMION PORTER.

"YORK, *this 20th of September*, 1640.

"See that you keep a careful watch for therein

consists your safety ; sleep in the day and watch the nights.

"*(Endorsed) To my dear son Captain George Porter these.*" [1]

In spite of his failing health and press of Irish work, Strafford had hastened to the King at York and was urgently declaring to the Yorkshire gentlemen that they were no better than beasts if they hung back from the King's service now.

The inhabitants of Newcastle had at last done a few days' work on the fortifications, but there was no chance of being ready to meet the Scots, either on the walls or in the field. Strafford's fiery spirit could not understand such delays. Colonel Arthur Aston wrote to Conway from York, on the 29th of August, describing an interview with the Lord-Lieutenant of Ireland, "who, being still in bed, commanded me to sit down and read your letter to him. He said he was glad I had come that he might be resolved of some things concerning you. He asked various questions about Newcastle, and Endymion Porter being present was very well pleased with what I said, and instantly told the King I was come, and would satisfy his Majesty in all particulars." [2]

But even while Porter was carrying the news to the King, at low tide on the 28th the Scots crossed the Tyne at Newburn, and the insufficient defences which Conway had thrown up at the ford were quickly deserted when the Scotch ordnance began to play from the opposite hill.

The Scotch charged the English Cavalry, which

broke, but was rallied again by Astley.   Leslie
in person then charged a second time, and the
English forces fled and did not draw rein till they
reached Durham.   Some of the English officers
remained prisoners in the hands of the Scots, and
some, worthy of better comrades, were to be found
neither among the prisoners nor the fugitives.   Of
them a mourning friend writes, "It is whispered the
English was too resolute : there fell Endymion
Porter's second son, a youth as much pitied, as
famed, for his brave carriage and valientness." [1]

No letters are preserved to tell of the father's
sorrow, but no doubt Olive's sharp words in the
following letter to George came from an aching
heart. She had lost the best of her sons, the one who
old Mrs. Porter had said most resembled his father.
Whom the Gods love die young; Charles was brave,
affectionate, and dutiful ; too good to live to be the
companion of his brother George, and share his
drunken revels and futile campaigns.

George Shaw, one of Porter's agents in Brussels,
writes sadly enough to Harvey, " Send me word
how Captain George Porter does and where Giles
Porter is.   My dear comrade Charles Porter ! I
have no words to express my sorrow for that brave
young cavalier of so great expectations." [2]

"GEORGE,—I am very sorry that you continue
still your disorder without having any sense of
Almighty God that hath preserved you from so
many dangers, and if that would not move you, if
you had any good nature or sense of the affliction

[1] Sir E. Hartopp to Coke, Hist. MSS. Com., vol. xii.
[2] Cal. Dom. S. P., Nov. 6, 1640.

your father and I suffer, you would not do it, you knowing I love you more than my soul. Dear child, do not add to my affliction, for if I fail of having comfort in thee there is not (nought?) for me in this life. Farewell, my heart, and make haste home.

"Your most affectionate mother,

"OLIVE PORTER.

"*The fourth of October.*"

"GEORGE,—I could not get that drunken slave Hobdie out of town, but at last I told him that if he would not carry the dogs I would send them by another, he doth nothing but complain of your ill-usage of him; I gave him thirty shillings, and I entreat you to let me have the two large young dogs, for I believe they will not be for your purpose, and I would wish you to try them, and such as you like not send back to me; and indeed if you send them all away now I shall thank you, for you shall not stay there long. Though you take your pleasure in the day, yet see you be vigilant in the night, for now upon treaties they will be aptest to take revenge of their last affront; this I charge you now to look to, and see that you obey me in something, for your own good and your honour. I have opened your mother's letter, the which I here send you. Farewell, I am very ill of a cold.

"Your truest friend,

"ENDYMION PORTER.

"YORK, *this 28th of September,* 1640.

"*(Endorsed) To my worthy friend Captain George Porter, these.*" [2]

---

[1] Dom. S. P., vol. cccclxix. 32.   [2] Ibid., vol. cccclxviii., 75.

The Scots soon pushed on to Durham, but the united armies of the King and Conway were equal to them in number, and were on the whole really in a better position than they had been before the enemy had crossed the Tyne. The Scots now sent in a humble supplication begging that their grievances might be redressed with the advice of an English Parliament, and the Peers in London also forwarded a petition begging for a Parliament and the punishment of the "authors of their grievances." The petition was drawn up by Pym and St. John, but was signed by twelve peers, and in Dr. Gardiner's words, "behind them stood England." Then came yet another petition, this time from the City of London, and from the far north came news of more Scotch victories. The King was driven to take some steps, and he resolved to call a Council of the Peers, hoping to find them manageable in the absence of the Commons. These Peers are the Lords alluded to in Porter's letter of October 5th.

" GEORGE,—You never write to me how you do, and I fear that you mistake the medicine I sent you. My brother Giles was ill, and with taking the Cashew and using that other four or five times, he is now well. I have sent you two pasties of venison, the overcast one if you heat it in the oven will be excellent hot, and the upright one is to eat cold. I pray you send me word how you like them, for I have sent this bearer of purpose with them. Your mother tells me that the Queen hath written to the King to send you home, but I hear nothing of it yet. The city hath lent the money to the King, but what the Lords will do at Ripon I know not. I hear of cessation of arms, if it be so your sergeant-major will give you leave to see your mother, and then we will do well enough ; I pray you send me the two young hounds by this bearer, and that which Sir William Penniman promised me, and so praying to God Almighty to bless you, I rest,

"Your loving father,

"ENDYMION PORTER.

"YORK, *the 5th of October*, 1640.

"*To my worthy friend Captain George Porter, these, at Worsall,*[1] *within two miles of Yarum.*"[2]

But the Lords gave the King no satisfaction ; they echoed the general cry for a Parliament, and the King, unable to resist longer, issued his writs, and the famed Long Parliament met on the 3rd of November, 1640. Endymion sat in it as member for Droitwich.

The English army left in the North soon began to find the new Parliament intended to treat them with complete neglect. The Scots, who had entered England as invaders, and were still in arms on English soil, were its favourites, and Londoners were even indignant that the King should speak of them as rebels. The army of the Scots really stood behind the Parliament, as the Irish army, organised by Strafford, stood behind the King.

But the English army was not clear that it stood on either side ; it was only clear that it wished to be paid. One of its officers, gallant young Edmund Verney, warned his brother, the Member of Parlia-

[1] On the borders of Durham.
[2] Dom. S. P., vol. cccclxiv. 43.

ment, that there would soon be a mutiny among the men for want of pay. The soldiers took the question of commissariat into their own hands. Twelve men of Captain Porter's troop, with their quarter-master, broke into Sir Robert Anstruther's house near Doncaster, and made use of what they found there, and Edmund Verney wrote, "The army are already notable sheep stealers." In November, George Porter's discontent with his position in the North came to a crisis. Orders came that all the troops were to be made complete in horse and arms at the captains' own charge before the 10th of December, and a certain amount was to be deducted from each man's pay to meet this expense. When the men's pay was in arrears this order was not likely to please the captains. To make matters worse, George disliked his commanding officer. Pembroke writes to Conway—"Though I cannot lay the sufferings of George Porter as set down in this petition to your charge, yet on your motion I nominated him for service in this action, and he, as being one of his Majesty's trumpeters under my command as Lord Chamberlain, I cannot but take notice of the injuries said to have been done him, please remit him back to his attendance on his Majesty here, he being now put from yours to the unpleasing service of one Captain Brough." [1]

George Porter's tastes did not lie in the direction of all these hardships and he resigned his commission.

Lady Diana seems to have been with George during part of this uncomfortable time, for on

[1] Cal. Dom. S. P., Nov. 12, 1640.

November 3rd Mr. Walls writes from Farforth that
he was sorry not to have been in the country when
Captain Porter and his wife were there.   Probably
George returned to his duties at the Court of St.
James, for in December a jovial friend sent up
an Oxford cake to Endymion, in London, praying,
if it proved good, " let Captain Porter have one
toast in a cup of Muscadine." [1]

[1] Thomas Williams to Porter, Dec., 1640.   Cal. Dom. S. P.

CHAPTER XII

THE LONG PARLIAMENT

ON November 3rd the long-desired Parliament
met at Westminster.

The story of the drama that was then to be
enacted in England belongs rather to history than
biography. Porter was never a leading actor in the
stately tragedy, but he was seldom off the stage,
and although he professed himself to be "no
politician," there was hardly a man in the country
who was not now ranging himself on one political
side or the other.

Parties were rearranging themselves and opinions
were crystallising into shapes that would hardly
have been dreamt of a few years previously. At
first some were for bishops, some were for pres-
byters, some were for Strafford, some were for
Pym; Porter only knew, "my duty and loyalty
command me to follow my King and Master," [1] and
gradually the line of public division followed that
of his private conscience, and it was only asked
who followed the King and who the Parliament.

The two men who had been the strength of the
King's personal government, Strafford and Laud,

[1] Letter of January 14, 1642, p. 200.

were arrested ; Finch and Windebank fled over-
seas, the Queen's confessor was threatened with
impeachment, her converts were summoned and
fined as recusants.

The Royal Family were in actual need of money
for household expenses ; the King had to cease
keeping open table for the members of the Upper
House, and the Queen's mother had to sell her
jewels and discharge her servants.

Alarmed and indignant, Henrietta Maria thought
it was time for her to take some active part in
mending matters. She sought help on all sides ;
she called on her brother of France, on the Prince
of Orange, on the Pope, " no enterprise seemed too
daring, no combination too extensive for her self-
willed inexperience."[1] She was not long without
finding councillors to her mind ; Jermyn, the self-
confident courtier ; Suckling, the feather-brained
poet ; Goring, " who loved no man so well but he
would cozen him first and laugh at him afterwards :"[2]
all these joined in reminding her that her best ally
might be the English army left facing the Scots in
Yorkshire, which was growing mutinous for want of
pay, and angry with the English Parliament which
reserved its money and favour for the invading and
rebellious Scots.

A splendid plot was soon concocted, which was
to place all the real power over the army in Goring's
hands. Led by him, the troops were to make a
dash on London, and there to join the Irish army and
an invading force from Holland.[3] The Catholics

[1] S. R. Gardiner, " History of England," vol. ix. p. 342.
[2] Bulstrode, " Memoirs," p 71.
[3] S. R. Gardiner, " Cromwell's Place in History," pp. 20, 21.

and foreign residents in London were to rise ; the Governor of the Tower was already won over ; Strafford should be delivered, and all rebels, both Scots and English, should meet with their due reward. Jermyn and Porter were commanded to convey their Majesties' wishes to the Northern army.

Never can royal conspirators have devised a more ingenious plot, or more coolly made preparations for plunging their dominions into civil war. Fortunately the English army was hardly ready to take part in a *coup d'état*, and the officers absolutely refused to entrust unlimited powers to the hands of George Goring.

This refusal wrecked the plot. Goring, as soon as he found the coveted honours would never be his, followed his usual course, " cozened his friends," and secured his own safety by betraying all to the leaders of the Commons. He was permitted by them to return quietly to his governorship of Portsmouth, and that important port was secured for the Parliamentary party.

Jermyn, Suckling, and their principal associates, sought safety in flight. Porter's share in the plot must have been very unimportant, as he was not called to account in any way, and on the day that the conspirators' flight was announced, he was in his place in the House, and there, with the other members, was signing the Protestation that he would, with his life, power, and estate, defend the Protestant religion expressed in the doctrines of the Church of England and endeavour to bring to condign punishment any one who should plot or conspire against it, or endeavour to bring about a misunderstanding between the Army and the Parliament." [1]

The discovery of the army plot decided Strafford's fate. Porter was in his seat two days later, on May 8th, when the Commons, weary of the long delays of Strafford's trial, voted by a large majority for a Bill of Attainder against the fallen Minister. Few ventured to vote against the Bill, and as soon as the names of that daring minority were known, they were posted up in Old Palace Yard by an enraged mob, with the epithets of "Straffordians and betrayers of their country." [2] Among those names are Selden, Hyde, Godolphin, and Endymion Porter.

Nine days later Strafford's head fell, and the King had lost the only man who might possibly have saved him. But whatever remorse and grief Charles may have felt at the sacrifice of his servant, the idea that Strafford's help was indispensable to him never seems to have troubled his fatuous self-confidence.

All through the earlier years of his reign, he had looked on the rival states of Europe as pieces in a game which he might move and countermove so as to check each other, and he still hoped he might carry on the same system in the British Islands. He had called a Parliament in Westminster because the Scots had proved too strong for him. Now that his English Parliament had become unmanageable he turned again to the Scots, and as a reserve in the background he still kept the Irish army,

---

[1] "Commons' Journals," vol. ii. p. 135.
[2] "Verney Notes," pp. 57, 66.

ready to be pushed forward if needful against either England or Scotland.

On August 10th the King started for Edinburgh, leaving the Queen as a hostage and almost a prisoner in England. The elder Vane followed the King to act as Secretary of State, leaving Edward Nicholas, one of the clerks of the Council, behind to forward news to him.

Porter was granted leave of absence from Parliament to attend on his Majesty, and his letters to Nicholas give various little hints of the intrigues that went on in the royal circle at Holyrood.

Porter was too prudent to mention names, but his allusion to " certain legislators who know how to handle the King," shows what he thought of the great Earl of Argyle. That wily nobleman had just succeeded in winning over the King's kinsman, Hamilton, to the Presbyterian side, and few men of any distinction were left to rally round the King. Traquair and the other Royalists had been dubbed incendiaries, and Montrose, who had not scrupled to charge Argyle with treason, was paying the penalty of his boldness in the prison of Edinburgh Castle. Loyalists began to murmur that while Argyle and Hamilton held the highest offices in the country there were three kings in Scotland.

Porter's letters to Nicholas are as follows :—

" MUCH HONOURED FRIEND,—We have no certainty of our return, for his Majesty's businesses run in the wonted channel, subtle designs of gaining popular opinion, and weak executions for the upholding of Monarchy. The King is yet persuaded to hold out, but within two or three days must yield to all, and here are legislators that know how to handle him, for they have his bosom friend sure and play their game as he directs them that sees both.   Traquair dares not appear ; and though Montrose be in hold, he is so gallant a gentleman and so well beloved as they will be fearful to meddle with him but will keep him up so long as the King is here, for they imagine he would turn Caesarian.

"I take the boldness to mention you now and then to his Majesty, and he speaks most graciously of you.   I pray God bless him and send him quickly and safe into England, where I am sure they desire him heartily at this time.

"Your faithful friend and humble server,

"ENDYMION PORTER.

"EDINBURGH, *this 7th September*, 1641." [1]

Porter wrote a second letter to Nicholas four days later, chiefly occupied with a grant of bog land in Ireland, whence grants of land and all other hopes of wealth were soon to vanish in the explosion of the Irish war.

The letter closes sadly enough.

"Since my last unto you there is nothing of news but only the same delay to bring the King to be weary of staying here and so to yield to all they desire (which he is most apt to do), and so to streighten time, as he must leave all such as have appeared contrary to the humours of the Covenanters to be judged by them, which may cost them dear.   And they that scape best will

---

[1] Nicholas Papers, Camden Society, p. 40.

repent that ever they shewed themselves for the
King : for the public applause opposes Monarchy,
and I fear this Island before it be long will be a
theatre of distractions.   God Almighty send you
much happiness and give every true-hearted English-
man a right judgment to study the preservation of
our nation, for we are like to see lamentable times ;
but if there be a fate in it, we cannot discover the
secrets of heaven but must submit to all.

    " I am sure I ever will be,

        " Your most affectionate friend and
           humble servant." [1]

But in spite of Porter's forebodings the first days
of the King's visit to Scotland passed gaily off.
Affairs seemed to take a hopeful turn, the King
was both prudent and affable, Argyle was con-
ciliatory and relaxed his severity to Traquair, and
even held out hopes of pardon for Montrose and his
followers.   The disbanding of both the Scottish
and Irish armies had begun, and orders were sent
to Ireland that four thousand of the unemployed
soldiers should be shipped out of the way to Spain.

Some members of the Irish House of Commons
urged, very reasonably, that if men were sent
abroad to learn the art of war under the enemies
of England, they might prove to be no peaceful
subjects when they returned home.   Cox says :
" These cobweb pretences of public good " delayed
the embarkation of the soldiers for some time. [2]

But the English Parliament was too busy at

---

[1] Porter to Nicholas, Sept. 11, 1641, Nicholas Papers, Camden
Society.
[2] Cox, " Hibern. Ang.," vol. ii. p. 71.

home to think much of "public good" in Ireland.
The future of that distressful country might take
care of itself; the important and pressing matter
was to put the sea between that terribly efficient
army of Strafford's and a King who might make a
dangerous use of it. Let the Irishmen go where
they pleased so long as they went quickly out of
Ireland.

George Porter was one of the few English gentlemen sent to take command of the soldiers destined
for Spain. Whenever there was Spanish business
to be done some of the Porter family generally had
a hand in it, which did not increase their popularity
with the Puritan party.

The King himself, before leaving England, had
condescended to recommend George to the Duke
of Ormond for this purpose :—

"ORMOND,—I have taken this occasion by the
recommending the son of one of my faithful servants to assure that I very much esteem you and
that I do but seek an occasion to show it you by
more than words, as I commanded the Vice-
Treasurer to tell you more fully, and in particular
concerning the blue ribbon of which you may be
confident : I desire you not to take notice of it until
I think it fit. The particular for this bearer George
Porter is to permit him to make up a regiment of
the disbanded army, and if he can do it by per-
suasion to carry them out of the Country for the
King of Spain. This is all, so I rest

"Your assured friend,

"C. R.

"WHITEHALL, 19 *June*, 1641." [1]

[1] Cox, "Hibern. Ang.," Appendix lxix. p. 210.

Few, if any, of those disbanded soldiers reached Spain. The delays interposed to prevent their embarkation gave time for their long smouldering hatred of England to burst into flame, and they were not long in finding congenial work in Ireland itself.

Tradition still shows the spot on Musselburgh Links where the King was playing golf when the first rumours of an Irish outbreak reached his ears. At first there seems to have been some hope that the tidings were too horrible to be true, but post after post hurried in to confirm the news that all the north of Ireland was in a blaze of rebellion.

To the other misfortunes of Ireland was added that of divided authorities, and it was only to Ormond, the King's faithful Commander-in-Chief, that Porter could write without reserve. But Porter, with the majority of the King's friends, was helpless. They could only stand on one side, like the chorus in a Greek tragedy, and lament the disaster which they were powerless to prevent.

" *To the Earl of Ormond.*

"MY MOST HONOURED LORD,—I would I had as much power and worth in me to serve your Lordship as I have ambition to be known to you ; then I am sure the obligations I owe you should not be long unrequited nor I fail in that I so much desire. But your Lordship hath a gallant disposition that looks upon truth and goodwill with equal eyes : and therein my condition may be compared with the best, for no man can love your Lordship better nor honour him more than I do.

"This gentleman will acquaint your Lordship

how the affairs do stand here, which rather recoil
than advance to his Majesty's service. But what
fate it is that rules us I know not ; sure it must be
an untoward one that hath put three kingdoms into
such a tottering disease, as at this day the King
himself cannot say he is absolute over either of
them. And if the news that is brought hither of a
revolt there [1] be true, unless his Majesty make use
instantly of your Lordship's wisdom and courage to
save Ireland it will quite be lost at once whilst the
other two moulder away. But I am no statesman ;
my course is in a lower sphere. I can wish well,
and pray for his Majesty : and whensoever your
Lordship shall be pleased to command me,

"I am, by conquest and free will,

"Your Lordship's most devoted humble
servant,

"ENDYMION PORTER.

"EDINBURGH, *this 29th of October*, 1641." [2]

The news of the Irish massacres aroused in
England a horror which was mingled with terrible
doubts and suspicions. It was well known that
Strafford had proposed to bring his Irish army
over to support the King against any antagonists,
whether Scotch or English ; the very terms of his
commission as Commander-in-Chief bound him to
do so.[3]

The King had promised that this army should be
disbanded, but his secret intentions were not always
the same as his public professions. The English

---

[1] *I.e.*, in Ireland.
[2] Carte's "Ormond," Clarendon Press edit., vol. v. p. 256.
[3] Gardiner's "History of England," vol. ix. p. 184.

army plot was too recent an alarm for England to feel secure from an Irish invasion.

A rumour was spread that the Irish not only announced that the Duke of Ormond was their future general, but also showed in their own justification a royal warrant under the Great Seal. Corroborative details were added. The Seal, it was said, was not that of England, but of Scotland, for the Great Seal of Scotland was at that time in commission and had been left by the Duke of Hamilton, with amazing carelessness, in the hands of two men, one of whom was "Master Endymion Porter," who "found it a fitting opportunity for such a clandestine action." [1]

How much foundation there was for these reports it is hard to say. Porter did affix the Great Seal to a secret warrant three years later when Glamorgan went to Ireland, but it is hardly likely that he was allowed a chance of doing so in Edinburgh, for, at this time, Hamilton was entirely devoted to Argyle's party and would scarcely trust the Great Seal in the hands of the King's servant.

As Miss Hickson suggests,[2] a Scotch royal seal might easily have been cut from one of Lord Antrim's family papers and affixed to the rebel's commission, or the seal itself may have been forged.

That matter is still in mystery, but it seems to be only too true that secret negotiations were carried on with Ireland by the King and Queen from the time of Strafford's imprisonment, while gracious words and hints of employment, if not

[1] "The Mystery of Iniquity yet working," 4to, 1643, p. 38.
[2] Miss Hickson, "Irish Massacres," vol. i. p. 120.

distinct promises, were conveyed later on to the disbanded Irish by the Earl of Antrim, the second husband of the widowed Duchess of Buckingham. To dally with those wild and discontented spirits was indeed playing with fire. The soldiers were soon weary of idle words, and, as Antrim wrote, "The fools, well liking their business, fell on it without waiting." [1]

No one was more likely to be employed in such a correspondence than Porter, and from this service of his might grow the more serious charge of mis-use of the Great Seal.

It is perhaps noticeable that the only letter of this autumn to be found among the Porter corres-pondence is from Ireland. Mr. George White writes from Dublin to Porter lamenting "the dis-tracted state of this country." [2]

Porter's forebodings in his letter to Nicholas proved to be too true, and the King did indeed yield to the Covenanting party all that it desired. He started on his return to England, leaving Argyle a Marquis and Hamilton a Duke, and having put off from himself all but the ceremonial part of the royal dignity of Scotland.

His game had failed in Scotland, yet with scarcely abated hopes he turned again to England, and endeavoured to form a new party of allies among the wealthy citizens of London. The compliment paid to the City by a royal visit to Guildhall filled all hearts with enthusiasm, but in spite of loyal demonstrations, neither the City nor the Parliament

---

[1] Dunlop, "Hist. Rev.," vol. ii. p. 527.
[2] Tanner MSS., vol. lxvi. p. 214.

were going to retire from the position won before the King's journey to Scotland.

Distrust and discord grew fast and culminated in the King's disastrous attempt to arrest the five members within the sacred precincts of the House itself and their flight to the security of the City. Charles had to bow before the storm he had raised, less in fear for himself than for the Queen, who had urged him to that last fatal step.

He left Whitehall on the 10th of January, never to enter it again till the day of his execution. So unexpected was the flight of the Royal Family, that no preparation was made to receive them at Hampton Court, and the elder children had to share the bedroom of the King and Queen.

Endymion Porter, hurried away from his wife and home, thought that even in those straits the King was rather to be envied than pitied, for he at least shared his exile with those he loved best.

Porter's letter to his wife is evidently in answer to one the forsaken lady had managed to send after him to Windsor.

" My dearest Love,—As for monies, I wonder you can imagine that I should help you, but you always look for impossibilities from me, and I wish it were a time of miracles, for then we might hope for a good success in everything ; whither we go and what we are to do I know not, for I am none of the Council ; my duty and loyalty have taught me to follow my King and Master, and by the grace of God nothing shall divert me from it ; I could wish you and your children in a safe place, but why Woodhall shall not be so I cannot yet tell ; I could likewise wish my cabinets and all my other things were at Mr. Courteen's, but if a very discreet man be not there and take the advice of the Joiner to convey them thither, they will be as much spoiled in the carriage as with the rabble ; dearest love, to serve God well is the way in everything that will lead us to a happy end, for then He will bless us and deliver us out of all troubles ; I pray you have a care of yourself, and make much of your children, and I presume we shall be merry and enjoy one another long. I writt to you and sent the letters by Nick on Tuesday, but that rogue is drunk, and I hear not of him. If you remember my service to Mrs. Eure and tell her that I am her faithful servant, I will give you leave to kiss Mrs. Marie for me ; I wish sweet Tom with me, for the King and Queen are forced to lie with their children now, and I envy their happiness. I pray you let this bearer come to me again when you hear where we rest, and so Goodnight sweet Noll.

> " Your true friend and
> " Most loving husband,
> " ENDYMION PORTER.
> " WINDSOR, *this 14th of January*, 1642."

" Sweet Tom " was a little fellow of six ; " Mrs. Marie " was already a maid of honour,[1] but her age is not known ; " Mrs. Eure " is possibly the lively Margaret Eure, Ralph Verney's cousin.

The valuables left with Mr. Courteen at Clapham

[1] Peter Cunningham. *Once a Week*, Jan. 31, 1863.

were only left unmolested till June, 1643, when a letter to the "Parliament man," Sir Ralph Verney, tells how Sir Roger Burgoyne was sent to search for the plate on the information of a perfidious servant.[1] Mr. Courteen did his best to save the valuables, affirming they had been given to him by Mr. Porter in payment of a debt, and Lady Catherine, when she could do no more, desired Sir Roger himself to overlook the opening of the plate boxes and take the responsibility. But it is to be feared that nothing belonging to so notable a malignant as Endymion Porter was ever let escape the clutches of the Parliament.

Many of those who had made themselves obnoxious to the popular party left the country at this period, and Endymion must have known that he was not likely to see his house in the Strand again for some time. Woodhall was not long to be a place of refuge, as Parliament deprived Endymion of his position as guardian of William, Lord Boteler, replacing him by their own partisan, Lord Howard of Escrick.

No doubt he accompanied the King to Dover to see the Queen sail for Holland under pretext of taking the Princess Royal to her young husband. The King then returned to Greenwich, and there he received a demand from the Parliamentary committee who sat at Grocer's Hall in the City "that the King would remove from his person and the Queen's, Mr. W. Murray, Mr. Porter, Mr. T. Winter, and Mr. W. Crofts, being all persons of evil fame and disaffection to the public peace

---

[1] I have to express my thanks to Lady Verney for giving me this extract.

and prosperity of the kingdom." This demand, it is unnecessary to say, was not granted, and Endymion was in attendance on the King when he left Greenwich for the North, and established his Court at York.

CHAPTER XIII

THE CIVIL WAR

WHEN the King was once established at York, the Lords and gentlemen who favoured his cause were not long in gathering round him, and even Lord Keeper Littleton himself soon followed his Majesty, a serious blow to the Parliamentary party.

By way of checking this exodus, a census of the members who still remained in London was taken, and an order was promulgated that all members should be in their places punctually by the 15th of June under a penalty of £100 each, to be paid to. the fund for carrying on the Irish War.

Endymion Porter had already been summoned to attend to his Parliamentary duties, but the King had answered by a warrant to Lenthall, saying that he required Porter's attendance with him as gentleman of the bed-chamber. The House rejected this excuse, and warned him to be in his place, a warning he was not very likely to obey.

As soon as it was known that the Court was settled at York, many ladies joined their husbands ; most likely Mrs. Porter was among the number, and plans were made for Miss Lettice to go to her parents.

" If you wish it," writes the steward at Woodhall, " I will use my best endeavours to get her up safe to you, and the course I conceive fittest is either by waggon or else by hackney coach, if we can conveniently hear of any." [1]

A letter from Porter to Chief Justice Bankes at this time probably refers to a petition from the Parliament, which the King received on the 15th of July.

" My much honoured Lord,—His Majesty hath commanded me to send your Lordship this book, which he would have you peruse, and when you have perfected it, he would have your Lordship return it to him, and with what convenient speed you may. This is all I had order to say from the King, and for myself I can only assure you that I am obliged to be,

" Your Lordship's humble servant,

" Endymion Porter.

" Beverley, *this 16th of July, at ten of the clock at night.*" [2]

The King raised his Standard at Nottingham on August 22nd, and from there moved slowly across the country to Shrewsbury, which he reached just a month later ; Essex, the leader of the Parliamentary forces, keeping between him and London, but not offering battle.

During this march Endymion and his son George were surprised by the Mayor of Derby at the house of " Mr. Poudrel, a great Papist." [3]   It had become

---

[1] Dom. S. P., May, 1642.
[2] From Bankes' " Story of Corfe Castle," Edit. 1853, p. 148.
[3] " Exceeding Joyful News."   King's Pamphlets, E $\frac{11}{13}$.

known in Derby that arms were collected in this house for the King's use, so the Mayor raised a troop of his own adherents, and made a night march on September 15th to the house, which they surrounded and broke open. There they found several Royalist gentlemen, including the two Porters, and on searching more closely they had the satisfaction of coming on a secret passage, and a Jesuit disguised as a serving-man. No narrative of the sort could be complete without a secret passage and a disguised Jesuit ; but although the accessories were in order, the arms, which were the real object of the visit, were gone, having been removed to Nottingham. The Mayor had to content himself with the Jesuit, who was sent to London. Probably the gentlemen settled matters privately with their captors, for we hear no more of them as prisoners.

Endymion was now Colonel of the 7th Regiment, with Lieut.-Colonel Vavasour, Major Stanhope, and seven Captains under him.[1] It very frequently happened that the colonels of Regiments did not go on active service, that duty being discharged by the Lieut.-Colonel, and doubtless this was the case with Endymion, who had to be in attendance on the King, instead of fighting in the field. In his petition to the Committee for Compounding Royalist claims, long afterwards, he asserts that he never bore arms against the Parliament. It seems a curious assertion for a man of his military rank to make, but it is quite possible that it is true.

"The Houses," says Clarendon, "that the King might know how little they dreaded his forces," now

[1] Peacock's "Army Lists."

sent Essex instructions, desiring him to rescue his
Majesty out of the hands of the desperate persons
who were about him, and offering clemency to any
who would within ten days return to their duty;
excepting Bristol, Newcastle, and some more Peers,
Mr. Secretary Nicholas, Mr. Porter, and Mr.
Edward Hyde.

Then came the battle of Edgehill, in October,
1642, and the King's march on London, followed
by his retreat from Turnham Green. During the
ensuing winter he made his headquarters in Oxford.

In the end of February, 1643, the Queen landed
at Burlington, in Yorkshire, and was received in
the North with so much enthusiasm that henceforth
the army collected there under the Duke of Newcastle was known as the Queen's army. Her
landing was, however, made under difficulties,
and, when she hoped to take rest after a stormy
voyage, the Parliament's ships, under Batten, were
so unchivalrous as to bombard the house where she
was lodged. A Scotch report tells of her Majesty's
danger.

"Aluises scho gettis up out of her naiked bed,
in her night walycot, bair feet and bair leg, with her
maids of honour (whairof one throu plain fier went
strait mad, being ane nobleman's dochter), she gettis
saiflie out of the hous while the schipps bring down
the roof of her lodging."[1] The Queen, like a worthy
daughter of the hero of Ivry, only laughed at the
danger, and even ventured back among the flying
shot to fetch her little dog, who had been forgotten
in the first alarm; and no accidents seem to have

[1] Spalding. Quoted in Warburton's "Prince Rupert," vol. ii.
p. 217.

happened among her ladies save to the poor girl
who was frightened out of her reason. Her name
is not given, but a sad guess may be made, from
finding, among the York registers of burials, that
Marie Porter was laid to rest in the Minster on the
15th of March, 1643. If it was indeed Endymion
Porter's eldest daughter who died from the terrors
of that night, she was but the second of the loyal
family who gave life and all for the royal service ;
more were to follow. Mrs. Porter was at York at
this time, so at any rate the poor girl had all the
care her mother's love could give. A letter from
Endymion to his wife was intercepted by Parliamentary agents and read in the House on the 29th
of March ; it seems rather hard that the poor lady
could not even have the comfort of a letter from her
husband at such a time.

A letter from Porter to the Duke of Newcastle
was intercepted at Coventry about the same date ;
it enclosed a cypher letter from the King to the
Queen, and also a libel in verse on the Parliament,
which no doubt would have delighted the loyal and
poetical Duke, but so offended the House that "Mr.
Porter was thereupon expelled," a punishment that
he probably did not lay very much to heart, if ever
he heard of it.[1]

The letter is dated Oxford, March 2nd—

" I beseech your Lordship not to wonder at this
tattered Mercury, for we have had such ill luck in
our Cavaliers as we thought this way the best to
secure letters.

" I am extremely glad the Queen is safe arrived

[1] Gardiner, "Great Civil War," vol. i. p. 110.

at York, and now I hope your Lordship will not suffer Tadcaster to be fortified nor the rebels to domineer as they have done.

"I have long wished to place my wife in the Queen's bed-chamber. I beseech your Lordship to do in it as you shall think best and oblige me according to your accustomed goodness. I have sent your Lordship the Queen's letter herein enclosed, and with it a copy of excellent verses." [1]

In July the King and Queen met at Edgehill, and there was a splendid state entry into Oxford. There can be little doubt that Mrs. Porter had joined her husband by this time, and that life went on at Oxford much as it had done in the Strand. Charles and Marie were gone for ever, and Philip was abroad, but "sweet Tom" and Lettice were probably there to cheer their parents, and for a time the circle must have included Endymion's unmarried brother Gyles, for he served in the King's army and died at Oxford, aged 32 or 33.

On the 3rd of December, 1643, the King summoned a Parliament at Oxford of the Lords and gentlemen who still adhered to his cause. One of its first acts was to send a letter of remonstrance to the Earl of Essex ; he simply forwarded it unopened to the Houses in London, who desired him to return it, which he did with a short note saying : "We are all resolved to spend our blood for the maintenance of the Parliament of England and its priviledges." [2] The letter of remonstrance was signed by Endymion Porter among the rest of the Members.

[1] Portland Papers, vol. i. p. 98.
[2] "Old Parl. Hist.," vol. vxiii. p. 75.

This Parliament was not longlived. As soon as it ventured to express a desire for peace the King dissolved it, calling it in private a mongrel Parliament.

Oxford during these years of war reminds one of the calm spot in the centre of a hurricane. It was the centre and heart of the war, and yet accounts of the life there are hardly to be found ; nothing seems to have been said, done, or recorded ; Lady Isabella Thynn's lute-playing in Trinity Grove was as important a matter as a cavalry skirmish. One scrap of information comes from a Cornish cousin, Erisey Porter, a fellow of Exeter College. He was one of the Porters of Trematon, and was afterwards appointed Rector of Butterleigh, in Devon.[1] Exactly what degree of cousinship he held to the Porters of Aston is not clear, but he appears to have been very intimate. He wrote on April 14, 1644, to Colonel Seymour,[2] telling him that the Queen, who was in bad health, and anxious to try the Bath waters, "has yet deferred her journey to the West, much against her will and content. Your noble friend and my dearest Endymion labours of an Ague, but hope he will ere you get this shake him off with a powder."

One of the best of the King's generals, stout old Sir Jacob Astley, seems to have been on friendly terms with Endymion Porter, and sent him a present to Oxford. Unfortunately, the terms of the following letter of thanks are too general to enable us to identify which of Prince Rupert's enterprises are alluded to—

[1] " Alumni Oxonienses."
[2] " Private Archives of the Duke of Somerset," vol. iii. p. 33. I have to thank Lady Gwendolen Ramsden for kindly verifying this reference

" My much honoured Lord,—I Give your Lord-ship infinite thanks for your kind letter, and by this I perceive that unexpected favours oblige more than those which by importunity are obtained.   Indeed, my Lord, you cannot imagine how much I honour your Lord-ship for this remembrance of me.   But what shall I return?   Faith, my Lord, an honest heart, as full of true love and gratitude as you can wish or I think, and with such a one I will pay interest on the debt till better times make me able to satisfy your Lord-ship to the full.   It is good news to hear how your army increases, and we all think it a happiness to that gallant Prince Rupert in that he enjoys your Lord-ship's company in those enterprises his Highness undertakes against the K's enemies, and by your Lord-ship's good advice I hope he will be able to curb the unruly ambition of distracted rebels and bring them quickly to a know-ledge of their errors which have brought our poor nation to a miserable condition.   I showed his Majesty your Lord-ship's letter and he charged me to remember him to you, and publickly expressed with large kindness the confidence he had in your worth and courage.

" I beseech your Lord-ship present my humble duty to Prince Rupert and Prince Maurice, and when your Lord-ship hath occasion to employ any body here in your service, I am your Lord-ship's first man and will never fail you, for both my (by?) predestination and free-will I must and shall ever be, my Lord,

" Your Lord-ship's most devoted
humble servant,

" ENDYMION PORTER.

" OXFORD, *this 26th of March,* 1645 (44 ?).

" To my dear Sir Bernard and to Colonel Appleby I drink your Lord-ship's health, and they may pledge me in ale, for wine you have none."[1]

During the earlier part of the Porters' stay in Oxford, George may occasionally have joined the family circle, as he was serving in the army in that neighbourhood under Prince Rupert. He does not seem to have been a favourite with that fiery general, who preferred officers who talked less and did more; George Porter's day was yet to come.

Botanists tell us that while summer leaves are yet green, the buds which shall be leaves next year are already fully formed. The germ of the new time is maturing while the old time seems full of vigour. Among the stately figures who surrounded Charles the First, Strafford, Falkland, Rupert, Ormond, each worthy to be a king of men, there drank and jested those who were to form the future court of the Merry Monarch. The period of the restoration was heralded by such rollicking blades as Goring, Wilmot, and George Porter.

While the old courtiers of the King were in the ascendant, George Porter's principal business seems to have been to make apologies; and perhaps in his secret heart he was not ill-pleased when, in 1643, he received orders to place himself, as Commissary-general of Horse, under the command of the magnificent Earl of Newcastle at York.[2] His

---

[1] Sloane MSS. Sir End. Porter to Lord Ashley. [Misprint for Astley.] Fontblanque, " Lords Strangford," p. 79.

[2] Warburton's " Prince Rupert," p. 507 ; " Life of the Duke of Newcastle," ed. 1886, p. 165.

brother-in-law, Goring, was there already, sending reports of the taverns, "the Nonsuch," "the Flying Horse," and the "Bull," in his letters to his dear partner, that same Henry Percy, whose army plot he had betrayed the year before. George Porter seems to have left the army near Oxford under somewhat of a cloud, as his apologies and protestations to Prince Rupert begin at once.

"MAY IT PLEASE YOUR HIGHNESS,—Though the frown your Highness was pleased to cast upon me at my coming away ought to forbid the presumption, the great affliction it hath caused me makes me forget all other considerations but what tends to the clearing me and the regaining your Highness' favour, which I so undeservedly lost. If your Highness did but conceive how near it came to me, you would pardon the boldness I have taken to excuse your justice and believe the passion I have ever loved and honoured your Highness with did not merit so severe a return ; and that your Highness might not conceive these professions proceed from design, I will acquaint your Highness with the condition I am in, which wants nothing but your Highness' good opinion to make me the happiest man in England, besides the backwardness your Highness knows I have ever found in the King to advance me is a sufficient reason to forbid me pretending anything at Court. Nevertheless I shall endeavour to perform that duty and obedience I owe him, and never value my life when the loss of it may any way advance his service. This place is so barren of news as I must be forced to end with

the profession which I fear your Highness will
hardly believe, that is of my being
                "Your Highness' most faithful,
                        humble servant,
                                "GEORGE PORTER.
    "YORK, *the 20th of December*, 1643."

George Porter had the opportunity, which he
professed to desire, of gaining Rupert's favour next
spring, and under such a commander he managed
to perform some service.

Newark was closely besieged by three bodies of
Parliamentary troops.   The garrison were starving,
and the Governor, Sir John Henderson, could hold
out no longer.   Rupert, on his way to relieve it,
was joined by Lord Loughborough at Ashby, and
soon afterwards by Porter.   One of the first successes was gained by Porter, who drove in a party
sent to oppose the Prince's army crossing the bridge
over the Soar.

The Prince was afraid of sending any clear
instructions to the besieged lest his letter should
fall into the hands of the enemy, but he sent the
enigmatic message, "Let the old drum on the
north side be beaten early on the morrow morning";
and being understood by the garrison they made
a sally on old Sir John Meldrum's forces which
soon resulted in a general battle.   A real hand-to-
hand struggle followed, when three Roundheads
almost pulled Rupert from his horse, and he was
with some difficulty rescued by his own troop.
Finally, Rupert succeeded in seizing the bridge
leading to the town and surrounding the besiegers
who, when evening fell, were thankful to make

terms. They were allowed to march away with the honours of war, but their artillery and ammunition remained as a prize for the victors.

The relief of Newark placed all the neighbouring country in the hands of the Royalists. Gainsborough, Lincoln, and Sleaford fell to them without a blow. Rupert was at liberty to hasten to the West and put Wales in some sort of order, before dashing to the aid of the Duke of Newcastle.

George Porter was dispatched to occupy Lincoln. The Sir Miles Hubbard, to whom he alludes in the following letter, had led one of the divisions of the Parliamentary army at Newark. Sir Fulk Hunks commanded a thousand volunteer foot from Ireland and a hundred and twenty musketeers, in the Prince's army at Newark.

"*George Porter to Prince Rupert.*
"LINCOLN, *March* 24, 1644.

" I am come into Lincoln and find some cannon, but no arms or ammunition. From the several relations of the people of this town, I collect that the enemy is possessed with so strange a senseless fear that they will not believe any place tenable to which your Highness will march. Sir Miles Hubbard did not march with above one hundred armed foot from this place, and those that came from Newark are most of them dispersed. I am employing as many men as I can get to slight the works about the base town, but those about the close are so very strong that it will require time, and I think it worth your Highness' consideration whether those works should be slighted or no. To-morrow I march towards Gainsborough and will send you these cannon. If you have any commands for me, I desire to receive them, and they shall be faithfully observed by &c., &c."

"NEWARK, *March 28th.*

"I understand since your Highness' departure how that you are very much offended with me for that I did not wait upon your Highness before you went, and [for] expressing an unwillingness to come under Colonel Hunkes his command. As for the first I have most just excuse which I am confident will prevail with your Highness when you shall remember the haste my letter from Lincoln required; notwithstanding I was to wait on your Highness, but your Highness was gone before, and I could not allow myself so much leisure to follow. Then as concerning Colonel Hunks, if your Highness would but be pleased to look upon me with an impartial eye, I should certainly be freed from your displeasure, there was so much justice on my side, for I offered him to resign half the command I had in these parts both of the horse and foot which I desired Major Legg to persuade him to, but he would not, and nothing would content the Colonel but the absolute command of all, which I now most humbly beseech your Highness would confer on him, and so I shall be free to march to the aid of Yorkshire, which your Highness by these enclosed will find stands in great need of it. I beseech your Highness let your good nature so rule your Highness as to send immediately Colonel Hunks, whose zeal for the King's service joined to your Highness' commands will certainly persuade him to make no delay. Your Highness, &c., &c.

"I beseech your Highness let me know your resolutions with all speed."

"NEWARK, *March* 30*th.*

"I find fortune is strangely contradictory, else 'twere impossible a discourse so little intended to your Highness could have been an occasion of barring me from it. For the passion I expressed was meant for those who, I was informed, had first persuaded your Highness to send Colonel Hunks as commander of all these forces in chief and next for furthering your Highness' displeasure against me, because I was importunate with your Highness for the recalling the commission you had given, and he that told your Highness part of my discourse might likewise have told you that at the time I named your Highness I only said I was accurst to find their tricks and desires could so prevail upon your good nature. I hope this will satisfy your Highness. However, I shall in my absence from your Highness endeavour to let you see how your Highness in your distrust, injures one who is most faithfully; &c., &c., &c.

"I have just now received an order from my Lord General to march with all the horse and foot I can get together to meet with Sir Thomas Fairfax who is in Yorkshire."

"LINCOLN, *April* 1, 1644.

"MAY IT PLEASE YOUR HIGHNESS,—Yesterday I received an order from his Excellency to march into Yorkshire, which I am preparing to do with

all expedition, but in the interim I thought fit to
represent to your Highness the advantage 'twould
be to the King's service, my stay here some small
time, if not longer, for whereas now I cannot move
with above six hundred foot and a thousand horse,
in that space might add at the least two thousand
foot and some horse.   This likewise I have made
my Lord General acquainted with, whose answer
I hourly expect, but I am sure would be pleased
to have me observe your Highness' directions
who best understands the state of these counties.
Wherefore I beseech your Highness consider on
these reasons are here represented to your
Highness by the Commissioners, and lay your
commands on him who will punctually observe
them, as being

   " Your Highness' most faithful and
      obedient servant,

        " GEORGE PORTER.

 " There is one Lieutenant Leelborne, a prisoner
at Newark by your Highness' command, who if you
please to bestow him on me will release Major
Wheeler whom Colonel Jerret will assure your
Highness to be very deserving." [1]

Newcastle was gradually falling back before the
advancing Scots who had at last crossed the border
to succour the Parliamentary army, and he was also
threatened by Fairfax, who stormed Selby on the
11th of April, a disaster which Newcastle wrote to
the King was entirely owing to the lack of assistance
from Lord Loughborough and Colonel Porter, as

---

[1] The above letters from George Porter are from a transcript of
the Rupert Correspondence, in the possession of Mr. C. H. Firth.

they had time enough, and orders too, to come to his aid.

The Scots and the two Fairfaxes now joined in besieging York with the aid of the Earl of Manchester. But, as Rupert drew near, they raised the siege in order to avoid being caught between two enemies, and took up a position on Marston Moor. Newcastle did not think it prudent to follow them up and force them to a battle until reinforcements arrived. Rupert, however, was in possession of a letter from the King, in which was expressed an earnest hope that he would be able to fight the enemy and beat them. The letter coincided exactly with Rupert's own feelings, and, appealing to it as being a positive command from the King, he overruled Newcastle's objections. The Royalist forces accordingly advanced to give battle to the combined armies of the Scots and of the English Parliament. Rupert and his hitherto invincible cavalry were posted on the right ; Goring led the cavalry on the left ; in the Royalist centre, which was marshalled by the experienced Eythin, George Porter held the rank of Major-General of foot.[1] According to the "Full Relation," which Dr. Gardiner attributes to Lord Eglinton, who commanded one of the Scottish regiments of horse, Goring, after scattering the cavalry on the Parliamentary right, assaulted the Scottish foot in the centre with the aid of Porter. Eglinton maintains that the Scottish foot beat off this combined assault by cavalry and infantry, but it is an undoubted fact that it went so hard with them that Lord Leven,

[1] 9th Report Hist. MSS. Comm. p. 435 ; Vicar's "God's Ark," p. 277.

the Scottish General, thought the day was lost, and
fled headlong from the field in utter ignorance of
what had taken place upon his left. Here, however,
a very different state of affairs prevailed. For the
first time Rupert met his match, and Cromwell,
after putting his cavalry to rout, was free to come to
the rescue of the centre with his victorious Ironsides.
By this most timely aid the tide was turned, and the
King's army was overwhelmed in utter ruin. More
than four thousand were slain, and George Porter
was captured along with many other Royalist
prisoners. After some discussion in Parliament
concerning his exchange, he seems ultimately to
have succeeded in regaining his liberty in the
ensuing winter.[1]

In the west the Royal arms were more fortunate.
The King in person chased Essex into the barren
hills of Cornwall, and compelled his army to sur-
render at Lostwithiel, a brief success which flattered
the hopes of the Royalists for a moment ; but it was
followed by the indecisive (second) battle of New-
bury in October, and in November Charles was
back in Oxford. Probably Endymion Porter was
in attendance on the King during this campaign,
whose one barren victory was far indeed from
counterbalancing the heavy blow of Marston Moor.
Charles found himself in sore straits, and decided
that he had now no choice but to seek what help he
might from beyond the Irish Channel. At this
stage he needed all that any of his friends could
do for him.

One of the most powerful supporters of the Royal

---

[1] "Commons' Journals," vol. iii. pp. 658, 709-11 ; Rep. Duke
of Portland's MSS., vol. i. pp. 192-6.

cause during the war had been the wealthy Catholic
Marquess of Worcester. Although he had spent no
less than £60,000 in raising an army of Welshmen
only to have them cut to pieces by Waller at
Highnam, the Marquess still undauntedly continued
to support the King with royal liberality. His
eldest son, the Earl of Glamorgan, had even larger
plans than his father's. A brilliant, imaginative, and
unpractical genius, devoted to the Catholic Church
no less than to the King, Lord Herbert, as he was
then, plunged into the whirl of civil war with all the
high ideals of a knight of romance. His second
wife was a daughter of the Earl of Thomond, and
his friendships among the Irish nobility made him
think it would be easy to draw the Catholic party
in Ireland to the King's side at the price of a
few moderate concessions—then Church and King
together might crush the Parliamentary party,
which was equally obnoxious to both.

The King, who had long wished, yet feared, to
make use of the Romanist force in Ireland, this
winter at last resolved to embrace Glamorgan's
proposal ; but, as the concessions made to the Irish
would have alienated many of the King's supporters
in England, the negotiations were kept secret, even
from the King's Lieutenant-General in Dublin,
the Duke of Ormond. It was promised that if
Glamorgan succeeded, as his services would be
great, his reward should be nothing less than
princely. A duke's coronet for himself, and a royal
bride, the Princess Elizabeth, for his son, should
testify to the world that a King knew how to be
grateful. But, for the present, he was only made
prospective Commander-in-chief of an army about to

be raised in Ireland and among his own tenantry in South Wales, and to be supported by strong reinforcements expected from the Continent. So deep and dangerous was this secret that it could not be divulged even to the Lord-Keeper, and the sealing of Glamorgan's warrant as general had to be managed in private. As might be expected, Endymion Porter was called in to help, and the warrant was sealed, some say with a seal cut from another patent; while others tell that Porter and the ingenious Earl succeeded in using the Great Seal by hand, as no press was to be had. The grant to Glamorgan of the Dukedom of Somerset was indeed sealed openly, yet even in this some preliminary formalities were omitted so that it should not be valid at once.

But not "all their piety nor wit," not Glamorgan's chivalry, nor his father's wealth, could save the doomed Royal cause. The Irish manœuvre was a complete failure. Glamorgan found himself distrusted by the Catholics, disavowed by the King in public, and actually thrown into prison by Ormond, so that his help, when it did come, came too late.

Meantime, the chief hope for the Royal cause lay in the winning in the West of England, and in March, 1645, the boy Prince of Wales proceeded there to take nominal command. Goring, however, was the real leader, and George Porter was lieutenant-general and commander of horse under him. There was no Rupert there to overawe George Porter, and the two brothers-in-law cared nothing for the young Prince of Wales and his grave old councillors. In his account of the campaign, Bulstrode has little good to say of either Goring or Porter. General Goring, he says, "strangely loved the bottle, and the great misfortune was, he had two companions, who commanded next under him, who fed his wild humour and debauch, and one of them, if not both, wanted his great natural courage. They made the general turn his wantonness into riot and his riot into madness." [1]

Goring wrote from Chard to Lord Culpepper, describing what he tried to pass off as "a fantastical incident," which kept him from destroying the greater part of the enemy's army.[2] He had attempted a night surprise of the rebels at a bridge over the Parrett: "I sent my brother, Porter," he continued, "with one regiment to fall on them." But, instead of falling on them, most of the Royalists fell on their own friends, and skirmished above two hours before they recognised each other, while the enemy got comfortably back to Lyme and Taunton. Prince Rupert had said grimly long before, "My Lord Goring will make a good story of it," and, as this story of his is flatly contradicted by other accounts, it may be concluded, as Dr. Gardiner gently puts it, "the truth did not *lie* on the side of Goring."

But worse was to follow, and even Goring could not make a good story out of the disgraceful surprise and rout at Lamport. This town was placed in a strong position, defended on one side by the river, and on the other by the marshes that stretched away to Bridgwater. Bulstrode tells the history of this rout very graphically. The day before the

---

[1] Bulstrode, "Memoirs of King Charles," p. 135.
[2] Cal. Dom. S. P., 1645.

battle Goring had sent Lieutenant-General George Porter with three brigades to the other side of the river, "who had his quarters beaten up at noon-day by General Massey for want of scouts being out, the Lieutenant-General being then in his utmost debauches with some of his officers. The enemy was seen coming from the hills a mile before them, and yet was upon our men before they could get to their horses, which were feeding in the meadows." The alarm being brought to General Goring, he immediately marched in person to his succour, rallied the horse that were flying, stopped the enemy's career, and made a handsome retreat. "When our General met Lieutenant-General George Porter in the rear flying with the rest, his Excellency turned to me and said, 'He deserves to be pistolled for his negligence or cowardice.' But being the general's brother-in-law, that fault was soon forgotten and pardoned; and yet I have heard the General say 'that his brother-in-law was the best company and worst officer that ever served the King.'" After this skirmish followed the battle of Lamport, when Fairfax chased Goring's troop right through the town and across the marshes to Bridgwater. Many Royalist officers were taken whilst endeavouring to cover the retreat of their men across the narrow tracks through the bog, but George Porter escaped, "room being made for him by the other officers."

Probably Goring had no objection to using George as a scapegoat; at any rate, when Clarendon was sent by the Prince of Wales to ask for explanations, Goring declared "his apprehension of his brother Porter's negligence or treachery in many particular instances, and that he was resolved to be quit of him." [1]

Whether faithful or treacherous, certainly George Porter managed to have some friends in both camps. Perhaps he shared the opinion of other jovial gentlemen, that "good wine is of no party," but his frequent meetings with the officers of the other side aroused grave suspicions.

Riot, insubordination, and quarrels were fast doing the work of the enemy among the Royalist troops ; the Prince was treated with the most careless disrespect, and the few sober councillors whom the King had sent with him were openly laughed at.

One of George Porter's quarrels is probably a good example of the temper of the officers. For some reason he had dropped a certain Colonel Tuke, who had formerly been his particular favourite, [2] and had another officer promoted over Tuke's head. Tuke instantly resigned and challenged Porter. The Council interfered, and with some difficulty prevented the meeting ; but Porter's delicate sense of honour being still unsatisfied, Colonel Tuke, who was ill in bed, sent him word "he would not fail to find him as soon as he could get on horseback, if the fear of the sudden ruin of his party did not make him go to the Parliament sooner," which remark shows that it was already well known that George Porter was tired of war and was only waiting for a convenient opportunity to make his peace with the winning side.

[1] Carte, "Ormond Letters," vol. i. p. 131 ; Bulstrode, "Memoirs," pp. 135, 137, 141.

[2] Ibid. A letter from Tuke to Porter is in the Pythouse Papers.

Ever since the disaster of Naseby (June, 1645), the King's cause had been really hopeless, and, when autumn came, Goring, weary of playing a losing game, decided to leave England, having, as usual, excellent reasons to give for his movements. He assured his officers that rest was needed in order to recruit his health, worn out by hard military service, and that he was shortly to return in command of an army raised by the Queen. Before he embarked he signed a money warrant for George Porter, who was left in command, but the latter had no more inclination to find himself in a position where he would be perpetually at odds with the Council and distrusted by his officers than had Goring, and a good Gloucestershire friend, Colonel Cooke, of Highnam, was near by in Fairfax's army to make matters easy. Colonel Cooke's letter is not quite what one would have expected from an officer of the pious New Model army. Men were much alike then, as now, by whatever different names they called themselves.

Colonel Cooke wrote on the 26th of November:—

" I have Sir Thomas Fairfax his passe for you, and as many officers and gentlemen and servants as will be with you, and if you will send me word by my trumpeter precisely when I will meet you at Stoke, I will not fayle to meet you and carry you to my quarters, where after one night of merriment, we will go to the General, when you may be sure of his and Cromwell's best service. Come ; the more the merrier."

George Porter went, and doubtless had his night

of merriment ; he then proceeded to London, and made terms for himself with the Committee for Compounding, saying that he had left offices of great profit on the King's side for the sake of the Parliament. The records of the Committee state that "being a gentleman very considerable on that side, he was sollicited by Sir Thomas Fayrfax and Colonel Cooke as very much conducing to the Parliamentary service."

In February, 1646, the Committee considered his case, and he was fined £1,000, but the fine was remitted as he pleaded that his estates in Kent and Suffolk were only held during the life of his wife. Both he and Lady Diana, however, were included in a list of persons sequestrated in Westminster in 1648.

CHAPTER XIV

ALL the King's servants did not desert the
sinking ship; it was not till the following
April, 1646, that all resistance in the field having
ceased, and a siege of Oxford being imminent, the
King fled, to yield himself a prisoner in the Scottish
camp; and then at last his most faithful followers
were scattered to the winds.

How and when Endymion Porter reached France
is not told, but he wrote a year later, "I am still
wearing the pore riding sute in which I came out of
England," which sounds as if he had escaped as
best he could. Mrs. Porter, confident in the good
usage that women received throughout this war,
appeared boldly within the Parliament's lines. But
she was considered such a dangerous lady that her
arrival was brought before the House, and it was
resolved on the 6th April that she should have the
Speaker's pass, to go to France, from Dover or
Rye; and that the Sergeant-at-arms should send
one of his servants to see her shipped. She
delayed, no doubt trying to collect some of her
property, and on the 25th she was peremptorily
ordered to leave the country before the 1st of May,

under pain of being treated as a spy. She probably joined her husband in Paris, where Endymion was meeting with that gratitude which Strafford had said, long before, might be expected by those who put their trust in princes. His letter to his old friend Nicholas, who was now in exile at Caen, tells of his poor plight.

"MAY IT PLEASE YOUR HONOUR,—I did receive your Honour's of the 3rd January, and yesterday I had likewise the other of the 14th, by which I understand your Honour hath mine that gave your Honour an account of the Queen's answer, and I forgot to send you then my cousin Grant's letter, which I have now inclosed in this. I am a sad man to hear your Honour is reduced to want; but it is all our cases, for I am in so much necessity, that were it not for an Irish barber that was once my servant, I might have starved for want of bread. He hath lent me some money that will last me for a fortnight longer, then I shall be as much subject to necessity as I was before. Here in our Court no man looks on me, and the Queen thinks I lost my estates from want of will, rather than from my loyalty to my master; but God be thanked I know my own heart, and am so satisfied in my conscience, and were it to do again, I would as freely sacrifice all without hopes of reward, as I have done this. They discourse here of a journey to Ireland. I pray God it succeed better than the rest of the designs have done, and truly they had need to think of some course, for businesses go so ill in England, as I fear our poor Master will see himself in a worse state than ever he was, if Almighty God help him not. It seems your Honour's friends the Scots have sold him, and yet they are his White Boys.[1] And our Grandees lay the fault on his not taking the covenant and signing the propositions, yet I am of opinion they would have done like Scots had he done all the unworthy acts they could have desired of him. If your Honour remembers the second letter I wrote your Honour at Oxford from hence, I told you in that how you were to expect nothing from hence, though at that time they made believe here that we should have ten thousand men presently, and named officers, and sent Sir Dudley Wyatt to secure the loss of all the remainder of our horse, which without hope of such a supply might have made their escape and have kept on foot to this day. But I am of opinion the French Ambassador and Montreul went to the Scots and not to his Majesty, and your Honour will see that when we fall out among ourselves the Scots and French will fall upon us and divide us.

"The Spaniard and Hollander have made peace, and these people here are much troubled about it, and no question but it may be an occasion of rebellion here, and those that have fomented all the uproars of Christendom may by the Tyler's law be paid in their own kind, for in this country there is as much combustible matter to take fire as in any place of the world, the whole kingdom being discontented.

"Both our Court and the French Court are vehemently angry with my Lord of Norwich, and say he hath been a main stickler in the agreement between Diego and Haunce.[2] But why should we

---

[1] *i.e.*, his favourites.
[2] The Spanish and Dutch plenipotentiaries at Münster.

be angry at it I know not, for that peace can no ways retard our Master's, and in my mind that is the only thing that all honest English hearts should look after. So soon as I can get a small sum to carry me into Flanders I resolve to go thither, and I shall not starve there ; beside I may be able to do my Master some service in those parts, and when I go I will advertise your Honour of my departure, for by your Honour's good advice I may do something for our King's good, and that I will study all the days of my life, whether I be commanded to do it or no, and if the Independents would but alter their opinions a little, and say they would have a King, I would go to them presently and kiss their feet, for that were the right way to dispatch the business ; but a pox upon the Presbyterians and them too ; they will not fall out till it be too late to do our Master good, or to save our nation from general ruin, which I am afraid will be the end. I am so retired into the skirts of a suburb that I scarce know what they do at the Louvre, and I want clothes for a Court, having but that poor riding suit I came out of England in, which shows I am constant in my apparel as I am in my respects to your Honour, and I am confident that when your Honour shall take a survey of all my actions you will find that I never altered, nor was fantastical in seeking after new friendships ; I ever profess't to love and honour you, and I am and will be

"Your Honour's most faithful

"humble servant,

"ENDYMION PORTER.

"PARIS, *the* 19*th January*, 1647.

"P.S.—This epigram was sent me from London.

' The Scots must have two hundred thousand pound
To sell the King and quit our English ground.
And Judas like, I hope 'twill be their lots
To hang themselves, so farewell, lowsy Scots.' " [1]

From Paris, Porter moved to Brussels. He had
visited it so often in more fortunate days, that it is
probable he was welcomed there by old friends, and
his worst necessities were at an end ; his letters
certainly grew more cheerful. There he also found
" my sweet Marquess of Newcastle," and William
Aylesbury, the translator of Davila's " History of
the Civil Wars in France," and brother-in-law of
Hyde. One of the pleasantest features of that time
is the brotherly feeling shown among the exiled
English. As soon as one Royalist gentleman
escaped from starvation he immediately turned to
share his crust with some countryman in distress.
A sign of Porter's better fortune is that he was
able to be of some use to the Marquess of Newcastle.

The Duchess tells,[2] in her memoir of the Duke,
how " My Lord, notwithstanding that little provision of money he had, set forth from Rotterdam
to Antwerp, where for some time he lay at a public
inn, until one of his friends that had a great love
and respect for my Lord, Mr. Endymion Porter,
who was groom of the chamber to his Majesty
King Charles the First (a place not only honourable, but very profitable), being not willing that
a person of such quality as my Lord should lie in a
public-house, proffered him lodgings at the house

---

[1] Nicholas Papers, p. 73.
[2] "Life of William, Duke of Newcastle," 1886. Edited by
C. H. Firth, p. 97.

where he was, and would not let my Lord be at quiet until he had accepted of them." The Duke was still, however, in great difficulty about raising money, till " Mr. Aylesbury, a very worthy gentleman, and a great friend to my Lord, having some monies that belonged to the now Duke of Buckingham, and seeing my Lord in so great distress, did him the favour to lend him £200, which money my Lord since his return hath honestly and justly repaid."

The following letter from Porter to Mr. Aylesbury refers to this loan :—

" BRUSSELS, *the* 19*th of August*, 1648.

" SIR,—I received a former letter from you which I did answer and send you word therein of an indisposition I had which kept me from waiting on you, and to tell you the truth I expected you here before this ; but by yours of the 18th present I find you have not received mine, and that you continue your desire of speaking with me concerning some business of my Lord's wherein I shall be ready to show all the love and duty my heart can afford, and I would it were large enough and joined with such a capacity of understanding as might show me a grateful man ; I find by your letter likewise that you have a desire to see your brother Hyde, and to tell you the truth I was engaged to my wife to wait on her in a journey which she goes to-morrow, and is to return hither on Saturday. If you by that time think you can be back from Middleburgh let me know by Father Clayton to Father Darcey, who kisses your hands, and would have done it by letter, had he known

of your being in Antwerp.   He is with much
affection your servant, and he will at my return
on Saturday deliver me your desire of what I am
to do and when I am to meet you, for you shall
dispose of

"Sir,

"Your most affectionate humble servant,

"ENDYMION PORTER.

"If you see Mr. Chancellor assure him that I am
one that loves and honours him with all my heart.

"*For my much honoured and noble friend Mr.
Aylesbury, these.   Antwerp.*"[1]

The following letter is written to Sir Richard
Browne, of Says Court, Deptford, the father-in-law
of John Evelyn.   Sir Richard was sent as resident
to the Court of France both under Charles I. and
Charles II., and it was in his chapel, at the
Embassy, that the Duke of Newcastle married his
second Duchess, the writer of his memoirs.   Lady
Browne was Elizabeth, daughter of Sir John
Pretyman, of Dryfield, Gloucestershire.   No doubt
Endymion had known her as a child, as he was a
man of twenty-three when she was born.   She died
in 1652, aged forty-two.   Sir Richard Browne's
tomb may be still seen in Deptford Church.

"*To Sir Richard Browne.*

"BRUSSELS, *this 29th November*, 1647.

"MOST HONOURED SIR,—I write not often to you
for fear of troubling you.   But I wish myself often
in your company, because I love it as you do pie,
and God send me but good news next week of our

[1] Clarendon Papers, Bod. Lib., 1648, 2,859.

poor Master's safe delivery from his enemies the Agitators and I will be merry with you in my next. Was there ever so cursed a nation as we are, that must be thought murderers, for a company of fellows that are possessed with legions of devils and would make us believe they have the Holy Ghost. I hope the Lord will serve them, one of these days, as he did those whom he sent a-fishing in the Swine! For unless there be some such course taken with them we shall never live at quiet. I beseech you buss my sweet country-woman for my sake, with such a buss as made the lass turn nun. Come, Sir Richard, if our Gloucestershire mistress were out of the verge of wife, she is worth one thousand drabs that make you believe the moon is made of green cheese. I thank God I am now past these things, paternoster and good wine are the pastime of the aged. Present my humble service to Mrs. Evelyn and to the sweet Lazala of Deptford, and be pleased to assure yourself that

"I am, honoured sir,

"Your most affectionate humble servant,

"ENDYMION PORTER.

"I beseech you convey this inclosed to my Lord Marquess of Montrose, and this other to my sweet Marquess of Newcastle." [1]

"*To Sir Richard Browne.*

"MOST HONOURED SIR, AND MY DEAR RESIDENT, —I wrote unto thee last week, but we have a cooler from England this, and therefore I cannot be so merry as I thought to have been : yet methinks Sir William Fleming and William Murray should not

[1] Add. MSS., 15,858.

come hither empty handed.   I hope they bring you chirping news, and that you will give William a rouse at the 'Spread Eagle' and not forget me, but dash me in one glass as you do an orange peel, and I believe William will not like the wine the worse. We are here in a state of grace with the taking of Coutraye and are confident to relieve Ypres, which if we do, let me tell you, there will be trouble at Paris, for all the huge bang the Swedes have given the Emperor ; but why should we English hearken after what other nations do.   I would we were quiet at home and let them fight dog, &c.   Kiss my sweet lady and country-woman for me, and assure her I love her with my whole heart : and you may be confident that I am,

> "Dear sir,
> "Your faithful and most affectionate
> humble servant,
> "ENDYMION PORTER.

"BRUSSELS, *May* 30, 1648.

"I beseech you command this letter to be sent to my Lord of Newcastle." [1]

The task of negotiating with those in power in England, and of collecting the wrecks of royalist fortunes, was generally at that time the part of the women.   Mrs. Porter, like Mary Verney and many other anxious ladies, came over to London for the purpose.   In the winter of 1647–8 she had managed to procure a pass, but it was revoked in January. She begged leave to remain longer in England to arrange for her husband compounding, and in

[1] Add. MSS., 15,858.   Printed in Bell's "Fairfax Correspondance," vol. ii. p. 30.

November, 1648, she seems to have succeeded in her negotiations, for Endymion himself was given leave to come to England, and in April, 1649, he compounded, being only fined £222, probably in consideration of his property being mortgaged and himself penniless. His house in the Strand was half-ruined by the soldiers who had been quartered in it; one would like to know if a corner of it was made habitable, or if George took care of his parents as he had taken good care of himself.

Porter's ruling tastes were not quenched by his misfortunes. The last we hear of him is from Evelyn's "Diary," May 12, 1649, "In the afternoon went to see Gildron's collection of paintings, where I found Mr. Endymion Porter, of his late Majesty's bed-chamber."

But Endymion did not long survive his royal master. He was buried at St. Martin's-in-the-Fields, August 20, 1649. He died a bankrupt; his creditors, Sir W. Cooke Russell and Edmund Cooke were his administrators, with George, his son and heir. His will cannot be found.[1] The executors are, however, said to have been the Duke of Newcastle and the Marquis of Worcester. The late Lord Strangford preserved an extract from it, which contains a graceful tribute to his early benefactor.[2] " I charge all my sons upon my blessing, that they, leaving the like charges upon their posterity, do all of them observe and respect the children and family of my Lord Duke of Buckingham, deceased, to whom I owe all the happiness I had in the world."

[1] A note in the possession of Mr. Ernest Leggett says it was dated 1639.
[2] Fontblanque, " Lords Strangford," p. 82.

It is easy to pass judgment on the Courts of the Stuart kings, and laugh at the coarseness of King James and the debaucheries of the " godless Cavaliers," yet the gay and accomplished Endymion and his spirited wife were not the only married lovers of their day.   A Court and time cannot be all evil that can show such men and women.

CHAPTER XV

THE YOUNG COURTIERS OF THE KING

IT is a dangerous experiment to raise the curtain once more after the hero of the play has fallen, and it is not cheering to turn from the brilliant servant of King Charles to follow the fortunes of the shabby actors who played the part of Royalists on the Commonwealth stage. They seem to have consoled themselves for the dulness of life under a Puritan Government by fighting as many duels as they could arrange, and personal squabbles, abortive plots, and ignoble misdemeanours make up the history of most of the English followers of the "king over the water." Among these surroundings the once proud and admired Olivia Porter lived out the last years of her life. Four of her sons were still with her, and probably more than one daughter was living.[1]

It may be believed that George Porter's easy good-humour aided him to assume the duties of an elder son with a pleasant grace, and brighten the loneliness of her widowhood with the joviality for which he was famous. But George's own life was

[1] There is no record of Lettice's death, and there seems to have been an elder daughter, Mrs. Grenville. See Appendix.

not exactly a peaceful one, and he was several times imprisoned, not for his Royalist convictions, but for his invincible taste for fighting duels.

Tom Porter was as pugnacious as his brother, and narrowly escaped being hanged for running a soldier through in Covent Garden in 1655. He admitted the manslaughter, which he could not very well deny, as the gentleman, Mr. Salkeld, died of the wound, but he pleaded that he was innocent of murder. He was lucky enough to save his neck by the strange old legal fiction that any one who could read was a clerk and free from the authority of the common law, so he "read his verse and pleaded his clergy," and was only branded in the hand.[1]

The only other of Tom Porter's duels that need be mentioned was one he fought long afterwards with Sir Henry Bellasis, which Mr. Pepys noted in his "Diary" was worth remembering for "the silliness of the quarrel, and," he continues, "is a kind of emblem of the general complexion of this whole kingdom at present." The pair were most intimate friends, but once being merry in company, Tom Porter said he should like to see the man in England who would dare to give him a blow, and with that Sir Henry Bellasis gave him a box on the ear. For this folly they fought and wounded each other, but Sir Henry, finding himself severely hurt, called Tom Porter and kissed him and bade him fly, "for," says he, "Tom, thou hast hurt me ; but I will make shift to stand upon my legs till thou mayst withdraw, for I would not have thee troubled for what thou hast done." Tom profited

[1] Middlesex Sessions Rolls, vol. iii. p. 233.

by his friend's generosity and escaped to France, but Sir Henry died a few days later, "and," Mr. Pepys concludes, "it is pretty to see how the world do talk of them as a couple of fools that killed one another out of love." [1]

But foolish as this story is, it is not so hopeless as what is perhaps the saddest bit of the Porter family history—the story of the third son, Philip. On the outbreak of the civil war he was on the Continent, under the care of a tutor, who proudly termed the boy his "masterpiece." But life abroad was not the strictest sort of training, and Philip returned to England one of the worst of the "Deboshed Cavaliers" who gave the Commonwealth magistrates so much trouble. In 1652 he was bound over to keep the peace towards his mother, after which he "again, in a very rude and unnatural manner and with wicked oaths before her door, did disturb and threaten her and her friends," and was finally committed to Newgate, there to remain till discharged by due course of law. [2]

Later on he was again imprisoned, at one time for debt, at another for duelling, and lastly for being privy to a plot against the life of the Lord Protector. [3] In 1655 his short and sorry life came to an end. He probably died reconciled to his family, as he left his little all, one thousand pounds, to his "dear mother, the Lady Olivia Porter, and his brothers Thomas and James."

Thomas Porter's life was rather less squalid than

[1] Pepy's "Diary," vol. iv. pp. 140, 141, 150.
[2] Middlesex Sessions Rolls, vol. iii.
[3] "Com. Journ.," vol. iv. pp. 486, 511 ; Cal. Committee for Compounding, p. 1,097.

that of his luckless brother Philip, and as he inherited his father's literary tastes, he devised other and more romantic fashions of breaking the commandments than by swearing at his mother or even fighting duels.

His first performance was to elope with his cousin Anne Blunt, daughter of Lord Newport,[1] a girl of eighteen, who left her father's house with her too fascinating cousin and was contracted to him in the Inn called the "Catherine Wheel," in Southwark, that they might afterwards be married in St. George's Church. Her father did his best to prove that the marriage was invalid, as Anne was under age, and St. George's was not the parish church of either of the contracting parties. Perhaps he succeeded in postponing the acknowledgment of the marriage till Anne was of age, for her son George was not born till several years later, and a Chancery suit mentions that Anne married without her father's consent.

Lady Anne Blunt cannot have long survived her marriage, as in 1659 Tom Porter married as his second wife, Roberta Anne Culpepper, one of the most uncanny of that odd and clever family.

This marriage was also petitioned against, as Roberta's brother wished to justify his refusal to pay her dower, but he failed in proving his case, and probably had no foundation for it, for he is said to have been nearly out of his mind, though a man of considerable learning and talent.

Lady Fanshawe, who loved ghost stories, spent a Sunday at Canterbury and there picked up a

[1] Middlesex Sessions Rolls, vol. iii. p. 237; Cal. Dom. S. P., 1645, 74, 577; Merc. Polit., 5,164.

ghastly legend about Roberta Porter, which was told by the Dean of Canterbury himself and confirmed by many other gentlemen.

Roberta was daughter of Sir Thomas Culpepper, second husband of Barbara, Lady Strangford, whose son, the second Viscount Strangford, married Mary, daughter of the first George Porter, in 1661.

"Roberta and her brother were atheists," said the good Dean, "and living a life according to their profession, went in a frolic into a vault of their ancestors and pulled some of their father's and mother's hairs. Within a very few days Mrs. Porter fell ill and died. Her brother kept her body in a coffin set up in his buttery, saying it would not be long before he died and then they would be buried together; but from the night after her death until the time we were told the story, which was three months ago, they say that a head, as cold as death, with curled hair like his sister's, did ever lie by him wherever he slept, notwithstanding he removed to several places and countries to avoid it, and several persons tell us they have felt this apparition." [1]

Thomas Porter does not appear to have been troubled by the ghost, and married as his third wife his cousin, Anne Canning, of Foxcote.

With the Restoration the good fortune of the Porter family returned.

Tom gave up eloping and settled down as a successful literary man. His three comedies, "The Carnival," "A Witty Combat," and "The French Conjuror," all drew crowded houses.

[1] "Mem. Lady Fanshawe," 1830, pp. 156--7.

D'Avenant was still alive and showed his interest in the son of his old patron by writing an epilogue to his play "The Villain."

But George Porter was the great man of the family. His chance had now come, for he matched the humour of the second Charles as well as his father, Endymion, had suited his own stately master. He returned to Court as Gentleman of the Bed-chamber to the Queen Mother, Henrietta Maria, and the world went well with him.

Many of the royal grants to Endymion were now renewed to his widow, and George's name is generally associated with his mother's in the deeds.

Aston had been sold directly after Endymion's death, but other valuable property was recovered, and George succeeded in recovering Alfarthing from the hands of the mortgagees.

It is probable that Olivia lived in her house in the Strand for the two years that she survived to enjoy the return of prosperity, and she was then laid to rest beside her husband in the Church of St. Martin's-in-the-Fields on December 13, 1663.

That same year, George was honoured by a commission to the Court of France, £200 being allowed by the Privy Seal for his expenses. Anne of Austria, the Queen Mother of France, was dying, and George was to carry letters of condolence from Queen Henrietta Maria and King Charles II. to Henrietta of Orleans, the King's lovely and favourite sister.

"I send the bearer, George Porter," wrote Charles, "with no other errand than upon the

subject of the Queen Mother's indisposition, who,
I fear by the nature of her disease, and what
I find by letters from thence, will not long be
in a position to receive any compliments. This
bearer will tell you of our fleet being gone out
to seek the Dutch, and you know him so well
that I need say nothing more to you. He will
play his own part and make you laugh before
he returns, which is all the business he has
there, except to assure you with how much kindness,

" I am yours,

" C. R." [1]

In 1665 George Porter was in attendance on
the Duke of Monmouth, in company with the
Duke of Buckingham, evidently on a round of
visits, as Lord Arlington reported that they were
" all engaged in warm country dances." [2]

In fact, George seems generally to have been
selected whenever, in King Charles's words, "all
the business is to make you laugh," but we
really know little else of this merry servant of
the Merry Monarch. Even the poem D'Avenant
addressed to him gives no further information,
being chiefly concerned with a certain " fair Chlo-
rinda."

George did not live to see the dethronement of
the last Stuart king, and was spared having once
again to choose between his loyalty and his
comforts. He died on the 11th of December,
1683, aged 63.

His brother James appears, as far as his life

---

[1] " Madame," J. Cartwright, p. 215.
[2] Cal. Dom., S. P. Dec., 1665.   Arlington to the King.

is known, to have been the most worthy of the Porter sons. Through good and evil fortunes he was true to James the Second, acting as colonel to a troop of volunteers raised to oppose Monmouth's rebellion, and as lieutenant-colonel in the Irish war which ended his Royal master's reign in the British Islands. Just before King James landed in Ireland he had been dispatched to beg assistance from Pope Innocent, and when the battle of the Boyne drove the King into exile, James Porter followed him to France and resumed his duties as Vice Chamberlain in the English Court at St. Germain's. There he remained till the King's death, and fulfilled his last duties by collecting the materials for a funeral oration.[1] Endymion's youngest son, at least, lived true to his father's creed, " My duty and my loyalty have taught me to follow the King my master, and by the grace of God, nothing shall divert me from it."

[1] Dedicated to the King of France. Translated into English, 1702.

APPENDIX

APPENDIX

I

EPITAPH ON DR. DONNE BY ENDYMION PORTER, PRINTED WITH
VERSES BY MANY OTHER ADMIRERS IN THE EDITION OF
DONNE'S POEMS IN 1639.

THIS decent urn a sad inscription bears
   Of Donne's departure from us to the spheres ;
And the dumb stone with silence seems to tell
The change of this life, wherein is well
Exprest, a cause to make all joy to cease,
For us it is impossible to find
One frought with virtues to inrich the mind.
But why should death with a promiscuous hand
At one rude stroke impoverish a land ?
Thou strict attorney unto stricter fate
Did'st thou confiscate his life out of hate
To his rare parts ? or did'st thou throw thy dart
With envious hand, at some plebeian heart
And he, with pious virtue, stept between
To save the stroke, and so was killed unseen
By thee ?   O 'twas his goodness so to do
Which human kindness never reached unto.
Thus the hard hands of death were satisfied
And he left us like orphan friends, and died.
Now from the pulpit to the people's ears
Whose speech shall send repentant sighs and tears?
Or tell us if a purer virgin die
Who shall hereafter write her elegy ?

Poets, be silent, let your numbers sleep,
For he is gone, that did all fancy keep.
Time hath no soul but his exalted verse
Which with amazement we may now rehearse.

II

DESCENDANTS OF ENDYMION PORTER

George, eldest son of Endymion Porter, left three sons, George, Endymion, who died aged twenty-three, and Aubrey. The latter was made a " page of honour " in 1671.

He had also five daughters, of whom Mary married Philip Smyth, Lord Strangford, as his second wife ; Isabella married Edward Bedell, of Woodrising, Norfolk ; Anne married Thomas Condon ; and Olivia and Diana appear to have remained single.

It is not always easy to distinguish between George Porter and his eldest son George. The latter was made Gentleman Usher to the Queen in 1663, and later on Vice-Chamberlain. Young George married Mary, daughter and heiress of John Mawson, and left several children, his eldest son being seated at Alfarthing.

Thomas, Endymion Porter's second surviving son, left one son George, by his first wife Lady Anne Blunt, who inherited Newport House from his grandfather, Lord Newport. In 1678, while still a minor, George endeavoured to gain permission to sell the house, saying it was unfit for his habitation, but the House of Lords refused him leave to do so. In the year 1659 he was left £5,000 by his godmother, the Countess of Portland, and in December, 1684, he was indicted at the Old Bailey for killing Sir James Hackett in a scuffle outside a theatre. He was found guilty of manslaughter, as there was no evidence of premeditation, but less lucky than his father he was for some reason not allowed the benefit of the legal fiction of " reading his neck verse," and was " barred his clergy," and stood a good chance of being hanged. However, the King was merciful and granted him a royal pardon. Perhaps to show his gratitude to the House of Stuart, he was, after the Revolution, involved in a plot to assassinate William III. But he soon thought better of his Jacobite schemes, and betrayed his associates to the Government, bringing two of them to the gallows as traitors in 1696, and earning a pension of £260 a year for himself. He died in 1726, apparently leaving no children, as his widow, Elizabeth Porter, of St. James', Westminster, was his sole executrix. In the report of the trial of Rookwood, Fenwick, and other conspirators, he is called Captain Porter.

James, third surviving son of Endymion Porter, left no children.

It is not known who Endymion Porter's daughter Lettice married. No record is to be found of the birth of any other daughter, whether in the registers of St. Martin's-in-the-Fields, or of Aston. The registers of Hatfield do not begin at so early a date, so it is possible that another daughter was born to the Porters at Woodhall, and afterwards married with the Greville family, for an undated letter to Endymion is signed by his grandson Richard Greville.

Sir Edward Greville, of Mickleton, and Fulke Greville, Lord Brooke, were old friends of the Porters, and a match between one of Endymion's daughters and a member of the Greville family was a very probable thing, but it is at present only a supposition. The letter itself gives no clue.

"MY UNFEIGNEDLY HONOURED GRANDFATHER,—I must heartily beseech you to favour me in so acceptable a kind as to command me in all or any occasion to give yourself most assurance of my faithful heart's desire to be approved most covetous ·of your service, and it is and daily shall be prosecuted by my prayers to God for yourself and my Grandmother's happy long life. I have here inclosed sent you all my receipts and rules for shooting, that I can call to mind without book, some more I have which shall be all yours when I can come into my country to send them to you, in the mean time I must crave your excuse, and so according to my beginning, my continuance, and last end, shall testify these words, that you have not any one friend in the whole world that more fervently and faithfully loves you than myself.

"Your constant devoted servant,

"RICHARD GREVILLE.

'(Endorsed) For my dearly honoured Grandfather Mr. Endimeon Porter, these." [1]

[1] Dom. S. P., vol. cccclxxv. No. 91 (endorsed in pencil "try 1640").

III

PORTRAITS OF THE PORTER FAMILY

There are so many portraits scattered through public and private galleries that only an attempt can be made to give a list of them.

Besides those reproduced in this volume, some of the best known are the Vandyke portrait of Endymion owned by Lord Mexborough. It "is life size, wearing a red doublet slashed with white under a dark orange cloak which is worn over the left arm, seen to the knees and turned to the left, in three-quarter view of face and figure, pointing downward with left hand." [1] Lord Hardwicke possesses another Vandyke portrait of Porter. Another interesting Vandyke portrait was in Sir T. Phillipp's collection at Middle Hill, and is now in the gallery of the Rev. J. E. A. Fenwick, at Thirlestaine House, Cheltenham; it much resembles the Dobson portrait engraved in this work.

A group by Vandyke of the whole Porter family, which seems to be identical with that reproduced on page facing 125, was once in the collection of Sir P. Lely, and is now in one of the Royal collections. [2] A sketch of this picture in grisaille is in the possession of Mr. Ernest Leggett, of 62, Cheapside.

Another portrait of Olivia Porter is at Petworth.

There are two portraits of Porter by William Dobson, whom King Charles named the English Tintoretto. The one in the National Gallery has rather a self-conscious expression, he is bare-headed, dressed in amber-coloured doublet and point lace collar, he holds a fowling-piece in his hands, and is attended by a page carrying a dead hare. The other portrait by Dobson is reproduced as Frontispiece.

The portraits of Endymion vary greatly. Engravings are even more perplexing than paintings, as engravers had a way of altering the name under a picture, and then selling it as a portrait of whatever distinguished personage might be most in request. One portrait of Endymion, engraved by Faithorn from a painting by Dobson, is suspiciously like Lord Fielding, and is actually known to have been sold for the Earl of Essex.

There is also a miniature engraved in Mezzo by Earldom

---

[1] Notes on Vandyke Exhibition, 1887. F. G. Stevens.
[2] Ibid.

showing a young man, smiling, but not very attractive. Also a
Mezzo by Richardson, a side face view of a stout somewhat Italian-
looking man. In the Sutherland collection at the Bodleian there
are drawings by Bulfinch and Flight, and a coloured drawing by
W. W. Gardner from the picture at Wimpole, a handsome Vandyke
type of face, light brown hair, hazel eyes, light beard and
moustache, and red dress. The Print Room at the British
Museum has several reproductions of the Madrid portrait by
Vandyke.

INDEX

INDEX

18

UNWIN BROTHERS, THE GRESHAM PRESS, WOKING AND LONDON

www.ingramcontent.com/pod-product-compliance
Lightning Source LLC
Chambersburg PA
CBHW030632030726
47497CB00006B/1754